'Be quiet and listen.'

His chin tilted down. His brows rose. 'Yes, Miss Cherroll?'

'I will not stay here.'

He waited, his gaze locked on to hers.

'My sister needs me for the children,' she said.

'I understand completely,' he said, his voice agreeable, and stepped to the door. 'You can take my carriage to visit them as often as you wish.'

One stride and he would be out of her vision.

'It is not a problem at all. Send your maid in Warrington's carriage for your things. The housekeeper will be with you shortly to help you select a room.'

He was gone by the time she opened her mouth.

Author Note

Bellona's story was formed while I was writing my previous book, *A Captain and a Rogue*.

I first envisaged her as wanting to be like the Grecian heroine Laskarina Bouboulina, who owned a large warship and would have been active around 1822, when *Forbidden to the Duke* begins. I also planned for Bellona to be a bit of a Robin Hood in spirit. With knife and archery skills that can protect her from many dangers—except the most surprising ones.

But Bellona became a different character from the warrior I first imagined. When this story begins she's on the path to separation from the security of her family and making her own world. The new hobby she finds at the end of the book wasn't planned until the words were being written, but I feel it truly expresses who she was meant to be, and the part of her she's hidden from herself.

I hope you enjoy Bellona and Rhys's journey, and that you see them as I do— two people who have to step out of the roles they were born into and rise to be the beginnings of a new legacy.

FORBIDDEN TO THE DUKE

Liz Tyner

MILLS &
BOON®

First published in Great Britain 2015
by Mills & Boon, an imprint of Harlequin (UK) Limited,
Large Print edition 2016
Harlequin (UK) Limited, Eton House, 18-24 Paradise Road,
Richmond, Surrey TW9 1SR

© 2015 Elizabeth Tyner

ISBN: 978-0-263-26274-2

Printed and bound in Great Britain
by CPI Antony Rowe, Chippenham, Wiltshire

Liz Tyner lives with her husband on an Oklahoma acreage she imagines is similar to the ones in the children's book *Where the Wild Things Are*. Her lifestyle is a blend of old and new, and is sometimes comparable to the way people lived long ago. Liz is a member of various writing groups and has been writing since childhood. For more about her visit liztyner.com.

Books by Liz Tyner

Mills & Boon Historical Romance

English Rogues and Grecian Goddesses

Safe in the Earl's Arms
A Captain and a Rogue
Forbidden to the Duke

Visit the Author Profile page at
millsandboon.co.uk.

Chapter One

The pudgy-eyed gamekeeper pointed a flintlock straight at Bellona's chest. His eyebrows spiked into angry points. 'Drop the longbow.' His gun barrel emphasised his words and even without the weapon his size would have daunted her. He'd not looked so large or his stare so bloodless from a distance.

Noise crashed into her ears—the sound of her heart—and the beats tried to take over every part of her. She forced the blackness away and locked her stare with his. Charred hatred, roughened by the unshaven chin, slammed out from his face.

She nodded and tossed the bow into the twining berry thorns at the side of the path. The canopy of sycamore leaves covered him in green-hued shadows.

He put one hand to his mouth, thrust his fingers

to his lips and whistled loud enough to be heard in Greece. The shrill sound jabbed her, alerting her that he wasn't alone. She'd never seen anyone else in the forest but this devil. She would be fighting two men and at least one weapon.

'…shoot at me…' He spoke again and the words snapped her back into understanding.

She cursed herself for not taking more care. She'd not heard him behind her—but she should have smelled his boiled-cabbage stench.

'I be bringing his lordship,' he said. 'Your toes be dangling and the tide be washing your face before they cut you down. You won't be shooting at me no more. You're nothing more'n a common wench and people in lofty places be wantin' you to hang.'

Her fingers stiffened, her mind unable to send them commands. She held her chin high. She'd thought she was in a safe land. She'd thought she'd escaped men who wanted to hurt her. Showing fear would be dangerous. 'You—' She couldn't have taken her eyes from his. 'I'm a guest of the Earl of Warrington and I have misplaced myself.'

The man's nose bunched up as he talked. 'But you ain't on the earl's land now, Miss Lady

Nobody. You're no better'n me.' He waved the gun. 'You're a poacher and I've seen you here aplenty times before. I just niver could catch you.'

'The earl will be *thymomenos*, angered.'

He snorted. 'But this is the duke's land. His Grace don't lose no sleep over what an *earl* would think.'

She forced her fingers alert. 'You are the one who should think. You must know I live near.'

'But you ain't no real lady. I already told the duke all about you and how you been scattering my traps and he thinks I'm imaginin'. Your eyes is even uncommon dark like some witch borne you. I told him you're half-spirit. They hanged Mary Bateman. If they don't be hangin' you, you'll end up lyin' with vermin in gaol. Good 'nuff for you.'

He indicated the trail behind himself by swinging the barrel of the gun towards it. 'Don't move a feather.' The gamekeeper swaggered. 'His Grace be right behind me. I told him I set my traps near and this time I be catchin' somethin' big. You've ruined your last snare.'

Footsteps in the leaves signalled the approach of another. Bellona rested her left hand on the top of arrows tucked into the quiver strapped around her waist. 'You can go to the devil.'

The shoulders of another man came into view, and Bellona swallowed. She needed all of her strength. Two men to fight.

The gamekeeper stepped off the path so the other one could see her.

The duke stopped beside the gamekeeper and the scent of the air became clean. The newcomer examined her, not scowling or smiling.

She would not have thought this man a peer had she seen him without introduction, but she would have known him for a gentleman. His neckcloth looped in a simple, soft knot. His boots reached his knees and his dark riding coat had plain buttons. He wore every thread as if it had been woven to his own order. Sunlight dappled over lean cheeks. His eyes were the same colour as her own.

Her stomach clenched, but not with fear. She'd made a mistake. She'd looked into his eyes. For the first time in her life, she was afraid of something inside herself.

She stepped back.

'Your Grace, I caught the murderous culprit

what's been stealing the hares from my traps and wishin' curses on us all. She be a common thief, a murderous woman and full of meanness, just like I said.' The gamekeeper's words spewed out, leaving even less air for Bellona to breathe. 'You want I should send the stable boy for the magistrate?'

The duke gave the slightest shake of his head. 'You are mistaken, Wicks. I will see her back to my estate safely and ensure that she is escorted on her way.'

'She be a thief, Your Grace, and a bewitched woman. Why, see how her eyes be puttin' evil my direction now. She be tryin' to burn me into ash right where I stand.'

'Miss—' the newcomer directed his words to Bellona and he leaned forward as he peered at her '—have you been poaching on my land?'

She sensed somehow that he jested with her. 'No. Never,' Bellona said, shaking her head. The knife was in her boot. But she didn't want to attack. She only wanted to flee.

The duke's lips firmed and he took in a small breath on his next words. 'Wicks...'

The gamekeeper's stance tightened and he

rushed his words. 'She tossed her bow into the briars. She'd kill a man herself for blood sport. She'd cut out his heart and cook it.'

The duke's lips tightened at one side and his eyes dismissed the other man's words.

'I don't eat hearts,' Bellona inserted, directing a look straight into the vile man. 'Only brains. You are safe.'

'Your Grace,' the gamekeeper sputtered, outrage and fury mixed. 'She's—'

'Quiet.' The duke's words thrust into the air with the seriousness of a sword point held to the throat.

He stepped towards her, moving over the fallen log in the path, his hand out. 'The lady and I have not been introduced, but as this isn't a soirée, I think—'

Instinctively, she pulled an arrow from the quiver and held the tip against the duke's grey silk waistcoat—pressing.

His arm halted, frozen.

'Do not touch me.' Her words copied his in command.

His eyes widened and he straightened. 'I was

going to take your arm. My pardon. It's usually received well, I assure you.'

She kept the arrow at his stomach, trying to keep the spirit around him from overtaking her.

The gamekeeper moved so the weapon again pointed at her. 'Just give me the word, Your Grace, I'll save you. She be tryin' to kill a peer. No sense wasting good rope round that boney neck.'

'Put the flintlock away, Wicks. Now.' The duke didn't take his eyes from Bellona. 'This woman and I have not finished introductions yet and, by my calculation, the arrow tip isn't exceedingly sharp.'

'It's sharp enough,' she said.

'Miss…' He blinked. He smiled. But they were just outward movements. 'Most people get to know me a little better before they think of weapons. Perhaps you should consider that. It might make an attempt on my life more enjoyable for you if there were some justification.'

She never saw his movement, but his hand clamped around her wrist, securing her, not tight, but shackle-strong.

'My property.' He stepped back from the arrow. Then he extricated it from her fingers, the warm touch of his hand capturing her in yet another way before he released her. 'My rules, Huntress.' He studied her face. 'Or if my observation is correct, should I refer to you as goddess?'

As he examined the arrow, she took another step back. She gave the merest head toss of dismissal and readied her hand to the single arrow left in the quiver.

His eyes flickered to the sharpened tip of the projectile he held, but he wasn't truly examining it. He twirled it around, tipped his head to her and held the feathered end to her. 'I have met the lovely Countess of Warrington and although you resemble her, I would remember if I'd met you. That means you're the sister named for the goddess of war. The woman hardly ever seen.'

'You may call me Miss Cherroll.' The rules she'd studied fled from her, except the one about the curtsy and she could not force herself to do it. She took the arrow.

She only wanted to leave, but her limbs hadn't yet recovered their strength. She controlled her voice, putting all the command in it she could muster. 'You're not what I expected.'

'If you've been talking to Warrington, I suppose not.' He tilted his head forward, as if he secluded them from the rest of the world. 'What is he fed for breakfast? I fear it curdles his stomach—daily.'

'Only when mixed with entertainments not to his liking.'

'Well, that explains it. I can be quite entertaining.'

'He claims you can be quite...' She paused. His eyes waited for her to continue, but she didn't think it prudent, either to Warrington or the duke.

The duke continued, taking in the words she didn't say. 'Not many are above him, and, well, I might give him the tiniest reminder of my status, when it is needed.' He shrugged. 'Our fathers were like brothers. He thinks he has become the old earl and I have not attained the grandness of my sire. My father did limp—and that knee was the only thing that kept him from perfection. The injured leg was the price he paid for doing the right thing. He once thrust himself between someone and the hooves of an angry horse.'

'I would not be so certain of the earl's opinion.' She paused, softening her words. 'He says you are quite the perfect duke. A duke from heel to head.' Warrington had stared at the ceiling and grimaced when he spoke.

'A compliment. I'm certain. From Warrington.' He shrugged. 'Too many things distract me from perfection. I just trudge along, doing what I can. Hoping to honour the legacy my father left behind.'

He turned to the other man, sending him along. 'I'll see Miss Cherroll home.' Taking a step towards her, he paused when she moved the pointed tip the slightest bit in his direction. 'Assuming she doesn't do Warrington a boon and impale his favourite neighbour.'

When he stopped moving, she relaxed her hand.

'I will manage well enough on my own.' She turned, pulling the skirt's hem from a bramble, and moved closer to the bow. 'I know the way.' She heard her own words and turned back to the duke and leaned her head to the side. 'I have been lost here before.' She pulled the bow into her hand, freeing it from the thorny brambles clasping it.

'I would imagine so. Wicks claims you are here more than he is. I might call on you,' he said, 'later today to assure myself you arrived safely home.'

She shook her head. 'Please don't. Warrington is always claiming I bring home strange things from my walks.'

'My dear, I'm a duke. He won't be able to say a word. It's a rule of sorts.'

'You truly don't know him well, do you?'

'Well, perhaps he might grumble, but his good breeding would insist he appear welcoming. At least in your presence.'

She held the nock end of the arrow as if she were going to seat it against the bowstring. 'You're right in that my English father named me for the Roman goddess of war. And, it's said I'm completely lacking in the ways of a proper Englishwoman. But I do remember one phrase. "I am not at home."'

'Miss Cherroll. I would think you'd not mind sharing tea with me seeing as you have already shared my property.'

She shook her head. 'I have been called on before. I have not been at home.'

'Ever?'

She firmed her lips and shook her head.

'Why not?'

She didn't answer his question. She could not speak of her memories aloud. Putting them into words brought the feel of the rough fingertips to her neck.

His brows furrowed. Even though she knew a proper lady didn't scurry along the trail, she did, leaving the duke standing behind her.

Rhys Harling, Duke of Rolleston, sat at his desk, completely unmoving. Wicks stood in front of Rhys, repeating the same words he'd said two days ago and the two days before that. Rhys hoped the air would clear of the man's dank scent when he left.

Wicks waved the arrow like a sceptre. His lips didn't stop moving even when he paused to find new words.

Wicks rambled on, falling more in love with his discourse as he continued. If the gamekeeper were to be believed, the woman created more mischief than any demon.

It had been five days since Wicks had caught the woman. The gamekeeper had approached him twice to discuss the lands and could not keep from mentioning her.

Rhys interrupted, his voice direct. 'She did not try to impale me. Neither her teeth nor her eyes—which are not rimmed by devil's soot—show brighter than any other's in the dusk and she is not as tall as I am. You cannot claim her to be something she is not. I forbid it.'

'You can't be faultin' me for lookin' out for your lands, Your Grace.'

'I don't. But she's the earl's guest. You must cease talking at the tavern about the woman.'

'Who told you?' His chin dropped and he looked at the floor.

'Who didn't tell me?' Rhys fixed a stare at the man. 'Wicks, you should know that words travel from one set of ears to the next and the next and before long every person who has shared a meal with someone else has heard.'

'She does stick in my craw, Your Grace.'

He didn't blame the gamekeeper. Rhys couldn't remove her from his mind either. The quiver cinched her trim waist. A twig had poked from her mussed hair. The magical thing he'd noticed about her was the way her hair could stay in a knot on her head when most of it had escaped.

Rhys had known when the gamekeeper first mentioned the trespasser who it would most likely be. He'd wanted to see her for himself.

Wicks wasn't the first person to discuss her. Even the duchess, who talked only of family members who'd passed on, had varied from her melancholia once and spoke of the earl's sister-by-law Miss Cherroll. The foreign-born woman rarely let herself be seen by anyone outside the earl's household and that caused more talk than if she'd danced three dances with the same partner.

'Forget her,' the duke said. 'She's just an ordinary woman who likes to traipse the trails. I can't fault her for that.'

He couldn't. He'd travelled over those same trails countless times, trying to keep up with his brother, Geoff.

Looking for the woman had been the first time he'd been in the woods since Geoff's death. The gnashing ache grinded inside him again, but the woman's face reminded him of unspoiled times.

But she was…a poacher of sorts. Nothing like her sister—a true countess if tales were to be believed. He wouldn't put it past Warrington to keep this bow-carrying family member in the shadows, afraid what would happen if the woman met with members of the *ton*.

'You didn't feel she could near strangle a man with one look from her eyes?' Wicks asked. 'I could feel that devil in her just trying to take my vicar's words right from mind. She still be trespassin' ever' day. Taunting me, like. She tears up my traps and she lurks out in the wood, waiting until I check them and then she tries to kill me.'

'I'm sure she's not trying to kill you.'

'This arrow weren't whipping by your head.' He pulled every muscle of his body into an indignant shudder. 'And since I caught her last time, she stays too far back for me to snatch her again.'

'You will not touch her.' Rhys met Wicks's stare. Rhys stood.

Wicks's lips pressed together.

'You will not touch her,' Rhys said again and waited.

'I don't want no part of that evil witch,' Wicks said finally. 'I looked at her and I saw the Jezebel spirit in her. I be sleepin' on the floor and not in my bed so she can't visit me in my night hours and have her way with me.'

Rhys put both palms flat on the desk and leaned forward. 'That is a good plan. However, if you sleep with your nightcap over your ears it will do the same.'

'You're sure?'

'Yes.' Rhys nodded.

Wicks's lips moved almost for a full minute before he spoke and his shoulders were pulled tight and he watched the arrow in his hand. 'Well, I'll be considerin' it. Floor's cold.'

'Do you think perhaps she is a normal kind-hearted woman, Wicks, and merely doesn't want little creatures harmed?'

'I wondered. But that seems odd to me. When I gave her my smile—' He bared perfect teeth except for one missing at the bottom. 'She didn't even note. Just raised her bow right towards me and let this arrow loose.'

Rhys rose, walked around the desk and held out his hand. Wicks slowly placed the arrow across Rhys's palm.

'If you see her again,' Rhys commanded, 'at any time at any place, you are not to give her one moment of anything but respect. You are not to smile at her or approach her, or you will answer to me in a way you will not like.'

'Not right,' Wicks said, his nose going up. 'Being shot at while doin' my work.'

'I will handle this. Do not forget my words. Leave her be.'

'I will,' Wicks said. 'I pity her. Has too many airs to settle into things right for a woman's place.'

Rhys glared.

'But I be keepin' it a secret.' He nodded. 'I ain't givin' her another one of my smiles. She missed her chance. And if she tries to have her way with me, I be turnin' my head and keepin' my night-cap tight.'

He used both hands to clamp his hat on his head as he shuffled out, grumbling.

Rhys studied the arrow and thought of his mother's melancholia. How she hardly left her room, even for meals. How she talked more of people who'd passed than of her own friends, and how she claimed illness rather than go to Sunday Services. His brother's death had taken the life from her as well. The one moment the duchess's thoughts had wavered into the present had been when she asked Rhys if he'd heard of the earl's guest, but by the time he'd answered, his mother's thoughts had wavered back into the shadows of the past.

He brushed his hand over the arrow fletching. Window light bounced over the feathers, almost startling him. Raising his eyes, he saw the sun's rays warming the room. He stood, walking to the sunlight, pausing to feel the heat on his face. He lifted the feathery end of the weapon, twirling it in the brightness.

Winter's chill had left the air, but he'd not noticed the green outside the window until now. The woman had also worn the colours of the forest, he remembered. She'd not looked like a warrior goddess, but a woodland nymph, bringing life into morning.

He snorted, amazed at the folly of his imagination. He'd not had such foolish thoughts in a long time. Nor had he longed for a woman's comfort overmuch in the past year. Now, he imagined the huntress and his body responded, sending reminders of pleasure throughout his being.

Leaning into the window frame, holding the arrow like a talisman, he tried to remember every single aspect of her. What she'd said and how she'd looked. Each word and moment that had transpired between them.

He pulled the soft end of the arrow up, looking at the feathers one last time before tapping the nock against the sill, staring at the reflections of sunlight.

This woman at the earl's estate, who was willing to fight for rabbits, but could keep the servants whispering about her, might be just the woman who could bring his mother back to life. She'd already reminded Rhys that he was still alive.

Within the hour, Rhys was in the Earl of Warrington's sitting room. The duke clasped an arrow at his side and waited as he expected he might. He moved to the window again, wanting to feel the heat from the sun streaming through the panes. Trees budded back to life. A heathen spirit might do the same for his own home.

The mantel sported a painting of three young girls playing while their mother watched. He wagered the painting was of Greece and one of the girls could have been the one on his property.

Except for the single painting, the room seemed little different than Rhys's own library.

Rhys looked out over Warrington's snipped and clipped and trimmed and polished world, almost able to hear the laughter from years before.

Only, the laughter was not his, but directed at him.

Of course, both he and Warrington had matured now. They had left foolish prattle and childish games behind.

Warrington strode in. Rhys could still taste the medicinal the others had found in the apothecary jar and forced into Rhys's mouth when they were children. That had to be his earliest memory.

'Your *Grace*,' Warrington greeted. The earl moved to stand at the mantel. He glanced once at the painting above it before he asked, 'So what is the honour that brings you to Whitegate?'

Rhys held out the arrow. 'I found this on my property and heard that you have a guest who practises archery. I'd like to return it to her.'

Rhys had never seen Warrington's face twitch until that moment. He studied Rhys as if they'd just started a boxing match. 'You are interested in talking with *Bellona*?'

Warrington's eyes flickered. 'I'm sure whatever she did—' Warrington spoke quickly. 'She just doesn't understand our ways.' He paused and then sighed. 'What did she do now?'

'I just wish to meet with her,' Rhys said, 'and request that she refrain from shooting arrows on to my property—particularly near others.'

Warrington grimaced and then turned it into a smile. 'She does… Well…you know…' He held out a palm. 'Some women like jewellery. Flowers. Sharp things. She likes them.'

'Sharp things?'

Warrington shook his head. 'Never a dull moment around her.'

'Truly?'

'Beautiful voice—when she's not talking. Her sister forced her to attend the soirée at Riverton's, hoping Bellona would find something about society that suited her. Pottsworth wanted to be introduced. She'd not danced with anyone. I thought it a good idea even though he is—well, you know Potts. She smiled and answered him in Greek. Thankfully none of the ladies near her had our tutors. Riverton overheard and choked on his snuff. We left before he stopped sputtering. He still asks

after her every time he sees me. "How is that re-
tiring Miss Cherroll?"'

'Can't say as I blame her. You introduced
Pottsworth to her?' Rhys asked drily.

'I'm sure she might wander too far afield from
time to time,' Warrington murmured it away, 'but
your land has joined mine since before our grand-
parents' time and we've shared it as one.' Warrington gave an encompassing gesture, then he
toyed with what could have been a speck on the
mantel. 'We're all like family. We grew up together. I know you and I don't have the very close
bond of our fathers, but still, I count you much
the same as a brother of my own.'

'Much like Cain and Abel?'

Warrington grinned. He waved the remark
away. 'You've never taken a jest well.'

'The bull,' Rhys said, remembering the very
incensed animal charging towards him, bellow-
ing. Rhys was on the wrong side of the fence,
his hands on the rails, and the older boys pushed
at him, keeping him from climbing to safety.
He'd felt the heat from the bull's nostrils when
they'd finally hefted him through to the other
side. Laughing.

He couldn't have been much more than five years old.

Warrington had instigated many of the unpleasant moments of Rhys's childhood. Actually, almost every disastrous circumstance could be traced back to War. Rhys had been lured into a carriage and then trapped when they wedged the door shut from the outside, and then he'd spent hours in the barn loft when they had removed the ladder. When they'd held him down and stained his cheeks with berries, he'd waited almost two years to return fresh manure to everyone involved. It had taken special planning and the assistance of the stable master's son to get manure put into Warrington's boots.

Rhys's mother and father had not been happy. The one time he had not minded disappointing his father.

War's face held camaraderie now—just like when the new puppy had been left in the carriage, supposedly.

'I must speak with your wife's sister,' Rhys said. 'I might have an idea which could help us both.'

'What?' The word darted from Warrington's lips.

'I thought Miss Cherroll might spend some time

with the duchess. Perhaps speak of Greece or...'
He shrugged. 'Whatever tales she might have
learned.'

'I forbid—' Warrington's head snapped sideways. 'No. She is my family and she must stay
with us.'

Rhys lips quirked up. 'But, War, we're like
brothers. Your family is my family.'

Warrington grunted. 'You didn't believe that
flop when I said it. Don't try to push it back in
my direction.'

Rhys smiled. 'I suppose it is your decision to
make, War. But remember. I am serious and I will
not back down.'

'I assure you, Rhys, Miss Cherroll is not the
gentle sort that the duchess is used to having tea
with.'

Rhys gave a slight twitch of his shoulder in
acknowledgement. Warrington had no idea his
mother was only having tea with memories of
death. She'd lost her will to live. With her gone,
he would have no one. No one of his true family
left. And he was not ready to lose the last one.
'Call Miss Cherroll. Let me decide.'

With a small cough of disagreement, Warrington shrugged. 'Speak with her and you'll see what I mean.' He reached for the pull. A child's laughing screech interrupted him. A blonde blur of a chit, hardly big enough to manage the stairs, hurtled into the room and crashed into Warrington's legs, hugging for dear life, and whirling so he stood between her and the door.

Bellona, brandishing a broom, charged in behind the little one and halted instantly at the sight of Warrington.

Rhys took in a breath and instantly understood Wicks's fascination with the woman. Her face, relaxed in laughter, caught his eyes. He couldn't look away—no man would consider it.

'Just sweeping the dust out of the nursery,' she said to Warrington, lowering the broom while she gingerly moved around him. The child used him as a shield.

Warrington's hand shot down on to the little girl's head, hair shining golden in the sunlight, stilling her.

Bellona's attention centred on the waif. 'Willa, we do not run in the house. We swim like fishes.'

The child laughed, pulled away from the silent admonishment of her father's hand on her head, puffed her cheeks out and left the room quickly, making motions of gliding through water.

Warrington cleared his throat before the chase began again. 'We have a guest, Bellona.'

Rhys saw the moment Bellona became aware of his presence. The broom tensed and for half a second he wondered if she would drop it or turn it into a weapon. Warrington was closer, and Rhys was completely willing to let her pummel him.

She lowered the bristles to the floor, but managed a faint curtsy and said, 'I did not know we had a visitor.' Her face became as stiff as the broom handle.

Warrington turned to Rhys.

'Bellona is… She gets on quite well with the children as you can tell.' His eyes glanced over to her. 'But she is not as entranced with tranquillity as her sister is.'

'I do like the English ways,' she said, shrugging. 'I just think my ways are also good.'

'But my children need to be well mannered at all times.' Warrington frowned after he spoke.

'I do adore the *paidi*. They are gold,' she said, voice prim and proper. 'But no little one is well mannered at all times. They have life. It is their treasure. They should spend it well.'

'They should also know the way to be proper and comport themselves in a lofty manner when they meet such a person as we are privileged to have in our presence.' He glanced at Rhys. 'His Grace, Duke of Rolleston. Rescuer of lost puppies, everywhere.' He turned to Bellona to complete the introduction. 'Miss Cherroll, my wife's kind and gentle-spirited youngest sister—' his brows bumped up as he looked back at Rhys '—who has called me a few endearments in her native language that our tutor neglected to teach us, and when her sister translates I fear something is lost in the meaning.'

Her eyes blinked with innocence at Warrington for a moment before she acknowledged the introduction with a slight nod.

'I believe the duke wanted to speak with you.' Warrington walked to her, took the broom and looked at it as if might bite. 'And I should see about Willa.'

The earl took two long strides to the door. 'I won't send a chaperon.' He smiled at Rhys as he left. 'You're on your own.'

Chapter Two

Pleased Warrington had left them alone, Rhys's attention turned to Bellona. She'd moved a step back from him and stood close to an unlit lamp on a side table. Her eyes remained on the arrow in his hand.

Perhaps he'd been mistaken about her. She might be unsettled.

Bellona nodded towards the arrow. 'I believe that is mine.'

Rhys grasped the shaft with both hands and snapped the arrow across his knee, breaking the wood in two pieces. Then he held it in her direction.

The straight line of her lips softened. Her shoulders relaxed and she moved just close enough so that he could place the arrow in her hand. Exotic spices lingered in the air around her and he tried to discern if it was the same perfume from a rare plant he'd once noted in a botanist's collection.

'Thank you.' She took the splintered pieces and increased the distance between them. Examining the broken shaft, she said, 'I feared you would not be so kind as to return it.'

'You could have injured someone. My gamekeeper.'

She raised her eyes to Rhys. 'The arrow did what arrows do. I didn't want to hurt him, but he—' Bellona dismissed the words. 'His voice… You should speak with him about *glossa*—his words.'

'Leave the poor man alone. He has been on my estate his whole life and feels as much kinship to the land as I do.'

'A man cannot own land. It is a gift from the heavens to be shared.'

'For the time being, it is my gift and I control all on it. You upset the gamekeeper.'

She shrugged. 'He upsets rabbits.'

'They are invited. You are not. However…' His next words were about to change that, but he forgot he was speaking when her hand moved.

Flicking up the notched end of the arrow, she

brushed the feathery fletching against her face. The arrow stroked her skin. One. Two. Three little brushes. Softness against softness.

His heart pounded blood everywhere around his body except his head.

He remembered where he was, but not what he'd been saying. He looked at her eyes, checking for artifice, wondering if she knew how he reacted to her.

'I do not know if this is a good idea.' He spoke barely above a whisper.

'The traps are a bad idea. Wrong. Thinking you own the earth is not correct.' She moved her hand to her side, the arrow tip pointed in his direction.

Traps? That problem was easily solved.

'At the soirée, what did you say to Pottsworth in Greek that was so shocking?' he asked.

She raised her brows.

'Never mind.' He turned away. Walking to the painting, he looked at it. An idyllic scene with a sea in the background. Waves lapped the sand and breezes brought the scent of moisture to him. 'Are you one of the little girls in the painting?' He raised his finger, almost touching the long-dried oils. She had to be the youngest one—the urchin had grown into the woman behind him.

'Miss Cherroll.' He turned back. 'Are you the little one in the picture?'

'It is just a painting. From my homeland.'

'Tell me about yourself.'

'No. You broke my arrow.'

'I beg your pardon.' He turned to her and locked his clasped hands behind his back. This intractable woman and his mother would not get on well at all. Such a foolish thought.

'You do not mean to beg my pardon,' she said. 'You just speak it because it is what you have always said.'

'I'll buy you a score of arrows to replace this one if you merely promise you will not shoot in the direction of a person. I was making a point.'

She waved a hand his direction. 'Keep your arrows. I have many of them.'

'Well, I must be going. You're not quite as I expected. Thank you for your time. I sincerely regret breaking your arrow.' He stopped. 'No, I don't. However, I will see that more are sent your way. Please be careful with them and do not practise archery on my land.'

She didn't speak.

He strode to the door. This woman could not reside with his mother. He did not know how he could have imagined such a thing. But he just did not know what to do. He turned back. He could not go out that door.

'You may visit my land whenever you wish.' He didn't recognise his own voice. His words sounded parched to his ears—the same as when he was little more than a youth and requested his first dance from a woman whose eyes glittered with sensual knowledge.

'I will not shoot near the gamekeeper any more unless he comes too close to me.' Her tone commanded, but underneath there might have been a waver in it. His thoughts raced ahead.

'But be aware he is not a nice man,' she continued. 'He has killed—he has killed them after taking them from the trap. With his foot.' Her voice dipped. 'It is—it is bad. He does not care.'

He turned away so he could concentrate and put his hand on the door frame, sorting his thoughts, listening with his whole body. 'He said you shot at him.'

'Yes. I was watching the traps to see if he'd caught anything. I was going to free the animals.

But he was early. He knew. He saw me and he walked closer and I thought of the rabbits. The rabbits. What man could do that to another living creature? I could not let him near me. I shot at the ground between us. He stopped.'

'It is his job to watch for poachers.' He slid his hand from the wood and moved just enough to hold her in his line of vision.

'Nothing should be trapped like that.'

He asked the other question again. 'What did you say to Pottsworth?'

'The man at the soirée?'

'Yes.'

'I was in the gardens because I did not want to be with the people. I heard him speak to another man and say I was ripe for his hands. I only told him what would happen if he touched me, although I did not say it pleasantly. I knew he could understand my language. Warrington had told us that most men at the soirée had been tutored in Greek.'

'I have heard that your parents are no longer with us,' Rhys asked, tactfully changing the subject.

She touched a finger to the tip of the arrow. 'My *mana* is not alive. I miss her still. I miss her more now than when she died, because she has been gone from me longer.'

He stepped closer, into the whiff of her perfume—until he realised it wasn't only the exotic scent around her, but that of fresh bread. His eyes snapped to hers.

The arrow tip followed his movement, but he didn't care about that.

'Have you been in the…cooking area?' he asked.

She waved her palm the barest bit. 'The staff here works hard. They do not need me watching over them.'

He edged forward and she stepped back. 'You have a dusting of white on your face,' he said.

She reached up, brushing, but missed it.

A duke simply did not reach out and touch a woman's face, particularly upon their first proper introduction. But he did. Warm, buttery sensations flowed inside him. His midsection vibrated, but it was with the outward pressure against his waistcoat. If he looked down, he knew he'd see the tip of the arrow pressed there again. But the broken arrow wasn't so long and it connected their bodies too closely. His blood pounded hot and fast. Blast. This was not good. He'd been too long in the country where he had to take such care because his movements were watched so closely. He needed to get to London soon and find a woman.

She smiled. 'I use the arrows as my chaperon.'

'Perhaps a maid would be better instead?' He reached the slightest bit to nudge the arrow away, but stopped before connecting with the wood. If his hand touched hers, that would be more than he wanted to deal with.

He moved back, freeing himself in more ways than one, and examined his fingers while rubbing the white powder between thumb and forefinger. He was fairly certain it was flour or some such. Something one dusted on the top of cakes or used in producing meals.

'You *have* been in a kitchen.'

'I—' Her chin jutted. 'I do not...visit the kitchen. Often.'

He shrugged. 'I do not mind. It just surprises me.' He lowered his voice. 'You shot at my game-keeper—I don't see why you'd have a problem with going into the servants' area.'

He wasn't in the mood to complain about her

at the moment. But he must keep his thoughts straight. She had put a weapon against his waist-coat. She ran through the woods, tormenting a gamekeeper. She'd traipsed in the kitchen with the servants, chased a child with a broom in the sitting room and probably would not be able to respond quietly in the bedchamber as a decent woman should. He clamped his teeth together.

This woman was as untamed as the creatures she freed. She might be a relation of Warrington's, but one always had an errant relative who did not do as they should.

'I—' She stepped back. And now the broken arrow rested against her bodice. 'I cannot let the rabbits be trapped. I cannot.'

'I suppose I understand.' He did understand. More than she thought. She had a weakness for rabbits and right now his weakness was for soft curves and compassionate eyes. He must clear his head. No matter what it took, he must clear his head.

'I would like to reassure you,' he said, 'that the rabbits will soon be holding soirées among the parsnips and their smiling teeth will be green-stained from all the vegetables they harvest. The traps are to be removed. You do not have to check my lands. No more traps.'

'Thank you.' She nodded. 'It is a relief.'

'In return, I would like very much for you to have tea with my mother tomorrow,' he said. He heard the youth still in his voice. That strange sound. Too much sincerity for the simple question. 'Please consider it. My mother is very alone right now,' he quickly added.

She moved, still grasping the arrow pieces, but her hand rested on the spine of the sofa. She studied his face. 'I don't… The English customs…'

She was going to say no and he couldn't let her. He had to explain.

'My mother will not know you are arriving and I will summon her once you are there. Otherwise she may not leave her room.' His chuckle was dry. 'She likely will not leave her chamber, unless I insist. But as you understand what it is like to miss a person you care for, I would appreciate your spending a few moments speaking with the duchess. Perhaps she will feel less alone.'

She didn't speak.

'My brother has passed recently. My father died almost two years ago, soon after my older sister and her new husband perished in a fire while visiting friends. My mother is becoming less herself with each passing day. She misses her family more with each hour.' He controlled his voice, removing all emotion. 'She is trapped—by memories—and only feels anger and self-pity.'

'I will visit your *mana*.' She spoke matter-of-factly. 'And if she does not wish to leave her chamber, I do not mind at all. I will visit her there.'

He turned, nodding, and with a jerk of his chin indicated the arrow in her hand.

'Would you really hurt me?' he asked.

Something flickered behind her eyes. Some memory he could never see.

'I hope I could,' she said. 'I tell myself every day that I will be strong enough.'

'You wish to kill someone?'

She shook her head, tousled hair falling softly, and for a moment she didn't look like the woman she was, but reminded him of a lost waif. 'No. I wish to be strong enough.'

'Have you ever…hurt anyone?'

She shook her head. 'No. I know of no woman

who has ever killed a man, except my grand-mother, Gigia.'

He waited.

'A man, from a *ploio*. A ship. He was not good. He killed one of the women from our island and hurt another one almost to her death. Gigia gave him drink. Much drink, and he fell asleep. He should not have fallen asleep. Gigia said it was no different than killing a goat, except the man was heavier. My *mana* and uncle were there and they buried him. I do not think the men from the ship cared about losing him. They did not hunt for him long. Gigia gave them wine and we helped them search.'

Rhys took a breath. He'd invited this woman into his home, where his mother would meet her. This woman who seemed no more civilised than the rabbits she wished to protect and yet, he wanted to bury his face against her skin and forget.

'I see.' He frowned, repressing his notice of her as a woman. He certainly did not need to be noting the insignificant things about her.

'From your face, I think you do.' Instantly, her eyes pinched into a tilted scowl, her nose wrinkled. She mocked him. His mouth opened the barest bit. Yes, she'd jested.

'Miss Cherroll,' he spoke, beginning his reprimand, holding himself to the starched demeanour his father had used, one strong enough that even a royal would take notice of it. 'Perhaps my mother could also be of some guidance to you.'

Lashes fluttered. A dash of sadness tinged her words, but the chin did not soften. 'I am beyond repair.'

Bits of words fluttered through his mind, but none found their way to his lips. He took a moment appraising her, then caught himself, tamping down the sparking embers.

This would not be acceptable. He had survived his sister's death. He had survived his father's death. Geoff was gone. The duchess was failing. Rhys's vision tunnelled around him, leaving only images from memory. He would take his own heart from his chest and wring it out with his two hands before he let it close to another person.

He turned his body from her with more command than he would ever unleash on the ribbons from a horse's bridle.

'I did not mean to anger you so…' Her voice barely rose above the drumming in his ears.

'I am merely thinking,' he said.

'You must stop, then. It's not agreeing with you.'

'I think you are the one not agreeing with me.'

'So it has never happened before?'

'Not recently.'

'An oversight?' Wide eyes.

'I can hardly believe you and the countess are sisters.'

'If you think we are brothers, then I do not know what to say.'

'You are—' He gave up. If she could use that same spirit to release his mother's mind from the memories snaring her, it would be worth the risk. He had no other options.

Chapter Three

Bellona took the carriage to the duke's house, frowning each time the vehicle jostled her. Darting through the woods would have been so much easier, but when the gamekeeper's eyes had rested on her the last time, a drop of spittle had escaped his lips when he'd smiled at her. The past had flooded back. She'd thought to put the memories behind her, but they'd returned like a wave, currents underneath tugging at her, trying to pull her to death.

Even now, looking out of the window, she could imagine a face peering at her from behind each tree. The eyes reflecting dark, evil thoughts, or no thoughts at all. Knowledge returned of looking into the pupils and seeing nothing human in a face she'd once seen innocently. Nothing behind those eyes which reasoned or thought, but only the same blankness from the face of an animal intent on devouring its prey.

She'd heard the tales of people being fed to lions. Telling the lion to think about the rightness of not clamping its teeth around her neck would do no good. Reminding the beast that she was merely wishing to live out her life wouldn't change anything. The lion might appear calm, but it would be thinking of only how to get a straighter lunge.

Bellona had known Stephanos before he killed—watched him dance and laugh and work as he'd grown older. Nothing had indicated how one day he would look at her with the harshness of death seeping from him like muck bubbling over the side of a pot left on the fire too long and too hot to pull away with bare hands.

The truth roiled inside her. She'd not escaped to a land where she could let her guard down. Men kept their power within themselves, behind their smiles and their laughter. Like a volcano, the fury could burst forth and take every being in its path.

The day her father had raged at her over a painting she'd accidentally knocked over, she'd known he would have preferred her to be the one broken in the dirt. If he could have traded her to have the painting back on the easel, he would have. He would have rejoiced if she could have been bruised and broken and his painting fresh and new.

Nothing had changed. She'd only lied to herself, hoping she'd be able to forget the past and sleep peacefully again, safe, in this new land.

Even the maid sitting across from her didn't give her the feeling of security she'd hoped. Moving her foot inside her boot, she felt the dagger sheath, reassuring herself.

She braced her feet as the carriage rolled to a stop. A lock of hair tickled Bellona's cheek as she opened the door and stepped out. Pushing the strand aside, she looked at the darkened eyes of the Harling House windows. Sunlight reflected off the glass and a bird flitted by, but the house looked no more alive than a crypt.

The entrance door opened before her foot cleared the top step.

The expanse of space between her and the stairway could have swallowed her former home. She could not blame the duchess for not wanting to leave her chamber. This part of the house, with all its shine and perfection, didn't look as if it allowed anyone to stop for a moment, but to only pass through.

The butler led her to a library which had more personality than she'd seen so far in the house. The pillow on the sofa had been propped perfectly, but one corner had lost its fluff. The scent of coals from the fireplace lingered in the air. The figurines on the mantel had been made at different times by different artists.

One alabaster shape had a translucency she could almost see through. One girl wore clothing Bellona had never seen before. A bird was half in flight. She noted a cracked wing on one angel. The hairline fracture had browned. This hadn't happened recently and been unnoticed. Someone had wanted to keep the memento even with the imperfection.

Then she studied the spines of the books lining the shelves. Some of the titles she could read, but the English letters her oldest sister, Melina, had taught her years ago were hard to remember. She asked the maid and the woman knew less about the words than Bellona did.

The open-window curtains let much light into

the room and the view overlooked where her carriage had stopped. A book lay askew on the desk and another one beside it, plus an uncorked ink bottle. The chair was pulled out and sat slightly sideways. Someone had been sitting there recently, able to see her arrive, and had left a few papers scattered about.

She settled herself to wait, the maid beside her on the sofa. The clock ticked, but other than that nothing sounded. Bellona stood again and noticed the walls. Framed canvases. These were not just paintings, but works of art. When she looked at each piece, she could see something else beyond it—either the thoughts of the person depicted, the way the room had felt that day, or the texture of the object painted.

They were nothing like her father's paintings. She'd had no idea that such wonderful art existed.

Bellona was seated when the duke stepped into the doorway. She'd not heard him, but the flicker of movement caught her eye.

He stood immobile for a minute, like the figurines, but everything else about him contrasted with the gentle figures on the mantel.

She tightened her fingers on her reticule. When

she met his eyes, her senses responded, reminding her of the times she and her sisters had build a fire outside at night on Melos. Sitting, listening to waves and staring at stars. Those nights made her feel alive and secure—the strength of nature reminding her something was bigger than the island.

Lines at the corners of his eyes took some of the sternness from his face, and even though he looked as immovable as the cliffs, she didn't fear him. Possibly because he seemed focused on his own thoughts more than her presence. When he spoke, his lips turned up, not in a smile, but in acknowledgment of his own words. 'I regret to say that my mother informs me she will not be able to join you. She is unwell today.'

Bellona stood, moving nearer to the duke. 'If she is unwell, then I cannot leave without seeing if I might be able to soothe her spirits as I did for my mother. I must see her. Only for a moment.'

The maid rose, but Bellona put out a halting hand and said, 'Wait here.'

A quick upwards flick of his head caused his hair to fall across his brow. He brushed it back. 'I may have erred in inviting you. Perhaps another day… Mother is fretful.'

'When my mother hurt, my sisters and I would take turns holding her hand or talking to her, even if she could not answer for the pain.'

'She's not ill in quite that way, but I think her pain is severe none the less.' Moving into the hallway, he swept his arm out, palm up, indicating the direction. 'The duchess is rather in a poor temper today. Please do not consider it a reflection of anything but her health.'

'My *mana* was very, very ill many days.' Bellona clasped the strap of her reticule, forcing away her memories. She raised the bag, bringing it to his attention. 'I brought some garden scents for Her Grace. I will give them to her. They heal the spirit.'

'If you could only coax a pleasant word from her, I would be grateful.'

Bellona followed Rhys into the room. He gave a quick bow of his head to his mother and the older woman's eyes showed puzzlement, then narrowed when she saw he was not alone. Her frail skin, along with the black dress and black cap, and her severe hairstyle, gave her an appearance which could have frightened a child. She pulled the spectacles from her face, slinging them on to the table beside her. She dropped a book to her lap. The pallor in her cheeks left, replaced with tinges of red.

'Rolleston, I thought I told you I did not want company.' The words snarled from her lips, lingering in the air. A reprimand simmering with anger.

Rhys gave his mother a respectful nod and looked no more disturbed than if her words had been soft. 'Miss Cherroll is concerned that you are unwell and believes she has a medicinal which can help.'

The duchess's fingers curled. 'I must speak with you alone.' She didn't take her eyes from her son. She lifted a hand the merest amount and then her fingers fluttered to the book. 'You may take whatever frippery she brings and then she can leave. I am not receiving visitors. Even the Prince, should he so enquire.'

Bellona stood firm, forgetting compassion. Her *mana* had been gentle even when she could not raise her hand from the bed or her head from the pillow. 'My own *mana* has passed and I have brought the herbs that made her feel better before she left us. And when their scent is in the air, I feel not so far from her. This will soothe your sleep.'

The duchess's brows tightened. 'I sleep well enough. It's being awake I have trouble with. Such as now. Leave.'

Bellona shrugged, looking more closely at the woman's skin. She had no health in her face. Her eyes were red and puffed. 'Then give it to a servant.'

'I will,' she said. She examined Bellona and sniffed. 'Go away and take my son with you. I am not having callers today. Perhaps some time next year. Wait for my letter.'

'I will leave the herbs with you.' Bellona reached for her reticule, opened it and pulled the other knife out so she could reach the little pillow she'd made and stuffed with the dried plants.

'Good heavens,' the duchess gasped. Rhys tensed, his hand raised and alert.

'It is only a knife,' Bellona said, looking at her, flicking the blade both ways to show how small it was. 'After the pirates attacked our ship, I have always carried one.'

'Pirates?' the duchess asked, eyes widening.

'I am not truly supposed to call them that,' Bellona said. 'I did know them, so they did not feel like true pirates, only evil men, and Stephanos was…' She shook her head. 'I am not supposed to speak of that either.'

'You are the countess's sister?' The duchess's voice rose, becoming a brittle scratch. She sat taller, listening.

Bellona nodded. 'We're sisters. She's more English than I am. Our father was not on the island so much when I was older. I hardly knew him. My second sister, Thessa, wanted to go to London. I did not. I like it, but I had expected to always stay in my homeland. But my *mana* died. Melina—the countess—had left and started a new life with her husband here and with Thessa determined that we should leave Melos I had no choice. The evil *fidi* would have— I could not stay on my island without either being killed or killing someone else because I was not going to wed.'

'*You* are the *countess's* sister?'

Bellona smiled at the duchess's incredulous repetition.

'Does *she* carry a knife?'

Bellona shook her head. 'No. I do not understand Melina, but she has the children and she did not have the same ship journey I had. She did not see the things I saw. I really am not supposed to speak of them.' Bellona bunched the things in her hand together enough so she could pull the pillow out.

Rhys reached out. 'I'll hold that,' he said of the knife.

She slipped the blade back inside and pulled the strings of the closure tight. 'I'm fine.' She gripped the ties.

Walking to the duchess, she held out the bag of herbs. Rhys followed her step for step and her stare directed at him did not budge him.

The duchess took the pillow, keeping her eyes on Bellona. She pulled the packet to her nose. 'Different,' she remarked.

'At night, you are supposed to put them near your head and then your dreams are to be more pleasant. I have one. It doesn't work for me. But my *mana* promised it worked for her.'

'I do not think it will work for me either.' The duchess sighed, letting her hand rest in her lap.

'The dreams. The dreams are the worst part,' Bellona said.

The duchess looked at the cloth in her hand, squeezing it, crushing the centre, causing the herbs to rustle. 'I know.'

'Some nights,' Bellona admitted, 'I dream my mother is alive and for those moments she is. But I dream she is the one being attacked by the men and I cannot save her. Those dreams are the worst. And they only grow and grow. I cannot breathe when I wake.'

The duchess nodded, eyes downcast. 'Do not talk of this to me.'

'No one wishes to hear it,' Bellona said sadly. 'I cannot talk about it with anyone. And not to be able to talk with Mana makes it so bad. I did not think I would live when she died, but my sister Thessa started slapping me when I cried. That helped.'

The duchess stared at Bellona. 'How unkind.'

'Oh, no. No,' Bellona insisted. 'I would get angry and I would chase her and chase her and want to hurt her. I will always love her for that.'

The duchess looked thoughtful. 'Child. Perhaps a pat or hug would have been better?'

Bellona squinted. 'That would have done no good. I would have cried more.'

A chuckle burst from Rhys's lips. A light shone in his brown eyes that she'd never seen before in any man's gaze and she could feel the sunshine from it. Her cheeks warmed.

'You might as well sit,' the duchess said. 'You'll make my neck hurt looking up at you.'

While she stood there, unable for the moment to think of anything but the duke's sable eyes, he slipped the reticule from her hand.

'Find me in the library when you leave so I may return this to you,' he said. 'I have some work to finish and I will have tea sent your way.'

He strode out through the doorway.

'Do not dare slap me,' the duchess warned.

'If you need it, I will,' Bellona replied.

'Do not try it. I will not chase you,' the duchess added, studying her rings, before indicating Bellona sit beside her. 'I would send servants.'

Bellona shook her head. 'You've lost enough family members for many slaps...'

The duchess nodded. 'It was not supposed to be

like that. My husband, I accepted he might die. He was much older than I. But my babies. My children. You don't know what it is like.'

'I know something of what it is like.'

'No. You don't.'

'Yes, I do.'

'You can't.'

'Then tell me.'

The duchess tossed the packet aside. 'My daughter had golden hair. I'd never seen a child so blessed…' She continued speaking of her past, taking tea when the maid brought it, and hardly pausing in her memories.

Finally, she looked at Bellona. 'You really must be on your way now. You've stayed much longer than a proper first visit lasts. One just doesn't act as you do.'

'I know. I do as I wish.'

'I can tell you have not had a mother about. You need someone to teach you how to act.'

'No. I do not. This is how I wish to be.'

'That is your first error.' She shut her eyes. 'Now go.'

Bellona rose. 'Thank you for telling me of your daughter.'

The duchess opened her eyes again and waved towards the door. 'I may send a note later requesting you to tea.'

Bellona left, hearing two rapid sniffs behind her. She shut the door, listening for the click. A dark hallway loomed, but she remembered her way to the library.

A few moments later, she found Rhys, sitting at his desk, leaning over papers. Her reticule lay at the side of his work.

'Where's the maid?' Bellona asked, walking into the room.

He twirled his pen between his fingertips as he stood. 'Below stairs speaking with the other servants. I think she is a cousin or sister or some relation to many of the women here.'

Bellona walked to the fabric bag, lifting it and feeling the weapon still inside.

He frowned and shook his head.

She ignored him and moved to the door.

'Wait,' he said. 'I'll send for someone to collect your maid.'

'I will find her. When I step below stairs and look around, servants will appear and the maid will rush to me. If it takes many moments, the housekeeper or butler are at my elbow, asking what I need. It works faster than the bell pull.'

'Perhaps you should leave them to do their jobs.'

'Yes. I should,' she agreed.

He smiled—the one that didn't reach his lips, but made his eyes change in such a way that they became like dark jewels she couldn't take her own gaze from.

'Would you wait here whilst I see how my mother fares?' he said. The words were a question, but he was halfway from the room before she could answer.

'No. I'll be on my way.'

He took two more steps, stopped, and spun around. 'No?' He stood in the doorway, almost taking up the whole of the space.

'You will ask her what I said. How we got on and make sure she is well,' Bellona said. 'I know the answers to that. She mentioned having tea with me again, but she will change her mind.'

'With me, she cannot speak for crying and it has been a year,' he muttered. 'A year... I think the honeysuckle was in bloom when they were taking my brother from the house the last time.'

'It is not quite a year,' Bellona told him, shaking her head. 'Your mother knows the dates. All of them.'

His eyes snapped to her and he pushed his hair from his temple. 'Of my father's and sister's deaths, too?'

'Yes. And her own parents.'

'You must stay,' he said. 'You cannot keep the knife in case someone accidentally gets hurt. But you must stay. I have tried two companions for my mother and she shouted one from the room and refused to speak with the other.'

'No.'

'Miss Cherroll, I fear you do not understand how trapped my mother is in her thoughts and memories. You must stay and see if you can lift her spirits. Otherwise, I fear she will not live much longer.'

She moved, putting the desk between them. 'I cannot.' She had grown up with the myths of her ancestors and tales of men stronger than storms and compelling forces. But she'd experienced nothing beyond the world of her birth until the duke stood before her. He changed the way her heart beat, the way she breathed and even the way her skin felt.

He tensed his shoulders, drew in a breath and his arms relaxed. She looked into his eyes, but lowered her gaze back to his cravat. She could not stay in this house. Not and be near the duke. He held the danger of the pirates, but in a different way. She'd seen her mother's weakness. Not the one taking her body near death, but the one that had locked her into a man's power. The power you could not escape from because it stole a person from the inside.

He strode to the side of the desk, nearer her. 'I will pay you whatever you ask. You can go to the servants' quarters ten times a day if you wish. You can have your run of the grounds. The entire estate will be open to you.'

She held the bag close to her body. 'I will not stay in your house.'

He held his hands out, palms up. 'It's— There's none better.'

'It's not that.'

He continued. 'You can have whatever rooms you wish if you stay as my mother's companion. Take several chambers if you'd like. You can have two maids at your elbows all day. And two at theirs.'

'Be quiet and listen.'

His chin tilted down. His brows rose. 'Yes, Miss Cherroll?'

'I will not stay here.'

He waited, his gaze locked on to hers.

'My sister needs me for the children,' she said.

'I understand completely,' he said, voice agreeing, and stepped to the door. 'You can take my carriage to visit them as often as you wish.' One stride and he would be out of her vision. 'It is not a problem at all. Send your maid in Warrington's carriage for your things. The housekeeper will be with you shortly to help you select a room.'

He was gone by the time she opened her mouth.

She stared at the fireplace. Warrington's estate was not far. She could return to take tea with the duchess every day if she wished; she didn't need to live in this house. Bellona did not care what this man said even if he was a duke. She did not follow Warrington's orders and he was an earl *and* married to her sister.

Slipping the reticule ties over her wrist, she walked to the servants' stairs.

The maid from Warrington's estate was whispering to another woman, but immediately stopped when she saw Bellona and bustled to her, following as they left.

'My cousin did not believe you'd stay such a long time,' the maid murmured. 'My cousin says the duchess will follow her family to the grave before the year's gone. The woman won't leave her chair except to weep in the garden. She gets in such a state that her humours are all gobber'd up. The duke is the only one can settle her at all and even he can't be around all the time.'

Bellona remembered holding her own mother's hand near the end. How cool her fingers were. So thin, and with no strength in them at all. The duchess's hands had felt the same.

'I will visit her again soon. Perhaps tomorrow. I am not certain. I am hopeful the herbs will help her.' She moved to exit the house.

'My cousin said the duke is right soured himself. Servants step wide of him since he became titled. Said he's wearing that coronet so tight it's mashed out everything not duke.'

'A man should take his duties to his heart.'

Her maid puffed a whistle from her lips. 'If he's got any heart left. My cousin says he don't care for nothing except for his duties.'

'He cares for his *mana*.'

'Simply another duty.'

They walked to the carriage. Bellona could feel eyes on her. She forced herself not to search the windows behind her to see if the duke watched her departure. But she knew he did.

She adjusted her bonnet and held the reticule so tightly she could not feel the cloth, but only the handle beneath. 'Tomorrow, when I return, I wish you to stay at my side.'

'What did you do to the duke?'

Bellona's oldest sister, Melina, stood in the very centre of the room. She tapped her slipper against the rug.

'I was nice to his *mana*,' Bellona said, adjusting the quiver at her waist. 'I am going to practise.'

'The duke is here, demanding to see Warrington.'

'Truly?' Bellona asked.

'But War is in London. So the butler said Rolleston demands to see you.'

'I am not at home.'

'I told the butler to tell him we will speak with him. The duke is our neighbour and War's parents and his parents were very close.' She frowned. 'Bellona. You just cannot tell a duke to go away, particularly this one.'

'Warrington does not like him.'

'They are quite fond of each other, in the way men are.'

'I am quite fond of the duke in much the same way,' Bellona said darkly.

'You can't be. You have to pretend to like him. We are ladies—as I must remind you as often as I remind Willa.'

'He wishes for me to move to his estate.'

Her sister's foot stilled. 'You are—imagining that, surely?'

Bellona shook her head. 'He thinks I can help the duchess. His Grace told me I would be her companion. I will visit her, but that is as much as I can do.'

Melina stepped near Bellona. 'She will see no one. It is said she is dying. How ill do you think she is?'

'I do not know. Bones covered in black clothes, with her face peering out. I would not think she would make it through a hard winter or a heavy wash day.' She forced her next words. 'Almost like Mana at the end.'

Melina's hand fluttered to her cheek. 'You must move in with her. It is the thing Mana would want.'

'I do not even want to visit her every day,' Bellona said, shuddering. 'She doesn't have the gentle ways of Mana.'

'You must. Besides, to live at the duke's house…' Melina put a hand at her waist. 'He might have friends visit. And you might meet them. You could learn a lot. The duchess is a true duchess. She could help you. You are not as wild as you pretend. Her Grace could teach you so much if you just watch and learn.'

'I already know how to say *I am not at home.*'

'Sister. A woman. Her husband gone. Her daughter and her oldest son gone, too, and you are asked to help her and you will not. Mana would weep.'

'I will help her. I just do not want to live in the duke's house.' Bellona turned to leave the room, but her sister's quiet voice stopped her.

'You do not like living here, either,' Melina said.

She couldn't tell Melina what she felt about the duke. Stone and towering and dark eyes. She remembered standing at the edge of the cliffs and looking at the ground far beneath, and knowing if she swooned she would fall—feeling brave and scared at the same time. The duke made her want to step closer and yet, if she did, the ground might crumble away. He reminded her so much of the stones she'd seen jutting from the sea and the cliffs.

'I wish to be here with the children. And you.' Bellona pleaded with her sister. 'I do not want to leave the little ones.'

'You'll never have your own babies if you do not learn how to mix with society. A footman will not do for you and you know that. The duchess could introduce you to someone suitable.'

'I went to the soirée. The men smelled like flowers.'

'Pretend you are a bee. You can sting them after you're wed. Not before.'

'I will not pretend to be anything other than what I am.'

'You cannot go back to the way we lived. You must go forward and the duchess could help. She could ease your way into society in a way that I cannot. They hardly accept me.'

Bellona hit her own chest with her fingertip. 'That is where we are different. I do not want to be in society. Bonnets pull my hair. Slippers pinch and corsets squeeze. The flowery world has nothing for me.'

'A husband helps if you want children of your own—and it is best for the child to be born within a true marriage, one with love. You know that as well as I.'

'Even children are not worth a husband. I have a niece and two nephews. They are my babies.'

'You are hiding. From everything. From the past and the future. The duchess needs you. You know how long the nights can be after a death and we had each other. We had the three of us, you, me and Thessa. You are just like our *pateras*, our father.' Melina crossed her arms.

'That is an evil thing to say. I am surprised your tongue does not choke you for forcing those words past it.'

'You are like Father. Of the three of us, you are the most like him,' her sister continued, pacing the room. 'Even Mana said so, just not where you could hear her.'

Bellona raised her voice. 'I am not like him.'

'When we angered him, he would go paint.' Melina swaggered with her shoulders as she walked. 'When he did not want to do something, he would paint.' She stopped and mused. 'Did you ever notice how paint brushes are shaped almost like little arrows?'

'You're wrong to speak so. I practise archery. I do not live for it.'

'Even the way you stick out your chin. Just like him.' She jutted out her jaw in an exaggerated pose.

'You always say that when you have no better words to fight with.'

Melina returned her stance to normal. 'I cannot believe my own sister has no kindness in her heart for a woman with no daughters or sisters.'

Bellona raised her chin. 'I will tell the duke I will stay a short time with his mother. It will be better than listening to you. *You* are the one like Father, insisting on having your way.'

'Only when I am right.' She examined Bellona. 'Please arrange your hair before you see the duke.'

'Of course.' Bellona patted both sides of her head, achieving nothing.

'Much better.' Melina paused. 'I expected you to pull a strand loose.'

'I thought of it.' Bellona sighed. But the duke probably wouldn't appreciate it.

Melina reached to Bellona and pushed her youngest sister's hair up at the sides, moving the pins around. 'There. Now you look as well as me.'

Bellona walked past her. 'Now you see why I do not show my face in society.'

Melina's chuckle followed Bellona from the room out into the hallway.

When Bellona reached the sitting room, the duke's gaze swept over her. The rock stood, un-yielding.

Even with a scowl on his face, she still wanted to look at him. The thought irritated her.

'I will return to your house,' she said curtly.

The flicker behind his eyes—the intake of breath. She would have imagined he'd just been hit, except his face softened much the same as Warrington's did when her sister walked into the room. The duke inclined his head in acknowledgment. 'It will mean a lot. To the duchess.'

Chapter Four

Bellona arrived at Harling House the next morning and the housekeeper appeared at her side almost instantly. The woman had a sideways gait, but moved forward so fast Bellona hurried to follow.

After being shown a chamber whose ceiling would need a heavy ladder to reach, she mused, 'I could put an archery target in here and practise without leaving the room.'

'We have no targets which are suitable for use inside.' The woman's face pinched into a glare that would stop any servant.

Bellona gave the woman the same look Warrington had given her countless times. 'I suppose if I asked the duke, he would arrange something.'

'Of course,' the housekeeper said. 'This was his

childhood room. Let me know if you need anything.' Then she darted away.

The room had the same scent of the storage rooms in Warrington's house and made her miss the sea air. No flounces and lace adorned it. Instead there were walls the colour of sand and darker curtains that required strength to move. She wondered if every trace of the boy had been removed, or if the room had never had anything of him in it.

The huge chamber didn't feel like home, but she was tired of looking for Melos in everything she saw and not finding it.

She placed her bow in the corner. Her mother would not have believed such a large room existed for one person to sleep in.

Someone knocked at the door. A maid, who looked almost the same as the one from Warrington's house, suggested Bellona go to the library to meet with His Grace. Curiosity and the desire to see more of the house pulled her straight to him.

'Miss Cherroll. Welcome,' the duke greeted her. Quiet words, almost cold, but his quick turn from the window, and one step in her direction, caused a flutter in her stomach.

The last year of his life might have been no easier than the duchess's, she realised. If Bellona had lost either of her sisters to death, the world would have become dark and bleak and suffocating.

He surprised her by the merest corner of his lips turning up at the edge. 'The maid who is unpacking for you will store your arrows and knives in a safe place. She will direct the footman to bring them to you each time you need to practise marksmanship and he will take them when you return to the house and make sure they are properly cared for.'

'You are most thoughtful of my property,' she said, thankful he did not know of the knife in her boot.

'Of course.'

'Then let us discuss payment for my stay.'

'Certainly.'

'I want another two score of arrows. The best that can be made. I also require a dagger perfectly balanced. And I must have a pistol that will fit my hand and someone to show me how to clean, load and shoot it. I have heard there is a Belgian hidden-trigger boot pistol in which the trigger does not fall down until it is cocked. I would like to see one of those. You can have someone bring selections of these things for me to choose from.'

'Ah.' The word wasn't clearly formed from his lips, but was more of a sound. 'No duelling swords? Fencing lessons? Cannons?' he asked, blinking once each time he named a weapon.

'Cannons are heavy, and—' she touched the bridge of her nose '—so are swords. A man with long reach can best me any day. I could not practise enough.'

'Miss Cherroll. Any necessities will be furnished to you and they do not include guns, knives, arrows or swords. You will accept the usual payment from me—enough to buy all the armaments you need and Warrington can help you choose the weapons after you leave. I will refrain from paying you until then because I realise what you might do with the funds. Since you do not like to see game injured, I fear what you might plan to do with any weaponry. You will not have such items in my home.' He stood with feet planted firm. 'I myself do not even keep them at hand.'

'No duelling pistols?' She raised a brow.

He looked aside and absently moved the pen at his desk on to the blotter. 'Yes, I have them, but they were gifted to my father and they are locked away. There is not even powder for them.'

'Swords?'

'Fencing is something we all had to learn.'

'Where are the swords?'

'I believe they are locked in a case in the portrait gallery. The butler has the keys and he will not be sharing them. With anyone.' His voice rumbled from his chest. 'I think you forget you are here to see my mother, a woman of trifling size who is stronger with her glares than most people are with their body.'

'Do you have daggers? Arrows? Flintlocks?'

His head moved enough so she couldn't see his eyes, then, before she could protect herself, he directed his full attention at her, consuming her with it. 'What do you fear?'

'Not having weapons.'

He shook his head. 'I am sure there is a bow and arrows somewhere. I don't think the bow has a string any more. No daggers.' Still standing alongside the desk, he splayed his fingers and gave the top several hard raps. 'Miss Cherroll, you do not have to concern yourself that someone will attack you in my home. I have footmen and stablemen no one would dare confront. I have had no violence on my estate, ever. That will not change while you are here. I realise you had a harrowing experience on your ship journey here and not a pleasant meeting with my gamekeeper, but you are now in what is the safest place in the world. My home.' For a second, he spoke with his expression. Relief. Thankfulness. 'I must let you know I was pleased to see you arrive.'

She didn't think any man, ever, had looked at her with so much hope on his face.

'You are in more danger from a fall on the stairs than anything else,' he added.

Or a fall from a cliff.

'I am exceedingly angry at the duke for bringing you here,' the duchess said to Bellona.

The duchess wore a fichu tucked into her bodice and the sleeves of her obsidian gown almost swallowed her hands.

The older woman had a maid at her side, holding a stack of four books. 'You must know that I cannot take my anger out on him, so it will land about your ears.' She pulled out one book and waved the servant away.

'I am not happy with him either.' Bellona sat in the matching chair. 'I will probably share that with both of you.'

The duchess frowned. 'Why are you not pleased with him?'

'He took my bow and a small dagger.'

'Your mother should have taught you better.'

'Why? I did not need to be better on Melos and I am fine enough to sit in a duke's home.'

She duchess snorted, just as Bellona's own mother might have. She held out the book. 'You may read to me.'

'I would rather talk.'

'I would rather hear what someone else wrote.' The woman thumped the book and held it out again.

'I am not going to read to you.'

'You have no choice. I have asked you to. I am your elder.'

This was not going to get any better. Perhaps his mother would summon the duke to complain about Bellona. That would tip his tea kettle over.

Bellona saw no reason to explain her struggle to read the English language to the duchess.

'It would indeed be an honour for you to read to me,' the duchess said, changing her methods, 'and might dispose me more kindly towards you.'

'I do not mind if you are not nice to me.'

'Well, I do. My prayer book is the only thing that gives me hope. My eyes hurt from reading it and the letters blur. The maid cannot read and I do not wish to replace her, though I might be forced to because I need someone who can see better than I.'

'You may replace me,' Bellona said. 'I do not read English words.'

'But your sister is a countess. And everyone knows she is from the best society in your home country.' The duchess looked at the book. 'So do not feed me such nonsense that you cannot read. Your family would not educate one sister and leave another unschooled. I have received notes from your sister several times. One she wrote when she visited me and I could not see her, so she must write them herself.'

'I am not my sister.'

The duchess shook her head. 'You do not read?'

'I know the English letters. Melina read our father's letters to Thessa and me many times and I could understand most of the written words. It has been a long time since I have looked at words, though. I do not like them on paper. I prefer a person's lies when I can see their face.'

'I do beg your pardon.' Words spoken from training. 'I cannot begin to imagine what my son was thinking to enlist a companion who could not read to me.'

'I do not dance or do any of the other things society women do, except archery. It is my favourite thing next to my niece and nephews. I sew, but only because one must have clothes. I do not like the nice stitches to make flowers. I like the strong sewing. I am from my *mana's* world.'

'I am from my mother's world as well,' the duchess said. 'Every day we had our hair dressed to perfection, our skin just so. We could not move if it might disturb our clothing. I sometimes hated it, but now I see the value of it. One must give others something to aspire to.' She leaned towards Bellona. 'Take a note of that. Because you are a companion only and from some foreign land, I will tolerate some folly on your part.'

'I am thankful I will not have to tolerate any on your part.'

'Child, I say again that I do not know what the duke was thinking to ask you to stay with me.'

'He was thinking I would be a slap for you.'

The duchess showed no outward reaction. 'Rolleston is making a good duke. He has always been a good son. Although he might have erred this one time.'

'He might have.'

'Do not be so quick to agree with me. Surely you have some accomplishments? What entertainments are you versed in? Recitations? Music? Song?'

Bellona smiled, tilted her head to the side and said, 'Would you like to hear a song the English sailors taught me? I am not sure of its meaning.'

The duchess's neck moved like a snake rising to eye prey, trying to get situated for the closest tender spot. 'Oh, my dear, I think you know full well whatever that song meant and I am not daft enough to fall for that one.'

'I already told you that I have no accomplishments,' Bellona insisted flatly.

'How do you spend your days?'

'Archery. The forest. I spend hours with my niece—I miss the little one. Her joy makes me laugh.'

The duchess opened the book. 'I know what it is like to miss someone.'

'You spend too much time with books,' Bellona said. 'If they make your eyes hurt it is not good for you. Poison in the stomach makes it hurt. The head is the same. Your eyes are telling you that you must not read.'

'Oh. Thank you for informing me.' The duchess digested the words.

Rhys walked into the room, greeting them both, a book under his arm. His eyes had a faraway look, but he settled into a chair and asked them to continue as they'd been because he needed to study the accounts.

But even though he stared at the volume in his hands, Bellona felt his thoughts were on her much the same as a governess might have her back to the children, but be aware of their every move. She felt the need to test her idea and knew she would before the conversation was over.

The duchess leaned towards Bellona. 'How did you learn to speak English?'

'My father was English.' Her father was alive, but he was dead as far as she was concerned. 'He insisted we only speak English when he was home. He made us recite to him. Yet he knew Greek well and if we spoke Greek in anger, we were punished. He is… It is hard to talk of him.' She sniffed and lowered her face. That would discourage any questions of him.

'At least you speak two languages.'

'Some French, too.'

The older woman nodded. She appraised Bellona. 'Did you leave behind family in Greece?'

'None close,' Bellona said. 'I have never wed. Marriage. It makes a woman change. And cry. Men are only good for lifting and carrying, much like the bigger animals that do not think well.'

The duke didn't respond to her deliberate prod.

'Well, yes, some of them can be,' the duchess admitted. 'But marriage is not all bad. Children make you change and cry, too. I do not know what I would have done without my own.' A wisp of a smile landed on the duchess's face. 'My three children were the best things that ever happened to me.' Then her expression changed with the memory and she began to sniff.

Bellona searched her mind for a distraction. 'At least I will not have to marry—like His Grace will have to before he gets much older.'

His mother's sniffle turned into a splutter. Bellona didn't have to turn her head to know where the duke was looking. She pretended to look like her own thoughts were far away.

'Yes. He will marry. Of course,' the duchess said. 'But that is not for you to discuss, Miss Cherroll.'

'I hoped that you would call me Bellona.'

'That is a strange name.'

'I was named for the Roman goddess of war. I remember that every day.'

'Perhaps you should put it from your mind. She doesn't sound like someone appropriate to be named after.'

Bellona shook her head. 'I'm proud of it. To get to England, I had to flee in the night. Thessa's suitor chased us.' She had slept though the final confrontation, unaware of all about her. Earlier, she'd fallen asleep with the rhythm of the ship and woken when her sister had shaken her awake. Thessa's rapid voice had fallen back into the Greek language while she'd told Bellona how the pirates from their homeland had followed the ship, planning to force the women into marriage.

She thought of what Melina had told her of Almack's—a marriage mart, her sister had said.

'Have you ever been pursued, Your Grace?' She turned to Rhys. He did have her direct in his vision, watching her without censure, but as if she were a very interesting…bee, and he wasn't afraid of getting stung.

'Not by a pirate,' he said. 'Only by a very unhappy bull.'

'I'm sure you could escape.'

'I have managed thus far.' He glanced at the book again, but even with his eyes averted, she could still feel his attention on her.

'My poor Geoff,' the duchess said, 'he was once chased by an angry dog and I thought—' Her lip quivered and she reached for a handkerchief.

Bellona did not want the discussion to return to sadness. A slap with words worked as well as one across the face. 'Reading does appear a good way to waste time. A way for people with no chores to be idle.'

The duchess's sniff turned into a choke.

She had the older woman's full attention and

Rhys's book looked to have turned humorous. For little more than a blink, their eyes met. Sunshine suffused her and didn't go away when he examined the book again.

After his morning ride, Rhys heard the clock as he strode into his home—the same peals he'd heard his whole life. The sounds didn't change, but if they clanked about in his ears, he knew the world felt dark. For the first time in a long time, the peals were musical.

His mother had spoken to him repeatedly about the *heathen*, informing him that the miss was beyond help. Each time she'd recounted the discussion between the two, her voice rose in anger. Not the bare mewl it had been before.

Finally, she'd left her room of her own volition to come and find him to complain with exasperation of having to deal with this motherless child who'd been left too long to her own devices. She'd wondered how he could possibly expect his own mother to correct such a tremendous neglect of education in the woman. 'It would take years, years,' she'd explained as she walked away, shaking her head.

He'd quashed his immediate urge to go to Bellona and pull her into his arms, celebrating with her the rebirth of his mother's life.

Thoughts of Bellona always caused his mind to catch, wait and peruse every action or word concerning her a little longer. The miss did something inside him. Like a flint sparking against steel. Made him realise that his heart still beat, his life still continued and that some day he'd be able to walk into a room and not be aware of all that was missing, but see what was actually there.

He turned, moving towards the archery target that now stood in the garden beneath the library window.

Disappointment edged into him when he did not find her near the targets she'd had placed about. He went inside the house, thinking of her hair and the way she reminded him of pleasures he did not need to be focusing on right now. As he passed the library door, he heard pages rustling.

He stepped into the library. Stopped. Stared.

She was lying on his sofa. Around her face, her hair haloed her like a frazzled mess, more having escaped from her bun than remained. This was the moment he would have walked to her, splayed his fingers, held her cheeks in both hands and kissed her if…

Ifs were not for dukes, he reminded himself.

She rested stockinged feet on the sofa. Her knees were bent and her skirt raised to her calves while she frowned into a book. His mind tumbled in a hundred directions at once, all of them landing on various places of her body. The woman should not be displaying herself in such a way.

Courtesans did not act so…relaxed and improper. Even the women he'd visited in London— ones without modesty—would have remained much more sedate in daylight hours.

But he remembered his manners. Perhaps he'd erred, not she. She had not heard him enter the room. He took a quiet step back because he did not want to mortify her by letting her know he'd seen her sprawled so indelicately.

But then he saw the books. A good dozen of *his* most precious books scattered about her. One was even on the carpet. How could she? It was one thing to trespass, another to shoot an arrow at a man, but…the books…

Books were to be treated as fine jewels— no—jewels could be tossed about here and there without concern—books were to be treasured, removed from the shelves one at a time, carefully perused and immediately returned to their place of honour. They were made of delicate materials. A nursemaid would not toss a baby here or there and books deserved the same care.

She looked up, swung her stockinged feet to the floor as she sat, dropped the book at her side. Her foot now sat on top of a boot, her skirt hem covering it, as she lowered her hand towards the remaining footwear.

Modesty. Finally. 'You may dress.' He turned his back on her slightly, so he would not see if her skirt flipped up while she put on those worn boots. He would have thought Warrington would have done better by her. He would put in a word to see that she had decent indoor shoes.

He heard a thump and the sound of pages fluttering.

'I cannot read this—this—'

From the corner of his eye, he saw the title of one of his father's favourite volumes disgracefully on the floor. He pressed his lips together and gave himself a moment. 'Why are you in the library since you disregard reading?' he finally asked.

'Your mother has insisted I pick a book, study it,' she muttered, 'and be able to speak about it. She is punishing me.'

He heard the sound of her fidgeting about and then silence. He turned.

She glared at him, but she only had one boot on and she held the other in her lap, her right hand resting on it.

'I do not think I like your mother,' she continued. 'The duchess told the servant who stores my bow I am not to have it. The servants are afraid to disobey her.' She stared at him. 'The duchess said it is good for me to learn to read English. That I should not be *unleashed on society* until I have better ways. I am fine with that, as long as they are my ways. I told her I do not wish to be *unleashed on society.*'

'The books?' With his hand, he indicated the floor.

'They have too many pages and not enough drawings.' She frowned. 'Melina taught me the words when I was a child and when I discovered I was not reading Greek, but English, I hid the books. I have only read a few letters since then and they are never more than three pages long.

This—' she stared at him as if he had written the offending length '—this has so many words I do not know how the man did not run out of them.'

She picked up the book, holding it in her left hand and shaking it in his direction. For a moment he forgot to be outraged. Her bodice bounced enticingly.

He pushed his thoughts in a safer direction.

He remembered how she'd helped his mother. He took a breath. He must remind himself that the duchess's health was more important than any book that had been in the family for near a century. Even one with hand-inked illustrations which Miss Cherroll had just waved about without any care.

He switched to a ruse she had used, turning it in her direction. 'Books are actually only meant for the upper classes. Only peers should have them. They are too much for the common folk to appreciate.'

'I agree. Only peers. Common folk have no time for reading. I sold both our books to a sailor,' she said. 'He knew how to read. It did not make him smarter, though, because he paid a good price for nothing.'

Her eyes sparked with a challenge that bolted inside his stomach.

She perched on the sofa like a preening bird and let the books rest about her like so many twigs.

'I suspect his purchase was not as much—' he eyed the books '—as my father and grandfather and I spent for those.' He walked to the sofa and picked up a tome from the floor. 'So when you are not casting jabs about the books, what do you really think of them?'

'They are too much to read. But very dear to sell. I was so happy when I discovered that.' Lifting one volume, she put it atop another. 'I would not damage such costly items.'

'That almost reassures me.' Rhys kept his face unmoved. 'What books did you sell?'

She held her chin high. 'I do not remember. But I remember the necklace we bought for our *mana*. She had it on when she died. We claimed our father sent it with a ship.'

Rhys imagined the three girls giving the gift to their mother.

'Your mother,' she continued, 'says I have been addled because I lost my own *mana* so young. She said I misled her about the pirates trying to capture our ship. She thought I lied about every-thing.' Bellona's lips firmed and she shook her head precisely.

'So I sang the sailors' song to her. She believes me now.' She lowered her eyes. 'I should not have done it. I do not like that song. It is *erotikos*.'

Damn. The song had probably singed the pages of his mother's prayer book and he would be hear-ing about it the rest of his life and on into eter-nity if he made it that far. He waved a palm about. 'You do not sing improperly—not to a duchess. My *mother*. Miss Cherroll, you are to be a com-panion, not—'

She sighed, shut her eyes and shook her head. 'I do not think she truly minded. I only wish I did not do it because it gave her a reason to trick me into looking at these infernal books.'

Dark eyes, more like some woodland pet than a woman's, took him in. She didn't say one word, but argument was in that gaze. He'd never seen eyes like those. His midsection jolted again and he looked at the floor to push his attention else-where.

In one stride he picked up a book and held it in both hands. 'This is Alexander Pope.'

'Well, that tells me nothing.'

Then he saw her eyes turn to the book at her feet. He gasped, and pulled it from the floor. 'You cannot place *The Life and Adventures of Robinson Crusoe* on the rug. I have read it three times.'

'I didn't like the first page. Warrington has a copy. My sister read the first words and I left the room.'

His head twitched to indicate the book. 'You simply cannot judge it by the—'

She contradicted him with her eyes. 'Why not? The first page of the book is about the rest of the story.'

'This one is about a man who lives on an island and learns to make do with what he has, and he is very happy because no women are about. Just cannibals.'

She snorted. 'I do not see how that makes fine reading. My sisters and I lived on an island.'

'He was marooned.'

'You mean he could not leave if he wanted. How sad...' She smiled. 'And is England not an island? I cannot return to Melos, which is also an island. Melina and Warrington refuse to let me go back home because of the Greek war for independence and they fear pirates.' She snorted again. 'And then there is the man on Melos who wished to marry me, but…one of us would not have survived the wedding night.'

'You were asked to wed?' He studied her, and, yes, he could see how a man might say anything to get her into his bed. She sat, wiggling that one stocking-clad foot, like an asp, tempting him to partake of forbidden fruit.

'If I had not hated him,' she said. 'I might have thought of it. I did not care for him and he had the mean eyes.'

'Marriage is an honourable state.'

'Your mother would be surprised to hear that from your lips. You should have married long before now. She has feared many times you would do as your father did and near destroy everything dear.'

'My father?' Rhys struggled over the words. 'My mother held my father in the highest esteem.'

Bellona nodded. 'Of course. But it was hard for her to love him at first.' She grimaced. 'When your brother was born and your mother became ill, your father stayed in London while she remained here. When he left, he told her he was a duke first, a man second and a father third. He did not mention being a husband.'

He heard her words. He saw her lips moving.

'Do not joust at me. My father is dead,' he said. 'His memory is sacred. I will not have you disgrace him.'

'Your mother said everyone knew. She felt abandoned. When she became strong again, she went to London and reminded him she was his wife.'

He picked up the volumes and placed them back on the shelf while he controlled his temper. Once the books were shelved he turned to her.

The rumours said Bellona's father had died young and left a wife behind who'd been descended from the Greek upper classes. Perhaps the sister Warrington had married was descended from some Aphrodite-like ancestor, but this one was from the wrong side of the clouds. It did not matter to him if she had been born on a gilded mountain-top. Once he discussed her with his mother and repeated what false tales Bellona had just spread about his father, the woman would be gone. He would have the carriage readied and escort her to it himself. A woman could not disparage the duke's father in his own home and expect to remain.

'Nothing my father ever did was disrespectful to my mother.'

Her eyes widened. Pity directed at him. He frowned.

'I must have misheard,' she said finally.

'I am certain you did.'

She glanced away. 'I am certain I did, too. Perhaps I do not understand English as well as I think.'

When she turned her head, he saw a flash of gold at her ears. His mother's earrings. He swallowed. He had unleashed the worst sort of woman into his very home.

'Your mother fears leaving her rooms,' she said. 'She knows when she does you will think she can manage on her own and abandon her for London just as your father did.'

'I would not *abandon* my mother.'

She looked down. 'She knows you would not mean to. It is your duty. She understands.'

'You are… I am… That is unacceptable. You are a liar of the worst sort. You will return to Whitegate.'

Perhaps that would be safest for them all. For her—because if she discovered how society would truly perceive her, she might be crushed. For his mother—because she did not need a woman near who would take her jewels while spreading lies. And himself—for a reason he did not wish to consider.

Bellona's jaw clenched. She jumped to her feet, and moved to the bell-pull, her boot under one arm. 'I will send for a carriage. I will not have to read at Warrington's house.'

He could *not* believe it. His bell-pull. In his house!

'Cease,' he commanded, hand out in a halting gesture. No one except he or his mother touched this bell-pull. And he would not let this thief leave with his mother's jewellery.

She stopped, still clutching the boot. 'I'm leaving. Even the walls are sad here. No one laughs. No one plays. It is all reading and embroidery and dressing of hair and clothes.' Her nose went up.

'I will see that you do leave. A carriage will be readied.' He waved an arm. 'Come with me. I want my mother to know what you have said about my father.'

'You first,' she said impudently.

He did not want her to dart away with the earrings. 'I insist. You first. I am a gentleman.'

'Then do as I wish.'

He would not stand and argue with her. 'Do not dare run for the door.'

'You tell me to leave and then tell me not to go.'

He stepped forward, but kept an awareness of her and held out his arm for her to precede him. She rolled her eyes, but flounced from the room.

He gave a quick rap on his mother's door and strode inside. She sat in her chair, but instead of the prayer book... He stepped closer. Fashion plates.

She glanced up at the two of them, but then returned to the books. 'Oh, Rhys. I do not know how this poor child will ever be saved from herself and I have such a short time to mend her because I am going to send her packing any day now. She does not listen. She is worse than you are and I never thought anyone could be worse than you...'

He stared at her.

She clucked her tongue, examining the engravings. 'I send her a maid to fix her hair and she complains. I gave her gold earrings and had to insist she wear them. Gold. What woman thinks gold is unsuitable?' She held up a plate so he could see. 'Child…' She held the drawing so Bellona could see. 'This is the gown I had made for me in blue to match my eyes. I don't want yellow for you, but I cannot decide.'

'I do not need any new clothing.' Bellona's words were clipped. 'I am leaving.'

'Nonsense,' his mother commanded. Then his mother's eyes caught on Bellona's boots. She gasped, eyes wide. 'Un-for-giv-able. Where are the slippers I found for you?'

'I hate them. They pinch. I cannot wear them.'

Rhys watched. He just watched.

His mother's fingers shook so that the papers in her hands made a fluttery sound. 'Your stockings are *dirty*. Were you raised in a stable?'

'Above one.' That goddess nose tilted up. Rhys thought she might not have any of the society airs about her, but her nose and eyes could manage well enough and needed no lessons.

'Now. Go. Put on fresh stockings and get those slippers and return to me. I wish to see you wearing them now.'

'You are just like Gigia.' Bellona frowned. She looked at Rhys. 'She is just like Gigia. I will never drink too much around her.'

'Then you were very lucky if you knew someone like me, but obviously you did not pay her enough heed,' his mother said. Her eyes tightened on Bellona. 'And you are just like my daughter was—may the angels hold her tight in their embrace. I thought never to get her wed to the right man.'

Bellona pursed her lips and blew. 'I do not need anyone to find a husband for me.'

'Bellona. I cannot believe it.' The duchess sat, closing her eyes. 'What did I tell you about being a lady?' She shook the paper towards Rhys. 'And you are in the company of a male.'

'But he is only the duke and has already tossed me out.' She shook her head. 'I must return to Whitegate. You must give me my bow and arrows so I can leave.'

Only the duke? Rhys tried not to be offended. That was a phrase he had never heard in his life.

'I forbid it,' the duchess said firmly. 'You are running amok and you have no mother to train you. You cannot leave until I tell you to. You will never have that bow and arrows if you do not do as I say.' His mother turned to him. 'Rhys. She cannot leave until I tell her.'

'I am not running amok,' Bellona said. 'I am doing as I please.'

'Exactly the same thing.' His mother turned to him. 'Tell her, Rhys. Tell her she cannot leave.'

'I believe she should,' he said stiffly.

'Nonsense. Why, no man of any higher level than a nightsoil collector would give her a glance as she is. And she has good skin and rather a star-tlingly good singing voice. I am teaching her a hymn.'

Rhys took in a breath. 'Is that what she sings to you, Mother?'

'Why, yes.' Her voice calmed and her shoulders relaxed. 'Along with a few old songs from her country.' She looked at Bellona. 'Run along and change those stockings, and hurry back because I want you to decide on a colour.'

'I will not hurry,' Bellona said, leaving.

He cleared his throat, giving the wench a chance to pull the door shut behind her.

He must inform his mother about the tales. Then he would explain to this miss the reper-

cussions of disrespecting a duke's household—
only a duke—and send her packing that very day.

Rhys forced himself to soften his words. He did
not want his mother upset more than she must be.
'She is a talebearer.'

'Nonsense,' her mother said. 'I am quite sure
she is honest. She told me the brocade in the sitting room is quite the wrong colour.'

'I am not talking of fashion. I am talking of the
deeper qualities of a person.'

His mother's eyes widened. 'She has some deep
qualities. They are just deeply common.'

'She has said—things about Father. Even suggesting he might have not seen you for a time
after Geoff's birth when you were ill.'

This time his mother put her hand over her open
mouth. Her eyes fluttered.

Rhys knew right where this was heading. Bellona would soon be waiting at the door for the
carriage to be pulled around.

The duchess clasped her fingertips as if her
hands were cold and then whispered, 'I do not
know how I am going to teach her what is proper
to speak of and what is to remain behind closed
doors. A servant could have overheard. Not that

I'm sure they… Well, you know how things get remembered like that.'

Rhys drew in a deep breath, studying the truth on his mother's face. His father? His father had behaved so callously? 'Mother. Did my father…?'

'Well…Rhys, I thought perhaps your father had mentioned it to you before his death, or even Geoff. I know Geoff and your father spoke of it. I heard them. So I assumed you knew as well.' She wilted against the sofa back. 'I have just had so much on my mind. It is hard to think of everything.'

His mouth opened. Bellona had moved into his house and discovered family truths even *he* did not know of. And his mother was discussing these things with her instead of with him.

He took the matching chair.

Then his mother straightened and pulled her handkerchief from inside her sleeve and refolded the fabric, her eyes on the cloth.

'Rhys, you understand…' She looked up. 'Geoff had just been born and it was a difficult birth. He was… I was… He cried so much and the nurse-maids didn't know what to do. My baby was small and didn't want to grow at first. I felt I'd failed my husband. Your father and I did not always get on well. I may have…been harsh in some of the things I said. Your father was angry because I could not think of anything but the babe, so he left me. But then, Geoff started getting bigger and I became better and your father returned home, after a nudge.'

She daubed the handkerchief to her eyes. 'That was a difficult time. And to think I would eventually lose them both… So near to each other.'

Rhys didn't speak.

'I had all a woman could hope for.' Her eyes filled with tears.

'My father…' He shook his head.

'Rhys, please do not tell me you are such an innocent. Sometimes, things happen.'

He stood again. 'I am not an innocent, Mother.' He straightened the sleeves of his coat. 'I am just surprised that I never knew of this. That no one told me. It's… You know how Father was. He was the perfect duke. Always.'

'Yes.' She straightened her shoulders. 'He was. And you know, Rhys—in some respects—nothing is forbidden to a duke.'

'Miss Cherroll—a woman we hardly know tells

me of this.' He shook his head in disbelief. 'How could you share this with her and not with me?'

'She lost her own mother and has had so many trials. I understood much of the pain she felt and I told her. The words just escaped my lips.'

Since Bellona had been correct about that, perhaps she had spoken truth on one other thing, too. 'You do not have to worry about my abandoning you, Mother, even when you become hale and hearty once more.'

'I know, Rhys. I understand completely. I know you would never wish to leave me.' She exchanged the fashion plates for the prayer book on the table beside her chair. Running her fingers over the lettering on the cover, she sighed. 'But, Rhys, if you do not… If you do not go to London and find a wife, you will be abandoning your title. Your duty to your family. Your brother's heritage. You have no choice.'

She raised her face. 'I understand you must go. I do not want you to marry a wife only to make her unhappy. Togetherness in marriage, I believe, is formed by people who have the same background and the same interests. You must marry a woman you have something in common with.

One who shares your dreams for the dukedom and can be at your side, a helpmate. I wish the same marriage for you that your father and I had, except, of course, for the one year when we could not stand the sight of each other.'

'I know what I have to do.' He did. A wife. House of Lords. A son to pass the title to. It did not have to be written in stone to be engraved in his head. Geoff's heritage.

'It's harder for a duke with all his duties and responsibilities and the stewardship of the estate,' she said. 'And women notice the duke, Rhys, rather than the man, as I am sure you are aware.'

Rhys remembered the last soirée he had attended with Geoff. The women had fluttered around Geoff, and the brothers had jested privately afterward about the peerage being far more handsome than any visage. The next event Rhys attended after Geoff's death, the perfume had choked him, the expanse of pale flesh had burned his eyes and the high laughter had been like spears in his ears.

Without Geoff, it was not humorous any more.

The door opened and Bellona walked in, wearing both boots and carrying the slippers. 'They bite my toes,' she insisted. 'I cannot wear them.'

'I know you must have slippers at Warrington's estate,' the duchess said. 'Send for them or trim off a few toes.'

Bellona put the shoes on the floor beside her. 'I will be considering which toes I can spare.'

'Of course,' the duchess murmured, 'you do want your little niece, Willa, to be proud of her aunt…'

The tousled head darted up and her eyes could have flailed the duchess. 'I do have some slippers my sister gave me. I suppose I could send for them and a gown that matches.'

'I have a tutor planned for you tomorrow in the ballroom. Do not be late. He will not.'

'I will not dance. I have a pain in my foot.'

The duchess spoke to Rhys. 'She can practise archery for hours. A few moments' dancing will not hurt her.'

'I will not,' Bellona said again, calling the duchess's attention back to her.

'It would mean a lot to your sister to know you are settled with a nice vicar or man of affairs. Perhaps a soldier who has returned and needs a wife to care for him? Your sister might even wish for a niece or nephew of her own. Someone her own little ones can call cousin. If you do not dance with a suitor… He will see you as thinking yourself above him and dance with someone more…pleasant.'

She held her fingers up as if dusting crumbs from them.

'I will dance the country dance if you insist.'

'Send a servant to me and I will give the order for your bow to be returned,' the duchess said.

'My foot is hurting more now and the pains are moving up to my head,' Bellona said, turned and left.

Rhys saw the jutting chin as she stepped his way, but as she passed by him, the tiny wink nearly did him in.

The door crashed behind her.

The wench would be the death of him.

'I would not say this in front of her, but if she carries on like this, that heathen child will never even be worthy of a tradesman as a wife. It's just…she did lose her mother, as she is *constantly* reminding me,' the duchess grumbled to Rhys. 'I cringe to think what would have become of your sister had it not been for my firm hand.' The duchess stared ahead. 'This one is more like your father's mother.' She nodded and her lips firmed. 'No one ever took that woman in hand and I will certainly not let this motherless child be so unruly.'

'You gave her the gold earrings.'

'Yes, and the matching necklace. I never really liked them. I'm trying to make a female out of her, Rhys. No man will ever give her a second glance if she does not present herself as a lady.'

Rhys turned to the door. He did not correct his mother on that point. But she was very, very wrong.

Bellona grabbed her cape, shaking it in her frustration. She had to escape the house for a few minutes and practise her archery. The first dancing lessons with the tutor had gone well, but today he had insisted on a much more difficult dance. Bellona had refused. She was determined the man would not touch her.

The maid returned and slipped into the room. 'Please, miss, the duchess is distressed.'

'She must get over her temper fit.'

'She is crying.'

Bellona stopped. 'Tears of anger?'

'Quiet tears.'

Bellona slipped the cape from her shoulders and tossed it on the bed. 'I'll speak with her.'

'Thank you, miss,' the maid said, backing away.

Bellona knocked on the duchess's door and walked inside. The woman sniffled, but didn't look at Bellona.

'You know I don't wish to dance.' Bellona shut the door.

'I know.' The duchess stared at the embroidered bit of linen in her hands. 'If you wish to be a heathen, then you may be a heathen. I wash my hands of you. My daughter. She loved to dance. Loved the dresses. The laughter. I just thought… I just thought you would, too.'

Bellona sighed. 'If you will help me, I will try.'

The duchess dotted her eyes dry. 'The tutor is waiting.'

'No. You must help me. I cannot do it without you. I *cannot*.'

'You are being ridiculous.'

'I am asking for no more than you are from me.'

'Very well.' The duchess stood. 'I am too old and tired to fight you any more.'

Chapter Five

Muffled pianoforte music wafted down the hall-ways. Rhys stopped, listening. That wasn't his mother playing. She'd long ago ceased, claiming her fingers hurt if she even looked at the piano-forte, though she wasn't above persuading some-one else to play for her.

Rhys trekked to the ballroom and then stared.

His mother sat in a high-backed chair similar to a queen's throne. She held her arm out and hummed above the sound of the music, as she grasped a fan like a sceptre and let it bounce in time with her hums. A man at the pianoforte had the music before him, but his eyes were closed as his fingers moved.

Rhys recognised the other man, the dancing master who had tutored every child from every estate in the area. The man danced, his lips in a grim line as he held Bellona and led her through the steps around the room. His hair was smooth at one side and the other stood out as if someone had tugged him around by the white locks. The wench had a disastrous effect on hair. Rhys's own was beginning to grey since he had met her. Only the duchess's hair stayed locked in place.

But when he looked closer, his mother's eyes were red-rimmed and he wasn't sure Bellona's didn't follow suit.

'Shoulders back,' his mother commanded, between hums, her voice reaching a crescendo. 'Bellona, the hand. Stop pulling your fingers from his. You are causing the tutor to miss his steps to keep you close. Hum-hum-hum. Hum-hum-hum. One-two-three. Feet. Feet. Feet. Remember the— Stop. Stop. Stop!' Her voice rose and her fan-tip jumped up.

Bellona immediately stepped back from the man.

Standing, the duchess moved to Bellona and the dance instructor. 'Bellona, you must simply refrain from pulling away from him. You were doing so well in the country dance, but you cannot manage one step of this dance.' She walked behind the man and straightened his back. He winced.

'Mr Mathers, you must, must, must pay attention as well. You do not have quite the grasp of the dance as I had hoped or Bellona would be able to do better. I will demonstrate for her. Dance with me, Mr Mathers…' She raised her hand and stepped into his grasp.

The dance continued, with his mother and the tutor.

Bellona stood at the side. Her eyes showed dark against wan skin.

The duchess and the tutor danced round the room. Bellona breathed deeply.

'It's not truly difficult,' Rhys said, walking to her side. 'Perhaps I could show you since the instructor is lacking.'

He would hold her only for a moment. That would not cause any problems within him. He could not even remember all the women he had danced with.

Her head jerked around, as if she'd not known he was in the room. She moved back, increasing the distance between them. 'I know. But I hate this dance. I hate it.'

'It's so elegant and the music is beautiful.'

'This dance is… Your mother said some people think it improper. They are wise. To be in a man's grasp like that…' She shuddered.

Rhys talked softly, leaning towards her. 'Has the tutor behaved badly to you?'

'Just in the same terrible way he is with the duchess.'

Rhys's head darted and he watched the couple swirl, his mother's voice slightly louder than the music as she instructed the tutor.

'They're just dancing,' Rhys said. 'If anything, Mother is holding him too close.'

'I cannot.' She shook her head slowly. 'I will tell her that I cannot do this…unsuitable dance.'

He studied Bellona's face and he reconsidered where his eyes had roamed on some of his dance partners. He raised his chin and slowly nodded downward. He moved his view over her shoulder and kept his eyes away from her breasts, but spoke in an undertone. 'I am sure, if you tell my mother, she will see that you have someone to fashion a gown for you with an adequate… bodice.'

She looked at him, studying his deliberately neutral expression. 'I don't understand?'

He furrowed his brows. 'Wasn't that what you were talking about?'

Her lids dropped a bit and her face changed. The eyes narrowed. 'What is wrong with my bodice?'

'Nothing.' It was the truth. He spoke dismissively and assumed the privileged bearing that usually stopped all questions. Whoever had fashioned her close-fitting garment should have been well paid.

Her gaze widened, and he could see the thoughts working away behind her eyes. She grumbled a word he could not make out.

'I thought,' he emphasised, 'you might prefer a more concealing dress—because you think the dance improper. A thicker fabric might give more of a feeling of distance—propriety—of all those things—important things—necessary for a dance. I am just trying to assist.' He heard the soothing tone of his voice and reminded himself he had meant no offence. He did not need to grovel to her.

One of her feathers unruffled. 'I will consider

what you said.' She crossed her arms, and patted one hand just at the top of her capped sleeve. Her arm now draped over her chest. 'I will never, ever dance in this dress now.'

'Just wear a dress that's more—less fashionable.'

Her eyes, if they could, became even more lustrous with disapproval. 'I was not speaking of that, although I will certainly take what you say into account when I choose my clothing.'

'Miss Cherroll… You must accept the norms of societal behaviour if you are to live in England.'

Her face didn't lighten. 'No. He holds my hand and around my waist and I cannot… In a moment he could clasp me tightly. I could not pull away if I wished.'

He looked at his mother and the instructor. 'The tutor did not hold you closer than that?'

'It was still too close.'

Oh, this woman was surely unsuitable for any man's wife. He felt sorry for her and the man she might wed, assuming she didn't geld him with an arrow first.

'I've held women in that manner and none seemed to mind.'

She shuddered. 'I cannot speak for them. But I cannot tolerate any more lessons.' The intake of her breath spoke of her determination.

She grasped her dress, lifted the hem enough to show those unsightly boots and darted from the room.

His mother must have been watching. She stopped in mid-step and shouted a command to the man at the piano. The music ceased. The two men and his mother were both looking at him.

'What did you say to send her away?' His mother stepped away from the tutor. She waved a hand. 'You would not believe how much effort this day has taken to organise.'

This was not the place to mention the bodice discussion. 'I may have made her…doubt her… ability to learn the dance.'

His mother's fingers splayed and her hands went up. 'Rolleston, I cannot believe…' She caught her words. 'I had to near drag her from her room just to get her here at all.' She pointed a finger at the ceiling. 'Just one moment.'

The tutor dropped his head, and a small moan fell from his lips. 'I so must beg your pardon, but I have another appointment, and I do not think

I will be able to continue… With the greatest of regrets and sadness. Not today or tomorrow.'

'See what you've caused…' She looked at Rhys. 'We had made an improvement.'

Before she'd finished the sentence, the tutor was out through the door. The musician stood and tucked his music under his arm, turning to leave.

The duchess raised her ringed fingers, stopping his departure. 'Stay. We will try again. Do not think to tell me you also have another meeting.' She turned to Rhys, her eyes showing the little lines at the side which could grow into quite huge ones depending on her temper. 'Rolleston, you do not realise how very important this is. Wait here,' she muttered. 'I will get Bellona and we will continue and, Rhys, you will show her that she is quite the dancer.'

Bellona sat in her room. She had taken country dance lessons at Whitegate with her sister and no one had ever minded that she did not participate in other dances. She'd merely taken the lessons to appease Melina and the women always practised together. Sometimes even the children partnered them.

The duchess didn't understand, and when she'd mentioned dancing to Bellona, Bellona expected no more attention to the matter than she'd given with her sister.

When the man touched her, she could not think of feet or music or dance. All she could remember was the feel of hands clasping her neck on the ship—all the more terrifying as it had happened after they had escaped Stephanos and his men, and the captain had promised her her safety. Or the night she and Thessa had escaped Greece— when Stephanos and his men had stolen her from her home.

She had made a promise to Melina not to speak of it. She said the things people whispered about, they overlooked. But if their suspicions were publicly confirmed and indiscretions admitted openly, then the *ton* could no longer ignore them. Nobody wanted to be seen as approving an open scandal as everyone wanted to uphold their place in society.

Bellona thought of a gasping fish lying in the sand, eyes wide, breathing air, but not truly breathing. That was how the dance instructor's hands made her feel. That was how she always felt when a man stood close enough that his hands could seize her neck.

Three quick raps on the door sounded.

Bellona forced herself to her feet, knowing the duchess would be on the other side.

The duchess stood there. 'I do not blame you for this, Bellona. I have explained to Rhys that he must mind his ways. The dancing master—I do not think he has even read Thomas Wilson's book or looked at the drawings. He does not know the correct method of dancing. He's left now and I'm sure—'

'He's left?' Bellona interrupted.

The older woman nodded. 'No loss. His posture was not good. Return and I will see that you learn properly.'

Bellona did not ever wish to attend another soirée—she hated them. Even the country dances caused her insides to ache when many people were together. Everyone moved this way and that and anyone could grasp her from behind. Breathing became impossible.

Almost before her thought was completed, the duchess fastened her hand on Bellona's arm and marched her out through the door. 'You must do this. Mothers need children. You must marry in order to have babies. You must attend soirées and dinner parties to meet the men. Even a vicar will expect a dance with his wife on occasion.'

Bellona walked back into the ballroom. Movement caught her eye. The duke stood at the side, talking quietly with the musician.

His gaze locked on her. He studied her—just a blink, but all the same, he'd already had too many thoughts she couldn't decipher. Too much intensity in his gaze.

The touch of the duchess's hand on Bellona's arm freed her to move again. 'Now, dear, don't be awed that you'll be dancing with a duke.'

Bellona paused, unable to take another step forward. He did not make her fear him as the other men did, but when his eyes raked over her, her strength waned.

Bellona spoke to the duchess. 'You must show me.'

She could feel the duke thinking about her, watching her.

'Nonsense,' the duchess said, waving Bellona's words away. 'Rolleston is a wonderful dancer. He knows what he's doing. With his height you might think his legs would get in the way or his feet would crush you, but he's quite graceful.'

Bellona moved her head sideways in refusal, as he stepped forward, movements slow.

'Miss Cherroll.' His words, rumbling just louder than a murmur, barely reached her ears above the sound of her heart beating. He stopped two arm lengths in front of her. His hands were at his side. 'I would be pleased if you would give me the honour of a dance.'

She could not speak.

'Child.' The duchess, all smiles, reached out to nudge Bellona forward. 'Do not be afraid you will step on his feet. He's quite able to withstand it, I assure you.'

'Mother.' Rhys raised his arm the slightest bit. His voice was quiet. 'I can help her. Why don't you ring for tea? Or some wine, perhaps? I'm parched.'

'That would be lovely.' She turned, signalling the musician to begin, before she moved to summon the tea.

'Listen to the music,' the duke said to Bellona. 'Just listen for a bit. Let it get into your thoughts.'

She nodded, unable to move her eyes from his

and trying to slow the roar in her ears. His mother stood near. The duchess. All was safe. Bellona knew it. But her body did not feel safe.

He raised one hand into the dance pose, but the other remained at his side. 'Step forward and put your hand in mine.'

She drew another breath into her lungs and looked into his eyes. They were not harsh or threatening or angry. They had softened at the edges, guiding her, and his head leaned forward the merest amount. Now she couldn't escape. She was trapped. But the snare was the velvety hue of his eyes and the rumble of his voice curling into her with the richness of a covering being wrapped around her on a cold day after the cloth had been warmed by the fire.

She moved towards him and put her fingertips in his palm, waiting for the moment when his hand would tighten over hers. The movement in his hand signalled to her that his fingers had flexed, but he didn't close them against her. He hadn't realised she wasn't scared by him, but was trying to keep from letting her life be changed in a way she'd never believed possible. This weakness she'd fought against because she'd seen her mother deserted by the man she'd loved.

'Now put your hand on my shoulder and I will rest my arm at your back, but I will not hold or clasp you tightly. It will be just the barest bit of my hand resting against you.'

Her throat tightened, and she tried to keep her breathing calm and the world from fading so that the only remaining thing was him.

'You will be safer than you've ever been before. I will let nothing hurt you. Mother is here. She's looking at the music and she is telling the man how she wishes to hear him play the piece.'

He stood, as if he were the one who couldn't move.

Bellona put her hand at his shoulder—wool soft beneath her fingers. The scent of shaving soap touched her nose.

He hadn't moved. 'Are you ready?' he asked.

She nodded.

She felt the flex of his shoulders and the slightest touch of his hand near her back.

'Pretend I'm not even here.' His words barely reached her ears over the tune the pianist just started playing. 'It will be simple as a stroll around the room.'

She nodded and he took the first step of the dance.

Bellona stumbled, managing to find Rhys's feet. He tensed his arms, but he didn't try to right her or gasp at her.

When she moved back into the dance, he looked beyond her and hummed a rich, soothing sound.

She listened to his voice, and thought of the music. She could still move. His eyes weren't on her and his thoughts looked far away. She forced herself not to move closer to him. The distance would save her.

The pianoforte music wafted inside her body and it was the same as being in the forest, free and alone—the moment of the leaves in the trees brushing the air over her and being safe, held by the forest.

Her arm barely contacted with his coat—a mountain of man moved beneath her touch, but instead of causing cold breaths inside her, the world invited her. She tightened the fingers of her raised hand, feeling his palm, and he responded with the merest pressure, silent reassurance passing between them.

She wanted to see his face, but she didn't dare raise her eyes. She didn't want to ruin anything about this moment.

The music stopped and their feet ceased at the same step. He did not move at all until he spoke to the duchess. 'I think she has the grasp of it.'

Then he ushered her to his mother and left the room.

'You did well enough,' the duchess said. 'I knew you could learn. Rhys is a much better dancer than the tutor, if I do say so myself. You should see the ladies at soirées beam when he asks them to dance. I'm sure it quite goes to his head, but it doesn't show. The dance is not so hard, is it?'

'No.'

She appraised Bellona's face. 'You need not concern yourself about the dance again. All it took was for Rhys to show you. Don't expect your next dancing partner to be like my son, though.'

Bellona nodded, and left the room. She didn't expect any man to ever be like him.

Chapter Six

Rhys stood just inside the open window. He'd had one of the servants move Bellona's target closer to the library window again. He suspected she'd lugged them away before because they'd slowly migrated from under the windows. He'd just wanted the arrows going away from the direction of the fields. *True,* he told himself, and the *thwack* of the arrow both irritated him and pulled him like a siren's song. *Liar,* he admitted.

A carriage rolled up. Warrington's.

The door opened, and Warrington stepped out, then turned to help Bellona's sister from the vehicle. His hand lingered in his wife's until a blonde bundle jumped from the opening and both parents turned to her in caution.

The little one dodged her parents and ran screeching to Bellona. Warrington reprimanded her, but his wife placed a gloved hand on his arm and then Warrington moved from view.

Bellona's bow and arrow slid to the ground and Willa bounded into her aunt's arms. The dark head and the light one bumped together. Bellona moved, hugging the little one in a swirling movement.

'Willa insisted her aunt is out with her bow and arrows slaying dragons. She claims you are doing so to rescue her.' Melina's voice carried through the open window.

'Only six dragons.' Bellona's excited voice was no quieter than her sister's.

'You killed six,' the little one insisted. 'But I killed ten for you.'

'What with?' Bellona asked.

The girl laughed, jumping back from her aunt. 'I stomped on them. They squished.'

'That is ugly, Willa,' her mother said.

'Yes,' Bellona agreed. Her hair had half-fallen from its pins. 'You must save them whole so we can have a feast. Dragon's meat is very tasty and is already cooked from the dragon's breath.'

'Bellona, stop adding to her imagination,' Melina said.

Willa shot an imaginary arrow into her aunt and Bellona was putting more drama into the play than any actress he'd ever seen at Drury Lane.

He wanted to join them. He wanted to hear the laugher around him, especially Bellona's.

'Sir,' a voice behind him interrupted. 'The Earl of Warrington did not bring a card, but suggested I tell you—'

'—To roll yourself out of bed—' Warrington stepped behind the servant '—because you are so tired from staying up late looking at your face in the mirror and wondering why the heavens have been so cruel to you.'

Rhys's quiet response would have earned him a fortnight of prayers from the vicar. The butler's lips quirked and he slipped out through the door.

Warrington walked to the other side of the window and looked out, viewing the same scene Rhys saw.

'Have you gambled away the inheritance yet?' Warrington asked.

'No.' Rhys turned to the earl. 'Do you need me to lend you some funds?'

'Like hell.'

'If you throw the first punch, you should be prepared with another one.'

'So how is the duke?'

Rhys tapped his boot toe at the base of the wall. 'It's been difficult managing the properties around London through my man of affairs instead of seeing for myself. I have had to depend on Simpson completely because the duties are so new to me and the duchess has been so distraught. I believe Simpson quite capable, but I need to take responsibility myself at some point.'

'It gets easier,' Warrington said. 'I was fortunate to have my brother Dane to help me after my father died. If you need anything, just ask. I'll send him.'

'Much better than having you around, I'm sure.'

'True,' Warrington said.

Both men stayed at the widow. All three females chattered and seemed to be having no trouble following every word spoken, mostly in Greek.

'So how are things here?' Warrington said. 'The duchess?'

'Mother is better.'

Warrington nodded, his voice soft. 'Bellona doesn't like quiet. My wife, fortunately, does. Hard to believe they are sisters sometimes.'

Rhys didn't speak, just watched the gestures

down below. Bellona unstrung the bow. The little girl wore the quiver. The women moved with each word they spoke.

'You'd think it's been years since they've seen each other,' Warrington said, moving away from the window.

Rhys still watched the scene. 'At least they get along.'

'They do. For the most part.'

Rhys stepped nearer the bookshelves, and considered his words while he looked at Warrington. 'Is Bellona truly nothing like her sister?' He waited for the response.

Warrington chuckled. 'Night and day. It's odd how they disagree on things, but never seem to argue. My brothers and I argued even when we agreed.'

'How did their father die?'

Warrington walked away from the window, and stood at the unlit fireplace. 'He's actually alive and I would prefer that to remain between us. I've been concerned word would get out concerning the pompous goat. That's what they disagree over. Melina wishes to keep him from all aspects of her life. Bellona has visited his wife secretly several times, though she doesn't like the man either.'

'Where does he live—in Greece?' Rhys knew her mother was dead and he'd thought her father was, too.

'On St James's Street in London. He's actually Lord Hawkins.'

Rhys relived the words in his mind. Yes, he'd heard correctly. Bellona's father was an English peer.

Warrington gave the smallest nod and studied Rhys. 'In his youth, he visited the island, married their mother and forgot to tell her he had a wife here. The second marriage was probably a farce to him, but still, the women didn't know of each other. Two families. Two sets of children. He sailed back and forth a few times. The children's ages are near the same.'

'Lord Hawkins?' Rhys could hardly stand to be in the same room with the man. His voice usually carried to all corners when he talked of the great art of the past and no one else's opinion on any painting came close to Hawkins's self-professed judgement skills.

'It's best that people think Melina's father is

dead,' Warrington said. 'Better than the truth and having to acknowledge him. Better for the women. For everyone.'

'I can see how that would be.' Rhys watched the women laughing. He could not connect them in his mind to Hawkins.

'My wife thinks Bellona wants so much to be different from her father that she almost becomes him. Hawkins has that nose up in the air, thinking he is above society's ways. Bellona can be uppity, too, around society. Can you imagine Bellona making morning calls or indulging in polite conversation at a house party? She's more likely to be asking the servants how many eggs a day the chickens are laying.'

'She's been a boon with the duchess, though. They have even looked at fashion plates together.'

'Bellona? That is not her normal way. My wife finally reached an agreement with Bellona so that at least her gowns are acceptable. I'm fortunate Hawkins spent more time with his eldest daughter. He insisted Melina act like a lady. When Bellona was growing into a young woman and should have been learning the same skills, Hawkins returned to England for several years. Probably hoped they would starve. I doubt he cared much either way as long as he didn't have to think of them. It's a wonder they survived into adulthood. I saw how they lived when I went to the island. I saw how hard it was for Melina to leave her two sisters behind, believing coming here was the only way to save her family.'

'Bellona has helped Mother think of something besides her grief.'

'That really doesn't surprise me.' Warrington stepped back to the window. 'One day, I smelled a stench in the hallway, but I ignored it, thinking a chamber pot had been dropped. Then I heard a strange noise and discovered Bellona had been keeping an orphaned pig in her chamber because she thought no one else could keep it alive. A pig. In the family quarters. Willa cried when I said little Snowdrop had to be removed. It was not leaving *snowdrops* in its wake. I was the only one in the entire household who didn't know of the creature.'

'Still, Bellona has something that...'

Her laughter trickled in through the window. Rhys head turned towards the sound.

'You need to watch yourself Rhys.' Warrington

shrewdly studied the duke's face. 'Don't make an error which might cause us to kill each other.'

Rhys didn't answer. London. He would have to go to London immediately. If even Warrington could sense his interest in Bellona…

Rhys couldn't even step away from the window.

Homesick. Heartsick. Bellona touched her stomach, before resting her hand on the fabric of the chair in the library. Seasick on land. She missed Melos, but she could not return. She missed her sisters, but they both had wed—Melina to the earl and Thessa to Warrington's brother, Captain Ben.

In the past, Willa and her brothers had always taken Bellona's mind from the feelings of sadness. Today, seeing her niece again had only heightened her loss. Her *mana* and sisters had laughed together so many times. Mana was gone for ever.

Now, instead of having her peaceful mother, she was sitting every day with a woman who could have tackled Zeus and made him leave the heavens. Bellona could not go back into the duchess's chambers right now. She had told the maid so— twice—when the duchess summoned her.

Bellona had chosen to sit in the library because

it had the largest windows, but now the evening shadows lengthened in the room, darkening everything. The duchess was suffering a fit of irritation. The older woman always became more cross as the sun set. She could sit it out alone this time.

Rhys walked into the library. He held a half-full glass of amber liquid. He sat it on a table, but his eyes met hers. 'My mother has asked me to collect you.'

Her chest constricted. She didn't know why she did not have the strength to make her body unaware of him whenever he walked into the room.

She was in the duke's chair. The arms of the chair seemed to grow bigger and the back taller. She rose. She had to free herself from the confines. 'Your chair.'

His head moved only an inch to each side as he shook it, but his eyes didn't move at all. They remained locked on her. 'Miss Cherroll. Please be comfortable. I am just as at ease wherever I sit.'

She raised her chin in acknowledgement of his words. 'I have been here too long. When I saw my family today, I realised how much I miss them.

I…' She moved back, planning to tell him she would have to leave.

'My mother just stormed into the dining room where I was eating,' he said. 'She insists you are being contrary.'

'I would not say I am the contrary one,' she said.

He turned to her, eyes shining, lips upturned. 'I would say you are, but with a definite purpose. You annoy her to keep her mind from dwelling on other things.'

'I suppose I must go see how she is faring.' But her feet didn't move.

'Please,' he said. 'Sit for a moment with me. I think you owe me,' he said. 'I soothed my mother and kept her from searching you out. She checked your room, by the way.'

She sat, but kept her back straight. 'I think you are contrary, too.'

'Very.' He sat on the sofa, legs stretched in front of him, one booted foot rocking back and forth on its heel. 'But you do not need to go to my mother right now. She is currently looking for my valet. I have told her when I go to London next, I am going to purchase a waistcoat and cannot decide on the right colour to go with yellow stripes. She is hoping to convince my valet of the proper garments I should buy so I do not look like I have lost my wits.'

'She tires me. All the sadness. It just reminds me of my own. I sit with her and have to remember that I am alive today. All of yesterday is gone. I must be alive for today or I will have nothing.'

'I just study the ledgers or read when I am lost in sad memories.'

'Or ride your horse, or check on the stablemen or write letters to your man of affairs.'

He stared at her. 'How do you know all that?'

'I wake many times in the night and it is too silent. My sisters were always with me when I was young. My mother near. Now I wake up and the room is so large and I am alone in it, so I move about the house. I was— I see you writing at night. I have been in the hallway many times and noticed the light from the open library door. I hear the shuffle of your papers and your sighs.'

'I do not sigh.'

She took in a deep breath, looked at him, parted her lips and imitated the sound of a weary sigh.

He shook his head in disagreement.

'And you grumble. I do not even have to be near the door to hear you complaining to the paper.'

'Next time, just walk into the room.'

She settled back into the chair and let her fingers rest on the arms. 'You must have many sad memories if you spend so much time working not to think of them.'

'A few. Mainly of my brother. We pretended to be jousting knights. We had fencing duels. We took our lessons together. He never was as robust as I, but I never expected him to die, even when he got very sick. I wasn't even here at the time. Now I ask myself, how could I have not known?'

'I hate sadness. Sometimes the duchess's melancholy almost swallows me.'

'She was not this way before. Not always gentle, but never was she like this. She's not the same person.' He raised a brow. 'I understand quite well. If you need someone to make you angry to take your mind from your sadness, search me out. I will do my best.' He gave a definitive nod of his head.

'That is kind of you.' She smiled. 'But I don't wish to be angry.'

'How does a person slap you with their words?'

'By criticising my clothes or my hair. Telling

me how I should act. Disparaging my boots.' She kicked out her hem of her dress. 'I like my boots even if no one else does.'

Her chest flooded with warmth. His eyes. He appraised her with something she recognised as laughter, but it was also mixed with the same look Warrington often gave her sister. In this moment, she could look at the duke directly and feel cosseted by his eyes.

'I cannot understand why your boots aren't revered. It's quite interesting how one even appears bigger than the other.' His voice flowed smoothly. 'And the toe appears to have a chunk out of it.'

'I disarmed a trap with it.'

'Perhaps you should have used a stick.' He studied her and, even as he commented on her footwear, he complimented her with his eyes and voice.

'I did the next time.'

'I will be happy to have those beautiful boots replaced for you with an even more lovely pair.'

'No. But thank you, Your Grace.'

'I assure you, I can have someone fashion such suitable, extraordinary footwear that your toes will sing.'

'You cannot have more *suitable* boots made for

me because these are perfect. And I hope you do find a yellow-silk waistcoat with something fashionable painted on it. Perhaps blue slippers.' She lowered her chin. 'You would like to discuss my hair next?'

'Hair like that...' His eyes wandered away. 'A man does not want to discuss it.'

She tightened her jaw.

But when he looked back at her, his eyes had changed. He'd lost the look that made her feel she knew him. 'I'm sure Byron could find something to say about your hair much better than I could.'

She wanted to bring back the feeling of companionship between them. 'Try,' she challenged.

He frowned. 'No. I am no poet.'

'You are every moment the duke?'

He gazed at her hair and his voice dropped to a whisper before his gaze took control of her. 'I do not have to touch it to feel it against my skin. A caress. Unequalled by any other woman's fingertips.'

The explosions in her body took her breath. 'I forgive you for what you said about my boots.'

'I am fond of your half-boots.' The seriousness left his face. 'They are quite serviceable, you do not have to have a valet to care for them and they do cover your feet well.'

She looked at her feet. 'That is the first nice thing anyone has ever said about them and I do think it might be the worst as well.'

He shook his head. 'It might be. But you find them comfortable and you wear them and you do not care if they are not quite the thing. You like them and so they are on your feet. That is all that matters.'

She half-nodded. They also held her knife. 'They are indeed serviceable.' But most importantly, they made her feel safe.

Only even with the knife hidden in her boot, she'd still not recovered her ability to sleep well after the attacks she experienced on the ship from Greece to England—first from Stephanos and his men and then later from the crewman who had tried to strangle her.

She'd been asleep when the pirate, Stephanos, had attacked the ship and she'd only woken when Thessa had burst into the room after everything had ended and Captain Ben had secured their safety. Realising she could have awakened to find her sister gone for ever had terrified her.

Stephanos had always watched every move

Thessa made when he saw her and when she and Bellona had fled Melos by swimming to the ship of Captain Ben—whose brother, Warrington, had taken Melina from the island—Stephanos and his men had followed them. The group had included the man who had wanted to marry Bellona… He had the demon's eyes. Eyes that darkened to a soulless pit. All the demons in her dreams had devouring eyes. And they always, always had the same scent of rotted eggs, while jagged-edged black earth crunched under her feet when she ran from a man with eyes growing darker and darker as he came closer and closer.

Captain Ben and his men had fought off the invaders and defeated Stephanos. The pirates had had no choice but to retreat and allow the Englishmen to leave with Thessa and Bellona on board.

'I must keep my boots nearby me at all times.' She studied Rhys's face.

'I feel the same about mine.'

She looked at his feet. 'Your valet is quite good.'

'I surround myself with the best.'

She gave the merest nod of acknowledgment and let the thoughts rummage around in her head. She chose something safer to mention.

'Your mother still says I must leave and when

I agree with her, she becomes even more angry. She doesn't want me to go, but she doesn't want me to stay.'

Nothing about him moved, except the rocking of his boot, until he spoke. 'Before you came here, countless times, every day, my mother said she prayed to die.'

He stood, towering up, but she did not feel frightened. 'I would like you to stay. You have no notion how much better she is today than the day before you came. She has not summoned any-one but me since Geoff died. She has not looked at fashion plates since my sister died. You have roused her spirit.'

His eyes stayed on hers. 'You've been a boon to me in so many ways.'

Looking up, she could only nod.

'If she becomes too much for you to bear, seek me out. Any time of the day or night.'

He left. The glass remained along with the lingering scent of shaving soap and leather from the chair. She'd not noticed it before. It had the same earthiness of the duke and it surrounded her on three sides—an embrace.

Chapter Seven

Bellona shut the duchess's door with the lightest of clicks and stood in the hallway. Then she made a gesture she'd seen the sailors use.

The older woman deserved respect, but certainly did not earn it. She'd called Bellona an ungrateful bumble-knot. A foreign muddle-mind. A featherhead.

The woman had been unwilling to accept that Bellona did not want to learn to read English, had managed just fine so far without such a habit, and the letters did not all stick in her head.

Bellona had explained she couldn't read that much in Melos as she hadn't had books and with so much work to do there hadn't really been time. Then she'd been told she was not in Melos now and discovered that the duchess and Bellona's own father had a similar way of expressing their ire. They waged a war on her ears.

Bellona had promised to search out a book and study it—because that was the only way to finally quiet the woman and escape.

The library was empty. Bellona pulled out the first book she saw, opened it, shuddered and, with a thunk, slid it back on to the shelf. That one was not even in English. She did not know the language at all.

Poetry might be ideal, she mused. That was why people liked poems. A poem did not require as much reading.

If she memorised a verse of a poem that she could recite in a mournful voice and become too carried away to finish… She could honestly claim it to be her favourite verse and favourite book and perhaps that would satisfy the duchess.

Bellona searched until she found a volume of poetry with a long introductory section at the beginning. She skipped that.

Bellona sat in the library with the book, staring at the few bits of words she recognised and the pleasant white space, knowing she would have to study the dribs of ink in more detail.

Pages. Pages and pages. Whoever invented paper must have hated everyone. Whoever decided to put words into sentences should have had to sit in a room with nothing else but paper and ink and a pen and write for the rest of his life.

But this family placed importance on books and if books meant something to them then Bellona would try to read. Especially if it might make the long stretches of night move more quickly.

She tried to sound out the first word. *E. X. P. O. S. T.* The next letter, *U*, she did not recall at all. *L. A. T. I. O. N.* She did not remember enough to read even the first word. She groaned at the fifth line. Books. That word she could read. This poem had books in it, which made no sense at all.

The duke strode into the room. He still wore the clothes of the day, but had discarded his coat. His sleeves would have been out of place on Melos, too much cloth and very white. The waistcoat, obsidian, and the night, took the lightness from his face, creating a cold look which reminded her of the marble pieces she'd seen on her island. They were all crushed and broken, though, and he didn't appear possible to shatter.

His face showed the beard trying to poke through for morning. He raked his fingers through his hair.

'I thought you did not like books.'

She could not make out the first word of the title. She held it up so he could see. 'I don't. This *biblio…*'

He walked closer, bringing all the pleasant scents of the outside with him. He'd been riding. Leather and wool blended into the air.

'Lyrical Ballads,' he read aloud.

She gave a sideways turn of her head. 'I have read enough of it.'

His eyebrows rose in question.

Nodding, she admitted, 'One word was enough. I even like embroidery better than reading. At least when you finish sewing you have something to show for it. When you finish a book, you still have the same pages you started with and tired eyes.'

'You've not read the right story.'

'I've not read any book.' She stood. 'I do not have to eat a tree to know if I would like how it tastes.'

'Sit for a moment,' he said, indicating the sofa. He walked to the shelves behind the sofa.

'Do not try to make me read.'

He tugged a book out and held it so she could see the title. 'This is a tale you cannot help but enjoy. I'll give you a primer on it.'

'Does your *mana* like the story?'

His jaw dropped. 'Of course Mother likes the book. Everyone does.'

'She expects me to read to her. She said when she holds out the book far enough to read the letters, her arms collapse.'

'She has spectacles. She refuses to wear them when anyone is near.'

'Spectacles? Then I will not worry about reading. If she wishes to read badly enough, she will do it herself.'

He rested the book against the top of the sofa back. 'Perhaps you could just read some *Robinson Crusoe* to her. If you do not like it, then you can truly say you do not like books.'

'If I do not like him, then you will believe me?'

'Yes.'

She settled into the edge of the sofa, her back straight. A crease appeared between his brows, but then his attention returned to the book in his hand.

Letting him worry about the words would be so much easier than doing it herself.

He moved to the chair across from her, whisking the lamp along with him and setting it at the side. He took up much more of the area than she'd believed possible. 'Listen.'

He read aloud for a few moments and his voice became like a soft thunder off in the distance when rain was needed. Something pleasant and hopeful. Her thoughts were pulled along with his words.

'Wait,' she interrupted.

He looked up from the words, his brows knit again, and that caused her own face to tighten.

'You are reading about a man who is being told to be happy he is not of higher birth—that to be born in a situation of middling life, not poor, not wealthy, is the best. Is that how you feel?'

'Of course not.' He turned back to the book, reading again. 'The writer was correct for Crusoe, but not for everyone.'

'Wait,' she interrupted a second time. 'The older man is crying. You cannot like that.'

'Perhaps you should not really listen,' he said,

not raising his eyes. 'But only sit there and pretend—to please me.' He took a breath, frowned and said, softly, 'Imagine I am enjoying reading the book and would like to have your company while I do so.'

He continued reading aloud.

Her company, she mused. What an odd thing to say. She intended to tell him she did not want to listen, but when she opened her mouth to speak, his voice increased and his words filled the air. She leaned back in her chair and his tone returned to normal.

She crossed her arms in annoyance, but the story wasn't so terrible. After a few moments she relaxed. If reading made him happy, she could pretend to listen.

The duke read of the man's age. He was only a few years younger than Bellona's age of twenty-two and he was planning to go on a sea voyage. Bellona shut her eyes and leaned back with a sigh the duke could not have missed. She'd been on a ship. If one liked bland sea biscuits and ale—in a gaol surrounded by water—then sailing was the best place of all to be.

Now, the tale told of the young man's *mana* trying to dissuade him from travelling. She nodded in agreement. If her own mother had lived, Bellona would never have stepped on the ship and left her.

Bellona shut her eyes and listened, letting her arms relax. His voice could make even the tale of sailing sound pleasant.

He paused a moment, but she didn't look at him and he continued reading.

She listened to every word and time vanished.

When his voice stopped, her eyes opened.

'See, reading isn't bad.' He handed her the book still warm from his hands. 'Finish the story and then tell me you don't like it.'

She challenged him with her eyes, and smiled. 'I really cannot read English.' She'd been so determined to forget every word of English her sister had taught her. Forced it from her mind, but now she wished she'd kept the knowledge. Not that she wanted to open a book any more than she wanted her skin scraped with thorns, but perhaps her mind might change.

'No matter.' He tossed the words aside. 'As a gift to you for spending your time with my mother, I will have a tutor installed here.'

'The dancing master didn't work out.' A tutor. She shuddered. Brambles in human form.

The duke's lids flickered just a bit. 'I am sure I can find someone you get on well with.'

'I am not educated. Warrington saw no reason for me to be taught if I did not wish it.'

'I do not care if that is how Warrington feels. It is a gift. From me to you.' He spoke as if the words were straight from some ecclesiastical scribe.

'I will consider it,' she said finally. It would not take her long.

'Yes. I am sure you will. In the meantime, I will have someone go to London tomorrow to collect a tutor for you.'

Bellona shook her head, eyes never leaving the duke.

'Miss Cherroll, if you are to move among society with your sister's family it would be an asset for you to be able to read. You may wish to look at the caption under an engraving to see what the ladies are laughing about in a shop. Or, like my mother, read your prayer book.'

She nodded. 'You are right. When that happens, I will learn.'

Three blinks of his eyes.

She smiled. 'Your Grace.'

'Miss Cherroll.' His shoulders relaxed and he leaned back into the chair. 'You did enjoy Mr Crusoe. I promise you would not need a tutor for very long before you would be reading for yourself.' He held out *Robinson Crusoe* to Bellona. She hesitated.

Rolleston leaned forward enough to put it in her hand.

She stared at the lettering and handed it back to him. 'I know most letters. I know some words.'

He turned the book around. 'Then why do you resist so much?'

'You have never met the first mate of the ship that brought me to England,' she said. 'I liked him. He does not read. He said he carries his knowledge here—' she pointed to her head. 'He does not have time to keep turning pages.'

'Some of us cannot carry all the required knowledge and would prefer to have more than is allowed in such a small space.'

'And you see what happened to your sailor,' she muttered. 'Crusoe.'

Rhys acknowledged her words with the merest smile. 'What would it take to convince you that you need this?'

'I don't believe you truly care if I read or not,' she challenged.

'Of course I do. You've helped my mother. I wish to return the gift.'

'Then—if it is so easy, teach me yourself.'

He coughed. 'I do not have time. I have duties. Tenants. Ledgers.'

'Then it is not important.'

She stood and moved to the door.

'I will do it.' His voice rumbled. Strong. Irritated.

She turned. His eyes did not match his face. For a passing second, the boy he'd been peeked out from his expression. Then he became the duke again.

'I must be daft.' He stood and *Robinson Crusoe* slammed back into the bookcase before Rhys stared her way again.

'You do not have to do it,' she said quickly. 'I don't wish to. You punish both of us for doing no wrong.'

'An unwilling teacher and an unwilling student should make a tiresome combination, so we will start tomorrow to finish all the sooner.'

She could change her mind. She could insist on a tutor. But the image of the boy behind his eyes flashed in her memory and tumbled about her body. He'd mentioned she was a boon in so many ways and she'd wondered about those words. He could be just as alone, in his own way, as the duchess. He'd even wanted to begin teaching her the very next day.

'The day after,' she asked, checking his response.

'Oh, no. Miss Cherroll. Tomorrow. I accepted your challenge. I dare say you will be reading quite quickly with me as a tutor.' He took the volume of poetry and walked to her, placing it in her hands. 'Look over this one, too. Mother can recite a bit of it from memory. She might like speaking it while you follow along with the words. It might help her as well.'

'You wish for your mother not to be alone because it will be good for her...'

'Yes.'

'You wish for me to read because it will be good for me...'

'Yes.'

'Have you thought about what you should do because it will be good for yourself?'

'Most certainly.' He stepped back. 'To be a

son my father would be proud of. To continue his legacy.'

She shook her head. 'You have only considered what your father's needs would be. Not your own.'

'My needs were formed the moment Geoff died. I cannot let him or my father down. That is what I am doing. And I thank you for reminding me that I should be about my duties. The most important thing I can do is have a son, because if I don't marry and produce a child, everything my father and grandfather did will pass out of their direct family line.'

She pressed the books together. 'Does that not feel as if you are being commanded to do something?'

'No. It is simply another duty. If a tenant's roof blows away, I must replace it. Now I must put another heir at the table.'

'I am fortunate that I do not have to consider such a thing. I was almost forced into marriage once. I did not like it.'

'A lot of women would wish to be a duchess.'

'I am sure they will also find you tolerable as well.'

Chapter Eight

The poems were mountains and crevasses of words. She could not make sense of them. She'd forgotten almost all of what Melina had taught her. She tried for hours to remember and not enough had returned to her memory.

The only good thing about this situation was that it gave her something to do in the long hours before dawn. She could not have read into the night on Melos, though. They only had the one good lamp.

After studying, she'd fallen asleep and dreamed of being chased. Again she'd awoken breathing fast, her throat hurting and her heart pounding. She'd sat in bed, clasping her knife. When the shadows in the room were replaced by sunlight, she felt herself nodding off.

The next thing she knew, someone knocked.

'Miss,' she heard a woman's voice call through the door.

'Enter.'

A maid, mob cap snug, walked inside. 'His Grace wishes that you might meet with him in the library.'

Bellona pushed herself up. The knife handle showed from underneath a fold in the counterpane. She swept the covers back over the blade. She closed her eyes and wiped her eyelashes with her fingertips, and yawned.

She could not learn the words when she was this tired. The duke would think her the same bumble-head his mother did.

'I believe I will sleep longer.'

'His Grace,' the maid said softly, as if the words should stand alone in the room, 'wishes you to see you in the library.'

'Please tell him I would be pleased to...' She looked back at the bed. 'But I cannot meet him now.'

The maid didn't move.

'Could you bring chocolate—several hours from now?' Bellona asked.

'If you are certain,' the maid said finally.

Bellona crawled back into bed and covered a yawn before speaking. She didn't know how she would inform the duke she could not read— ever—but she was too tired to tell him now. She could not even remember the letters of her own name, and could barely hold her eyes open. 'I am certain. I cannot see him now. I must sleep.'

The maid nodded. 'I will tell His Grace your head pains you.'

Rhys sat in the overstuffed chair in the library, a stack of unread newspapers on the table beside him. He'd changed from his riding clothes after he'd seen the maid, eyes averted, rush by the door with a tray. His mother had eaten. He had eaten. The tray could only be for one person who was not in his mother's room, nor in any of the common areas of the house.

He would not go to her chamber and find her. She would have to leave it some time. The woman did not sit about in her room with books or sewing or staring out of the window as his mother did. She flitted around the house and the gardens—a bird moving from one berry to the next with a flight of fancy behind her eyes.

He'd worked the ledgers and made notes for Simpson and now Rhys started with the oldest newspaper, more aware of the sounds of the house than the print before him. He tended to let them gather before he read them. Perusing them in the carriage on his trips to and from London didn't work out well. His eyes could not adjust to the jostling. He'd tried. Now he used the travelling time to review things in his head. On occasion he'd had his man of affairs ride with him so they could plan. The trip certainly went faster, but he didn't like to take Simpson from his home because he knew the man preferred staying near his wife.

The clock chimed one note.

He turned the page. The library had been both his mother and father's favourite place. To be allowed to sit there with his parents and older siblings had been a treat when he was a child. Whoever sat in the library could tell most of the movements about the residents on this side of the house.

He did not think he could have missed seeing Miss Cherroll if she had left her bedchamber. He snapped the paper straight. Five times servants had whisked by the door, certainly having been summoned by his mother or Bellona. The staff was well trained to stay invisible otherwise.

Even the paper didn't look to have been ironed properly. He'd smudged a word with his hand, and the smear vastly irritated him.

Something creaked. A door softly shut. No footsteps sounded, but he could almost feel her movements. He lowered the print enough so he could look over it.

'Miss Cherroll,' he said before she even appeared at the opening.

A rap sounded at the wall. He would wager that was a bow bumping wood.

She stepped to the threshold.

When she met his eyes, the bow was held in both hands, flat to her chest. The quiver cinched the dull fabric of her dress.

'Oh, Miss Cherroll,' he continued, 'I see you have arrived to practise your reading.'

He stood, folding the paper. Shadows rested under her eyes and her hair was more mussed than usual. Compassion touched him. Perhaps the maid had told the truth. Perhaps Bellona had really been feeling ill.

'Do you need a medicinal prepared?' he asked.

Puzzlement. He saw it. Puzzlement in her eyes and then the memory washing over her. The wench had forgotten she was supposed to be unwell.

'I am fine. Now,' she added. Her shoulders dropped and her chin weakened.

He looked at her the same way he'd reprimanded the gamekeeper. 'Wonderful. Then we will read.'

'I must practise my archery.'

'I am rushed for time. I think it would be best if we worked together first.'

'I should have a tutor,' she said. 'I cannot take you from your duties.'

He placed the paper on the desk as she spoke. Now he put a hand on his heart. 'I cannot think of any duty more important than your education, Miss Cherroll.'

'I have changed my mind.'

'I have not.'

'I cannot learn.' She shook her head. 'I have no mind for it.'

'Nonsense. You and I will have hours and hours of nothing but lessons until you learn.'

'You will be wasting your time.' The chin went up. 'I cannot even remember all the letters.'

'Then we will start there.'

She shook her head. 'I have already tried. I have tried and I have tried.'

'Last night?'

She nodded.

If the paleness of her face told the truth, then perhaps she had worried over it. He wanted to re-assure her. But he could think of only one way to do that. 'You will be reading in no time.'

'I know you have more important things to do,' she said. 'I will have the tutor.'

'I suspect you will not make progress with a tutor,' he said. 'I think you will somehow man-age to convince the man to quit his post. I have seen no dancing tutor of late.'

'You do not trust me?' Her brows rose.

'Should I?' he responded in kind.

The brows lowered. 'You do not know what you ask for.'

His eyes didn't leave hers, but he managed to take in her whole body. Warmth flooded him, and he felt he could conquer the world, but perhaps not stand upright any longer. 'I know what I am up against. I will fight the challenge.'

She glanced at the book he opened and the ink swirled into the dreaded confusing shapes. The duke stood, watching her. His hair curled the slightest bit at the end, brushing his ears. Some rested at the collar of his shirt, and some hid behind the cloth.

The currents in her stomach increased. How could she learn with the duke near her?

'I would prefer to stand,' she said. 'If you sit at the desk, I will watch.'

'You only want to be able to leave quickly if you can think of an excuse. You are scared of the words.'

No. His words flamed a challenge inside of her. She had survived far worse than this. 'We must start with the letters first.'

After putting the book away, he moved to one of the overstuffed chairs, grasping the back to move it near the desk.

'I will stand.' She shook her head.

He dropped the back of the chair. 'Very well.'

He moved to the desk, shuffled the ledgers aside and pulled out a paper and dipped the pen in ink.

As he wrote the alphabet, she spoke the letters she knew. When she didn't remember, he marked it and went to another one. Then he asked her to pick out her name and she did.

'You knew all but four of the letters,' he said, glancing at her. No smile. No frown. 'Memorising them should be easy. You also know your name. I'd say you're more than halfway there already.'

Then he sketched short, quick strokes on the page.

She leaned towards him, watching the movements he made and noting the scent of his hair, bringing back memories of the mornings by the sea, causing a stab of homesickness and a curling reassurance of home.

'And this is a pig,' he said of the drawing, jarring her mind back into the room.

He wrote the letters under it and spoke them aloud. She'd not remembered the G.

'We will name him Snowdrop.' He glanced up at her and she saw sparkling brown eyes and strong lips, half-upturned, and with a private laugh hidden behind them. Then he returned to his mission. He wrote the letters and called them out as he put them down. 'This is the W.' He tapped it with the pen, leaving a drop of ink. 'And Snow-drop wasn't quiet. So we'll have the Q and U.'

'How did you know of Snowdrop?'

'Warrington told me.'

'The earl was wrong. Snowdrop wasn't unpleas-ant. I kept her in a soapbox with oilcloth under her because the sow didn't like her. The stable boy could not have kept her alive, but I did.'

He digested her words. 'You must not only learn to read—you must let the servants do their jobs. Do you wish to live among the staff or with the people who employ them? If you do not keep your station, your children will not have the same op-portunities they could have. The legacy you cre-ate for them will follow for centuries. You do not want your children considered less than they could be. If you ignore society's ways, they will ignore you.'

She stepped back. 'I do not think they will ig-nore me. I think they will banish me. How ter-rible. No more dancing. No more maid putting her hands around my hair and pulling it tightly, trying to put a stinking mixture on it to make it stay in place. I do not want to anger people, but I do not like their discomforting ways.'

She lifted the hem of her skirt slightly as she retreated so he could see. 'These are my boots. I wear them comfortably in the house. And you spoke to me about them because they are not slippers. The more beautiful my clothes, then the more people will note my boots and talk of them. So I wear the plain dresses.'

'I noted your gown in spite of its plainness,' he said, almost under his breath, as he drew another line on the page.

'Without looking,' she asked, 'what colour is it?'

'Lighter than your eyes. Softer than your hair.'

Seconds passed. She spoke again. 'Brown. So my boots do not appear so different.'

'If you are saying you chose that gown so you would not be noticed so much…' He barely looked over his shoulder at her, but his lips caught her attention. 'You failed miserably. I hope you do better at reading or you won't learn a word.'

'My dress is the colour of leather.' She moved forward again, standing more at his back.

'Leather. Yes. Exactly the colour I meant. Just

couldn't think of the word.' He turned sideways in the chair. 'But you did succeed. I did not think of your boots.'

She touched his shoulder, pressing him to turn back to the paper, not wanting him to see the heat she felt in her cheeks.

He didn't continue writing. 'I cannot help jesting with you, Bellona. You need some escape from the sadness at Harling House. So do I.'

She made a light fist and rested the knuckles of her hand against his collar, just brushing at the end of his hair. 'You don't seem sad...'

His shoulders moved under her hand when he breathed out. 'I know. But perhaps I am. And perhaps I am not enough. You are right in what you said. My life is all planned for me now. I no longer have to think what I should do—I only have to think how I should go about doing it. Generations of people have decided it for me and how could they all be wrong?'

'Perhaps.'

'No. I have lived in this world my whole life. I have seen what has happened to those who do not see the failures of others and who do not learn. A person's mistakes are his legacy, too. His children can be lifted by their father's past or have to fight it.'

'I know that well.' She looked at him and let her breath flutter past her lips. 'If the wishes of others are so important to you, then you will have to marry soon. It is what you are supposed to do.'

His gaze looked through her. 'I, too, know that well.'

She tilted her chin. 'All you must do is seek out a woman who is fond of society. You have all that a woman might wish for and can put it at her feet.'

He frowned, but the words weren't from his title but from him. 'It is true, a woman may wish to wed me for the world I can give her, but how is that different from you?'

'My dowry is not so large it will choke a man.' She twitched her shoulders. 'But he may cough,' she admitted.

'I was not talking of funds. You could wed well without a dowry if you would just accept our ways. It is not much for a man to ask.'

'No. It is not much. It is everything. For my sister, she flutters about like a butterfly when people are about. For me, the eyes on me make my stomach feel seasick. The clatter at the soirée made my head hurt. Sitting with others with tea in my cup, pretending to like it, pretending to care about the brim of a bonnet, knowing I cannot even think of the right word to say something pleasant. I feel the same as a speck in the bottom of the teacup.'

Her hand fell from his back and she stepped closer so his gaze met hers. This time her chin tilted down and her eyes levelled at him. 'Would you give up all that you care for to sit and pretend to like the taste of a foreign tea that tastes like weeds on your tongue, while you discuss the brim of a bonnet, and only wear boots that do not fit? For the rest of your life?'

'Most women like bonnets and tea and those things.'

'Then they can enjoy them. I do not wish to take theirs. I am quite sincere in that.'

'Why do you not try?'

'I have. I have sat in my sister's house and I have seen her life. For the two years since I arrived in England.' She held up her fingers. 'I have travelled to London and made morning calls and walked in her steps. We returned home again. She flutters about there and her face shows that she has been in a garden of nothing but flowers. She says I can be a bee, too, and I understand, but her garden is wrong for me. And you—' Her voice slowed. 'You have not truly taken on your new duties. You have stayed in the country rather than go to town to find a wife. Do you not feel trapped?'

'Do not put words in my mouth.' He moved. His shoulders turned. He still sat, but his body faced her. 'There is nothing I want more than to accept my duties. Nothing.'

'You have not wed—'

'I merely have not had the time.'

'You are well over thirty. You've had more than ten years to look for a wife.' She waved an arm. 'Not enough time?'

'Apparently not.' His lips turned down. 'And I am not *well over thirty*. I am thirty-one. At *first*, I was the second son and Geoff was the shining star in the heavens. Every woman I thought fascinating only met me in order to speak with my brother. I could see where their attention went. I remember that well. I decided marriage was not for me—until I met one woman at a soirée and I thought she was the one.'

'Did she reject you?' Her voice wisped away at the last words.

'Not really. I have not asked her yet because… Geoff has not been dead a year. A respectful period of time should be waited. He is—was my brother. And truth be known, I pursued her before he died. Geoff just did not know it. He never missed a soirée where she attended that he did not ask her to dance. He told me he would win her some day—but that she thought him too rakish and said she could not imagine him forsaking his mistresses for a wife.'

Winter's chill settled in her bones, even though the temperature was warm. 'You and Geoff pursued the same woman and he did not know?'

'I have not had a woman in my bed since Louisa said a man must give up his mistress for her.' He picked up the paper with the alphabet and handed it to her. 'Geoff had told me what she'd said to him. I mentioned to Louisa, later, that I had made certain conclusions and that I wished Geoff understood my unwillingness to traipse about with him—to disreputable places. She certainly had to know what I meant.' He made a loose fist and tapped it on the table. 'I pursued her with more determination than Geoff. I selected every word before I said it to her. Now that he is gone, I don't know what I think any more. Except I do not like what I did to my brother. When he died, I received the message at her father's house.'

She looked at the page of letters and wanted to crumple it up, but she didn't. 'I believe I have met Louisa. She is one of my sister's closest friends. We went to the shops. She chose slippers with pink rosettes. When she laughs, no one near can frown.'

'That would be Louisa.' Rhys turned away, suddenly fascinated by the unlit lamp. 'When my brother left the room, I often talked with her. I made her laugh. I did whatever it took to get those smiles. I thought her worth the risk.'

'The risk of hurting your brother?'

She thought his silence meant he would not answer. He didn't need to. He'd not wanted to pursue the same woman as Geoff.

'The risk of—more than that. By then my sister had died. To lose her had been so unfair. I imagined the fire taking her. The pain of it. We'd all loved her so much. I still cannot dwell on it. I did not want to repeat such a thing, and if I married Louisa, how could I keep her safe? But I eventually pushed those fears aside. And then my brother died. And now that I am the duke…' He tailed off.

'You should always be a person before you are a title,' she said, then turned to leave. She'd reached the door when he responded.

'That is not how it works.'

The quiet emphasis of the words rang in her ears and when she looked back, he still gazed at the lamp.

She wondered if he imagined Geoff's face or Louisa's smile.

Chapter Nine

After his morning ride, Rhys walked to the library. A rustle in the room alerted him that someone stood inside.

Entering, he felt a surge of disappointment that Bellona wasn't there. Guilt replaced the displeasure, but then he truly felt pleased. His mother fussed with a curtain. She'd not shown any care of the house in a very long time and to have her standing with the sunshine about her brightened his own heart.

'You would think the maids would have learned by now how to arrange the folds.' She moved them this way and that, frowning.

'Now I am crushed.' He moved beside her. 'I thought you were here to see me and it is only the windows you wish to inspect.'

'Well, I might inspect you a bit, too. Now that

I see you in the light, it appears your valet does not know how to keep a man's hair properly trimmed. Or you have been leading him a merry dance again.'

'Guilty.'

She reached up and patted his cheek. 'Rhys. I am not here to merely note how you have let yourself go because it is possibly a good thing.'

He chuckled. 'How's that, Mother?'

'When you are truly well groomed, it would be so hard for a young woman to keep from losing her heart to you.'

'You must be sure to tell the young women this. I don't think they are able to realise it on their own.'

'Nonsense.' She frowned and fussed with the curtains again. 'I think we have one under our very roof who is becoming rather taken with you.'

'I am certain she might be a bit fond of me, Mother, but I believe she is also fond of the stable master as he has secured archery targets for her. She's also had Cook prepare a poultice for one of the footmen.'

'Your valet talks too much of the other servants.'

'Just as a lady's maid talks too much to the mistress of the house. You should not believe idle talk when someone suggests Miss Cherroll is taken with me.'

'This is not idle talk. It's from her own mouth.'

'Miss Cherroll?' He studied his mother's face, uncertain he heard correctly.

'Yes.' She nodded her head. 'She does not exactly say it in words, but a mother knows. A mother definitely notices when a woman's eyes change if the son's name is mentioned. If she speaks differently when he is discussed. It's obvious.'

'I've seen none of it.'

'I am not surprised. Only concerned. But please do not encourage this woman, Rhys. Such heathenish ways. But she does make the days bearable and she has a heart of gold underneath all that rubbish she spouts. I don't want more unhappiness for her. She's had enough. No parents. Not settled like her sister. I see a poor future for her and I don't wish more unpleasantness on her, especially not under my roof.'

'You have nothing to worry about.'

Her eyes batted his words back at him. 'If you say so. She's not right for society. You should hear the tales of her life. She is of a different world. If it were not for the earl, she'd be making her way at the docks.'

The image of Bellona walking among the toughs and cutpurses jabbed at him.

He pulled open a desk drawer, searching, for what he did not know, but he would know if he saw it. 'I am aware of the role I have to fulfil. I know how uncomfortable a woman as spirited as Bellona would be living this life.'

'How uncomfortable *she* would feel? The whole of the *ton* will be watching whom you choose as a wife, Rhys. They would not be pleased that you have turned your back on their daughters and sisters. They will think you married beneath yourself. And you will have. Remember your father's last request. He counselled all his children on the importance of marriage. He asked for his name to be carried on. He wanted the family to continue. *Wed a suitable duchess*, he said. He said that many times. It was one of the last things he asked for.'

'Those were not his final words to me. They were to Geoff.' His breaths were quick. Taking out a pen, he put it by the first one. He stared at them and then put one back inside the desk.

She walked to the window. 'I worry. I can't help it. I know how easily you could be taken from me. Everything has changed so much. Not quite a year ago, Geoff was here. A year before that, your father was here. He started failing soon after he told me of your sister's death.' She looked into the rain. 'It was like he died on purpose, so he wouldn't have to…'

'Mother. He was seventy-eight. I don't think he had a lot of choice in the matter.'

'Did you notice the honeysuckle blooming when Geoff died? I'd been in the garden with him the day before and we'd talked about how he loved the scent of them. So do I. His passing was so cruel—taking him in the spring when so much life began around him.'

She pushed back the curtains and didn't speak for a moment. 'He loved honeysuckle. When he was a boy, he'd pick the little flowers and bring them to me and I'd sniff them and exclaim to make him happy, but I truly was the most pleased. The two of you grew up so fast, Rhys. I remember how he felt as a babe in my arms. So many of the things I'd forgotten about while he was here, but after he died I remembered them all so plainly. The best children a mother could have. And the three of you so close. You and Geoff always watched out for each other and your sister. No rivalry at all. I couldn't have been more proud of my children.'

'Geoff was my only brother.' The words sounded normal enough—at least to her.

She turned. 'I wish for the family every hour. Every day I hear myself thinking about how I wish they would return. It's not asking much. To have my family. They were given to me once, but whisked away. Even the grandchildren they would have given me were taken from me. A home of this size should be filled with family. Instead we have servants and more servants and no one for them to take care of.'

Walking towards him, she smiled. 'I don't want you to think you're amiss. You're doing a fine job of managing things since they left, Rhys. I appreciate everything you've done to take over where your father and Geoff left off. I know how much you cared for them, too. How much you loved your sister. They would all be so proud of you. I am proud of you. I want you to know that.'

'Thank you.'

A maid crossed by the doorway with a tray, certainly taking it to Bellona's room. His mother's attention wavered and she waited until the woman could not possibly hear the conversation. 'Bellona must leave or you must go to London.'

He let out a loud breath of disagreement.

'Rhys. I am your mother. It is not only her acting differently. You are too aware of her. You understand quite well what I am really saying. A man's nature is such as it is. You could ruin her. She does not deserve that. You would hurt her. It is not the best situation for either one of you and you know it. She has told me how she is more comfortable with the servants at the earl's house than the guests. She has been there two years.' She paused. 'Think of her.'

His mother glanced at the statues. 'They're just bits of pottery. I don't know why we thought them anything else. Meant to hold memories of the past. They do. Soot left after the fire is gone.' She made a motion of sweeping them away before fixing her eyes on him. 'I don't know why I kept them.'

She stopped at his side, and reached to the loop of his cravat, straightening it. 'Think of *her*,' the duchess said again.

She left, skirts fluttering at her ankles. The maid moved by the doorway again, tray empty. Rhys called, stopping her.

'Inform the stable master to be ready to journey to London at a moment's notice.'

Rhys finished his meal, surrounded by empty chairs. The lamps lit the room as brightly as they always had. He sat at the same place he'd always sat.

He lifted his wine glass, sipped and put it down. Echoes of his sister's laughter, Geoff's jests and his father's half-hearted grumbles bounced in Rhys's memory. His mother, one brow raised in feigned dismay, or lips pressed to hide her smile, had presided over them all.

An infinite world at the time.

If he had known what was to happen, how could he have enjoyed the moments, knowing they were to end? But if he had known the future, the time with his family would have meant so much more.

Nothing could change one second of the time before or since. No oath was strong enough. He'd tried them all.

He stood, took the glass and finished it, sitting it back in the place it had always been and left the room.

No oath was strong enough.

Walking along the hallway, he stepped into the library and picked up one of the statuettes, turning it in his hand before putting it back on the mantel. His grandmother had owned one. His mother had added to the collection and his sister had given one to his mother. The women had thought them precious and he'd seen no value in them at all. None. Except now they'd somehow begun to matter a great deal to him.

Once he'd had to grab his mother's wrists to keep her from smashing them to the floor. They were supposed to have been passed to a daughter's daughter.

'What are you thinking of?' The question jarred him from his thoughts. He turned. Bellona stood in the doorway, staring at him. Yesterday, the message she'd sent to him had begged off reading practice because she said the duchess insisted on helping her. He knew why his mother kept Bellona at her side. He also knew just how long it had been since he'd been alone with Bellona. Two days. That he had kept count disturbed him. That his senses came alive when he saw her concerned him even more. His mother was right.

He watched her study his face. 'I was thinking of the statues on the mantel. How long they've been there. Most of them, my whole life.'

She walked into the room with the assurance of someone who'd never seen a cloudy day, but her eyes belied her steps.

'Your mother. I am concerned about her.'

'She is more demanding?'

Bellona shook her head. 'No. She's more pleasant, but still…'

'The woman you have met is not the woman she was before. She wasn't gentle, but she wasn't the same as she's been. The grief took over. Her worries surrounded her.'

'I run from mine.' She only touched her skirt long enough to hitch it up on one side, before letting it flutter into place. 'Sturdy boots, remember.'

'You can't always escape the things that trouble you.'

'If you say so.' She stepped to the books, grimaced and began to study the spines. 'I am thankful I ran from Melos. I am also making certain I do not have to stay in London if I don't wish it. If I cannot be in my own country, then I have no place to bind me to it. That is why I have decided to learn to read. Your mother said it might be needed some day to write to my sisters.'

'A good reason.'

She tugged at a book, looked at it and put it back.

'Where would you go?' he asked. He hadn't thought beyond the moment.

'I have a friend who thinks of me as a daughter, I believe. And she knows a woman who married well, but is lonely. They have written to each other and the woman says I might visit and, if we get on well, I can stay with her.'

'But you are already a companion to my mother. You must agree you take her mind from her grief.'

'I do. But she tells me she is so much better already and she is.'

She studied the books. 'Your mother said you had another book by the man who wrote *Crusoe*. I thought I might like it better. What was that man's name?'

'Defoe,' he said, not letting her divert his attention.

'I do not know how *Crusoe* ends,' she said. 'But he could not return to the same world. When a year passes. Two. So much changes if you do not see the people often. You cannot return to the same world as before. And neither can I. So I will move somewhere else. Somewhere smaller. While I have the chance to make a new life. I want children. But there are many motherless children. Many. I might gather some about me.'

'You could have your own. Marry.'

'Marriage.' She shook her head. 'Look at the grief that marriage has caused your mother. A husband and two children lost.' She paused. 'My mother did not truly have a husband. He was gone most of the time.' She took another book as she spoke. 'The woman who thinks of me as a daughter, her husband did not do right by her either.

Marriage—' She shrugged. 'The pigs and goats and chickens do not marry. And yet women do. They think they can change—' she looked at him '—nature. Yet the males of the species do not seem that particular.'

'I will be loyal to my wife. A vow is a vow.'

'You say that.'

'I know that,' he said. 'I have— I made no vow yet to Louisa. But for her I gave up other women…to prove to myself I could do it…' He had not thought it possible to go so long without a woman. 'I assure you it has not been easy, but I make no idle promise. I can be a true husband.'

'I am proud for you.' She looked at the book she'd taken out and her mouth formed letters, before she stopped, watching him. 'But I do not know if I can make such a vow.'

'You jest.'

She shook her head and held the volume towards him, letting it rest in the air between them. 'Sows. Ewes. Hens. They do not seem particular about their mates. Women, too, change their affections. Widows remarry. Women on Melos… I saw their hearts change. My mother's did not after she married my father, but I could see that did her no good either.'

'I pity the man who you might marry.' His fingers clasped over the leather, but she didn't release it and he didn't pull it away.

'That is why I should not wed. I wish to be happy. I like to smile.'

'I think you would like giving a man grief, too.' He looked at the book they held. Defoe. *Roxana.*

'Ochi.' A definite no. 'I do not want a man close enough to give him any sorrow. It would rebound double on me.'

'Your choice.' He slipped the book into his control and put it back on the shelf.

This woman was no society miss. The *ton* would certainly not accept someone so different, so free of restraints. He spoke his thoughts aloud, puzzled. 'Your sister cannot encourage your folly. She surely wants you to follow her example. I may not always agree with Warrington, but I believe he treats her well. Theirs is a good union.'

'Warrington is kind to her. Her heart is filled with him and the children. They are of such a similar mind.' Her eyes flicked up. 'Similar to yours. I have considered this life in England for two years, and after being at Harling House I know I may be wrong for others, but I am right for me.'

'You met me and decided marriage and society was not for you?'

'I would not say that.' He lips curved into a smile. 'I have been away from my sister and the children. I have missed them, but it is them I miss. Not just any baby or child. I see your mother and I see the damage even good love can cause in a person.'

'Your father. You are letting his actions rule yours. All your thoughts of marriage are coloured by the way he left you all.'

'No.' Her chin tilted and her lips thinned. She ducked her head, but not before he could read her face. Her next words didn't match her expression. 'I hardly knew him. I remember my mother crying more than I remember him. My uncle did what he could do to help when I was very young. But he died—killed for no reason. We had so little. I do remember that when my father came home, the food was better. Everything. But inside the house was not always better. Our life was a calm sea when he was gone even though my mother struggled so hard. But when he returned there was a storm inside our home. I only wanted the goods he brought. I did not care for him at all.'

Then she made a gesture with her hand. He didn't know what it meant, but he was certain it was not a suitable action for a lady. He'd noticed it before. Her wrist would turn quickly and her lips firmed and words formed in her mind, but her fingers executed the phrase he didn't know.

'You should not say such,' he said, testing his theory.

'A society woman would not,' she agreed. 'Another reason to remain as I am.'

'I surrender,' he said, moving to the desk. He caught her gaze and smiled. 'I have a surprise for you.'

He did not want to argue with her, but he did want to hear her voice. He had lost his mind somewhere among the pins in her hair, but as long as no one else knew and he recovered soon, all would be fine. He hoped.

He opened the desk drawer and pulled out a book, holding it aloft. *Cobwebs to Catch Flies*. He brushed a hand across the leather cover. 'I don't know where it was or which servant found it, but they have all been rewarded.' He smiled. 'Geoff, my sister and I all read this.' For a moment he was held by memories, all good. 'Sit near me.' He waved the book towards the cushions. '*This* one will have you reading.' He opened it, moving to the section with the three-letter words.

Bellona settled on to the sofa and he put the book in her hands and sat beside her. Spices flowed into the air. The memories and scent of Christmas around her made the present feel as good as the best of the past did. He could hardly wait for her to begin.

She took the tome and her lips moved the barest bit, saying the words silently while she studied the page.

Her mouth. He watched it, willing her to repeat the action. She didn't, but she still held the book.

A weakness plunged into him. He relived a memory that kept him strong.

He'd written some bit of fluff to the girl who'd given him his first kiss. The moment had been... a surprise.

He'd not really thought much about what a kiss could feel like. And he hadn't meant to be alone with the girl. They'd happened upon each other by chance. She'd rounded a corner and he'd caught her just as she stepped into him and then she'd trounced his boot and he'd been worried about his boot being scuffed. She'd purposefully rested her foot on his other boot and he'd meant to remove her, but her waist had felt more important than any new boot had ever felt in his life and he'd not been able to budge the little wisp of her. He didn't remember the conversation or how long they'd stayed there, but she'd reached up and kissed him.

His world had changed.

Later, he'd written to her about how her lips tasted—but the letter had been stolen from his chamber before he could give it to her and it had somehow ended up in his father's hands—thank you, Geoff—and his father had called Rhys into the library, told him to shut the door and they had had another talk. The letter had been returned to Rhys and his father said it was Rhys's choice whether he gave the letter to the chit or not, but to remember that words written could never be changed. He should consider how a wife might feel some day to read something which might concern her. Or how their servants might snicker to learn of such a thing about their master.

Rhys's father gave him the letter. Rhys threw it in the fire. He'd disappointed his father.

Just as his father would be disappointed now if he'd walked into the room. Rhys shoved the thought aside.

'Why don't you read aloud?' Rhys suggested, and she did.

Initially, she stumbled over the words, but she could understand them, slowly at first and then more easily.

She closed the book, but held the place with one finger. 'I did not know books were like this. Cats and rats and dogs.' She looked at him. 'I would wager there will be a pig in it, too.'

'I do not want to give away the ending.' He leaned closer, pretending to look at the pages. 'Keep reading. It is good for you.'

'I do not like to hear something is good for me. That usually means I won't like it.' But she wiggled a bit, reminding him of a hen settling into her nest.

Again she read the words aloud.

He watched, half his vision on the book and half

on her. The only other noise in the room besides her voice was the occasional sound of the page turning. He listened and then forgot everything else as her fingertips touched the paper.

His thoughts were much safer when he imagined only her hair. Now he watched her hands, heard her voice and could not stop his fascination from growing.

She reminded him of childhood and innocent times, and then she'd turn the page and he'd be ever so thankful to have left all that behind him and be alone with her. She made his chest feel broad and his skin vibrate just because her voice moved towards him through the air.

Her head dropped a bit to the side and her words wearied.

He wanted these moments. They were harmless. Nothing to be concerned about. Nothing he would remember later and feel guilty for, even when he was married to his duchess. No one would know that his mind wandered to places where it shouldn't. This was just a simple moment between two people who happened to be in the same room.

'I am tired of reading,' she said, closing the book.

He took it from her hands and put it on the other side of himself, causing him to move so close their sides brushed. Without her voice, it felt as if the whole world had ceased to have sound.

Rhys spoke softly, not wanting to disturb even a dust mote in the air. 'Tell me why you cannot tolerate dancing. Not the dance itself, but the holding.'

'It has always been this way.' The words were slow and barely reached his ears. She'd closed her eyes for a moment and she opened them when she answered. 'Or at least for a long time.'

'When did it start?'

'I'm not sure. But I know the dreams started on the ship to England. The first night I slept afterward.'

Her eyes flicked to his face. He didn't move, waiting.

'I told you that when I was on Melos...' The purr of sleepiness left her voice, but her lids dropped again. 'Men woke my sister Thessa and me during the night. They forced us from our rooms and one was going to wed my sister Thessa whether she wished it or not, and the other was going to—wed me, and I...could not have survived marriage to him. Or he could not have survived marriage to me. Snake. *Fidi*.'

'And…' he said, barely speaking.

'And Thessa and I swam to the English ship in the harbour. It left. We sailed here.'

He didn't want her to open her eyes, afraid if she did she'd pull back, taking him from this shared moment. He gave a soft sound of acknowledgement, looking at the shape of her face, and the skin, so delicate he feared even brushing his fingertip against it might be too rough.

He slid further from her on the sofa so he could put his hand along the back. His fingertips could have easily held her shoulder or dipped a bit lower and touched the bare skin where her sleeve ended. In his mind, he could feel her. Perhaps he truly did because the warmth of her body flowed outward. He was so close it had to be wafting to him.

'The island men pursued us, but the captain and his crew fought them off. I thought we were safe, but later on our voyage a man decided I was bad fortune.' She touched her throat, slender fingers resting against her skin. 'He tried to toss me overboard to drown in the seas. I couldn't breathe I was so frightened. Thessa pulled him from me.'

Spears of rage hit his midsection. Those words changed everything. They slammed into him as if his own body had been thrust hard against a wooden fortress. His temple pounded. He pulled back, not wanting her to sense the violence inside him.

How dare someone touch her so? He would have killed him without hesitation. He forced his voice to be calm, but it took a moment. 'I am pleased you were unhurt.'

Her lips turned up, not so much in a smile, but in some sort of inner amusement. 'I have a sword. I thought it would protect me, but I almost cut off my own nose.' Her eyes opened and she looked at him. In that second, he felt the same intimacy he might when looking across bedcovers at a woman, only it wasn't the same. This was more intense, deeper—something he hadn't known existed. It was as if she'd just taken over his whole body. As if her spirit was twice his size and had wrapped itself around him, cradling him. He never wanted to lose this feeling.

She leaned towards him, touching, perhaps not touching but brushing, just at the top of her nose, and he almost felt the sensation of her fingertips.

The trail of her hand lingering against his skin in the same way she swept her hand above her own nose. 'Can you see the scar?' she asked, voice husky. She slid more towards him. He could not move.

A tiny white line rested just at the bridge. 'How did you do that? Was it that man?'

'It wasn't him. This was when I was living in England. I was taking the weapon from the shelf where I had put it to keep it from my niece. It fell.' She shut her eyes again, only for a moment. 'I didn't know how I was going to tell my sister, since she'd already complained about the sword. But luckily, her babe chose that moment to be born and no one noticed my hand—' she rested her palm over her nose and peered out at him from around it '—covering my face. By the time my nephew was safely tucked into the family, the scratch hardly showed.'

She took her hand from her face. 'He was so tiny. I did not see why her *stomachi* needed to grow so big to have such a little babe.'

He studied her face.

'Your nose is rather a pleasant nose.' The words slipped from his mouth, sounding like a caress.

If he raised his forearm just the slightest bit and moved just the merest bit forward, he could be holding her.

'I didn't expect to like the babe.' She grimaced. 'He'd caused my sister such discomfort already and he wasn't a girl. Warrington already had a son and daughter, and I hoped the little girl would have a sister. I wanted another small Willa in the house.'

She pulled herself straight on the couch. 'I told Melina just a few days ago…about the mark. She thought it humorous that I could manage to sail from Greece to here, sleep when the pirates boarded the ship trying to take our other sister before being defeated in their efforts and have no marks to show for it. Then I wounded myself with the weapon I kept for protection.'

She looked at him. 'Let me try reading again. I like it much better when the words are small and the story is about children.'

He moved, securing the tome without looking at it. Holding it in her direction. Her hands skimmed over his as she took the volume, slowly, from him.

She turned the pages to the spot where she'd left off. 'The words are getting harder, though.'

His arm rested at her shoulders. 'Just hold your finger to the word and I'll help you.'

She began to read, and at the first stumble she moved into the cradle of his arm and pointed for him to read the word aloud.

She stayed where she was, and when she paused again he let go of the breath he'd been holding and helped her.

The book wavered because she pointed to another word. He took hold of the other side of the cover and held it.

As the words became longer and longer, he never realised when he became the speaker and she became the listener. His words lingered, so she could follow easily, and he read to her about the happy family of eight children and the merry-go-round.

He read more slowly as he neared the conclusion, and when the story finished they closed the book together, then he pulled back and she straightened.

'I did not want the story to end,' she said. 'I quite liked it.'

'I did as well.'

'A good tale,' she said. 'Better than *Crusoe*.'

He nodded, holding it with one hand. 'Though I enjoyed it as a child, I had not realised before how much interest it has.'

'Sometimes things more scholarly are not always the most enjoyable.'

'They are good for one, though.'

The flicker of her eyes when she heard the words acknowledged his jest.

'So true.' She stood and leaned towards him again, taking the book. 'Do you mind if I keep this in my room for a time?'

He looked up at pale skin, a long neck, a wilful chin and lips that he wanted to touch in all the ways that he could.

'As long as you'd like. It's yours.'

'Only for a short while and then I'll put it back,' she said and left the room.

He wondered if he would be able to move again.

Chapter Ten

Bellona fought, inside the dream, pulling hands from her throat, her grasping fists closing over emptiness. She struggled for air—ale-scented breath suffocating her. His darkened pupils expanded so that she could see nothing else. She scrambled back as her own vision clouded into black, reaching for her weapon, the world of the ship fading, changing to the bedchamber. The image of the crewman fell away into the recesses of the room.

Her eyes opened. She sat against the headboard of the bed, her heart pounding, fingers gripping the knife she'd had under her pillow. Her throat ached, the press of thumbs indenting her throat still choking her.

She swallowed slowly, trying to get air, but keeping her movements still so she could be aware of the room. Shadows brushed her skin with the lightness of spider's legs. Beyond the walls, something creaked.

Slipping one foot from the bed, she braced for her ankle to be clutched. She had to escape from the room, yet the hallway would be dark and someone could be waiting.

She dashed to the door, her back against the wood, the knife held close to her body. Listening. Watching. Waiting.

Wind blew against the window. She forced herself calm. Over and over the dream found her in the night.

Questions would throb in her head until morning. What if the pirates hadn't been defeated by Captain Ben and his crew? What if they had continued to pursue the ship intent on making another attempt to capture Bellona and Thessa? Or what if the gamekeeper had got angry at her because she had been accepted into the house as a guest and he broke in to attack her?

She touched the door latch with her left hand, gripping the cold metal. Listening. She had no reason to fear. None at all. But blood still raced in her veins.

She leaned back, feeling a vibration as she pain-lessly thumped her head once against the wood. She could not traverse the room and reach the bell pull. Her feet wouldn't let her.

The room didn't feel safe. She couldn't stay long enough to summon a maid. The pirates would not go away. She could not make them leave her dreams and in her dreams she had nothing to fight with.

Soundlessly, she opened the door and put one foot into the hallway. Nothing. Still darkness. No movement.

She couldn't shut the door behind her. Even though the room could trap her, she couldn't close even one possible way of escape.

Sliding her body out, she moved down the hall-way. If she called from the library for a servant, the butler would arrive. He stood tall and she could ask him to check her room for a mouse. She'd heard something. She'd heard a squeak or a creak. A noise had stirred her from the terror.

Or perhaps she'd only dreamed it. The figure of the man squeezing her neck had vanished as she woke, disappearing, as the nightmare always did, taking the stench of death with him. Leaving her room as quiet and still as a crypt covered in dust.

Standing, she waited, making sure she heard nothing again. She forced her imagination away. Those endless fears that plagued her had merely returned, but she didn't want to be alone.

She clutched the knife close to her body, and ignored the chills seeping through her thin shift.

'What—' A gruff voice—behind her—right behind her. Her mind froze, but her body did not. She swirled around, bringing the knife up. His hand rose, clamping on her own, holding her clutched fist with the strength of a vise. In the same instant her hand was caught, he moved forward, pushing her, her right shoulder crashing into the wall. He trapped her with his size.

Neither moved.

'Bellona,' the duke gasped out. 'What the hell are you doing?'

She could not speak. She could not.

'Bellona.' He called her name again.

It was Rhys. Her brain knew it. But her body wouldn't move. Her pounding heart took all the power from her voice. Pushing against him made no more difference than hurling herself at the strongest rock on Melos. Fear overpowered her, and her mind could not free itself from the terror.

'It's me. It's Rhys,' he said. 'Bellona.'

Shudders racked her body.

He still held her knife hand, but his other arm pulled her into an embrace. 'You're safe.' His voice rumbled softly, a caress in words. 'It's me. I won't hurt you. I'd never hurt you.'

The bulwark of his strength didn't frighten her, but terror still controlled her even though her mind translated the scene into the reality of the moment. She rested her head against his shoulder. The only movement she could make.

He pulled her even closer. He murmured to her and he lightened his clasp, cradling her now. Her body shook and he didn't speak again, just held her.

Minutes passed. The knife handle was pulled from her hand. She had no strength to hold it. She didn't have the ability to stand without his help. His other arm went around her.

Her face stayed buried against him, the silken threads of his waistcoat against her cheek. His male scent soothing her. He didn't clench her tightly, but she burrowed into him, regaining her composure as the shaking stopped and her heart-beats slowed.

'I thought…' she whispered.

'You thought to hurt me?'

'No. I did not know. I could not think,' she said. 'I did not know it was you.'

'Who else would it be?'

She whispered again, 'I did not know…'

He kept her folded into his arms, crushing her against the fabric of his clothing, surrounding her with the fortress of his strength.

His chin rested against her forehead. 'I didn't mean to frighten you.'

'I didn't recognise your voice at first.' She shut her eyes, taking solace from his hands clasping her back, holding her.

'Sweet, much as I'd like to hold you, I have something I must attend to.'

'I don't want to be alone.'

'I understand.' He squeezed her. 'We can talk about it later.'

She gripped him. 'I could have hurt you.'

'I know.' He mumbled the words, his lips against her hair. 'You could have.'

He pushed himself away from her. 'But you must get to bed now.'

She reached out, unable to let him go, and confusion hit her mind. She felt the sleeve of his arm, but he jerked back.

Something was wrong.

'I…' She clenched her right hand, letting her own fingers brush her palm. Wetness.

'I— Did I—?'

'Yes, I believe you did.'

'You're cut?'

'It does feel that way. I appear to have grasped the blade before I was able to get to your hand.'

She gasped. He stepped further away.

'Rhys—we must get a light. You're bleeding.'

'I'll attend to it. You go back to your room.'

'I'll summon help.' She turned to run, but he captured her arm with his right hand, grip warm and tight.

'Shh… I. Will. Attend to it.'

'But, Rhys… Are you hurting? We must—'
He must not be hurt. He could not be hurt. Her breaths gasped from her.

'Bellona. The servants. I do not want talk, but

really I should look at it. There is a light in my chamber.'

'Yes,' she agreed. She slipped from his grip and caught the fabric of his sleeve, pulling him in the direction of his room. 'Quick.'

Inside the room, the stain on his white sleeve looked like nothing more than a shadow until he stopped by the lamp.

Blood dripped from the hilt of the knife.

Red. She gasped. Death. She could hear the screams of the women of her homeland. She could have done to Rhys what the man who'd killed her uncle did.

Her knees weakened, but she did not fall. He put the knife on the bedside table and opened his hand. The skin parted where his palm had slid down the blade.

'You cannot die.' She appraised his body, looking for damage. 'You cannot.'

'I am not planning to.' He pushed the skin together and held it. 'Bring me a flannel. I need to stop the bleeding.'

She rushed to get the cloth and took the fingers of his hurt hand in hers, and he moved his free hand aside while she pressed the cloth against the wound.

'You must remove the blood from yourself as well,' he said. 'You look as if you have been in a fight. Are you cut?'

She noted the red splotches on her arm for the first time. Her own fingers showed red. She examined her arms and hands. 'No.'

'I'm thankful.' He shut his eyes briefly and shook his head. 'I'm thankful I am the one that felt the blade and not both of us. That would be hard to explain.'

'It should be stitched,' she said, bending over his hand. 'I will do it. I know I can.'

He took a step away. 'Damned if I let you near me with a needle. I've seen your embroidery.'

'I will be slow.'

'Bellona.' His eyes widened. 'We have a physician. I have been bled before and I survived. It is merely releasing some of the humours. I do not like it, however. Your method is a bit painful.'

'I will take care of you.' She moved to the washstand and splashed water from the ewer into the basin. She swept her hands through to remove the red. The water turned a bloody tinge, but no cuts showed on her own skin. She turned back. His eyes were on her and his gaze didn't move as she watched him.

She took a cloth, her hands dripping water, and rushed to his side. 'I'll care for it. Sit. Sit on the bed.'

Keeping his hand clasped over the cut, he held his elbows wide, still standing. 'Would you undo my cravat and the buttons on my waistcoat? I'd prefer not to get more bloodstains on the fabric…'

She wiped her hands dry, tossed the cloth to the bed and stepped closer. With a quick tug, she slipped the knot free. Then a swift snap.

The force of her pull on his neckcloth jerked him sideways.

'Damnation, woman. Do not break my neck.'

'Pardon. I did not realise it was wrapped around so many times.'

'You almost snapped my head from my body. You do wish to kill me,' he muttered, then leaned forward again. 'So unwrap it or merely slip it free by pulling *gently* at the sides and front.'

She finished her task, surprised at how comfortable she was this close to him. To be alone with him was quite different from anyone else.

She folded the cravat and put it on the bed.

Reaching up, she slipped the delicate buttons of his waistcoat free, moving back so he could raise his hands as she finished.

At the last one, she stopped, looking up into the dark eyes as she undid the final clasp.

'Are you…' she asked, 'in pain?'

The lightest nod.

When she turned, her eyes locked on his hand. She sucked in air through her nostrils.

'You look a bit rattled,' he said. 'Do not have the vapours.'

'Your Grace. Please. Sit.'

He looked at her. 'Bellona, I believe you can call me Rhys now.'

She paused. 'I am sorry I hurt you.'

'I know. I believe you.' He held his hands clasped a bit more and stepped away. 'What I don't understand is the knife. I thought your weapons were taken.'

'Not the one I carry in my boot.'

'Ah, yes.' He nodded. 'How remiss of me. The blasted boots. Your reticule knife was removed, but it was strictly an oversight on my part not to have someone collect the knife from your boots. That's their charm, isn't it? That's why you wear them?'

She answered with her eyes.

He stared at her bare feet and his eyes trailed up her body clad only in her thin nightdress, leaving warm currents in their wake, causing a *frisson* in her stomach. 'I would say that you do not have another knife hidden about you right now. Is that a safe assumption?'

'No—yes, I do not have a knife.' The words. They scared her. She'd just told a man she was unprotected. The walls in the upper rooms were solid… The duchess would not hear a scuffle. No one could answer her if she called out for help. In the servants' quarters, there was a chance someone might respond, but not here.

He watched her, but without the darkness she feared. 'You should go so I can summon assistance.' She lost all thoughts he could ever harm her. He was injured and he cared that she not be discovered in his room.

The red on his hand reminded her.

She had done that.

'I will summon my valet,' he said.

As he moved forward, she threw her body between him and the pull. 'I cannot go to my room.' He stepped to brush her aside, but she flattened her palms on his chest. His eyes widened. He felt rather like a wall. A wall of muscle and skin and male. 'Your Grace.' She thought it best to address him such at the moment. 'I will worry.'

He leaned close. He'd been drinking brandy some time in the evening. His eyes shone with an emotion that jumped into her and caused a heating sensation that somehow managed to touch her entire body.

'Sweet. It's his job. I will tell him that if I die he must alert the entire household. So, if you do not hear, then you will know I am well.'

'I am not leaving. He may care for you if you wish, but I am to stay and see that it is done right.'

'You cannot be found in my chamber in the middle of the night, particularly with blood on both of us. The man is discreet. He will not speak of it, but I fear he would have an apoplexy keeping silent on that. I would then have to replace him and I simply do not have the time.'

She lowered her eyes to her palms still resting on his chest and then slid her hands away, before looking up again. 'I will care for you.'

'You will?' He smiled. 'Just as you cared for me a few moments ago?'

Surely he would live if he could jest. She nodded and took the cloth from the counterpane, holding it towards his clasped hands. 'Yes, Rhys.' She daubed at the smears on him, taking the red from his knuckles.

When she indicated that she wanted to reach the cut, he did not open his grasp, but extended his fingertips to clutch the cloth.

'Let me,' she said, refusing to release it.

'You've already attacked me once in the night. Don't struggle with me now. I might stumble backwards and knock myself in the head.'

'If you stumble now, you will land on the bed. Sit on the bed so I can see the wound better.'

He sat on the edge. She was no closer than before until she perched beside him, her shoulder aligned with his. She wiped the cut clean.

'What happened to bring you out into the hall with a weapon?' he asked.

She pressed on the wound. 'I awoke from a nightmare and thought you were…someone evil.'

'And you only cut my hand?'

She pressed harder.

He flinched. 'Go more lightly with the cloth. You're making it worse. Leave and I will send for my valet. I just do not wish for him to know how this happened, but I suspect he will notice the cut and the shirt will have to be burned.'

'How dear are the lamps?' she asked.

'I have no idea. They're lamps.'

She sighed. 'Break the glass of one and tell him you stumbled.'

'I can do that. But when you turned to get the cloth, I noticed a bloodstain on your back. How will that be explained away?'

'The maid will not notice after I finish with the garment.' She peered at the cut. 'Move your fingers.'

He did.

She rested her forehead against his shoulder momentarily, then straightened again. 'That is fortunate. Now do not move them again.'

She held the flannel tight against his hand. He reached to pull it away, but she clasped it. Determined, he took the cloth and put it against his palm, closing the fingers of his right hand over it.

'You don't have to tend this. I'll break the lamp, call the valet and now you can go back to your room and get some rest.' Then he pushed her aside so that he could stand, reached with his left hand, picked an unlit lamp from the side of the bed and crashed the globe against the table. The glass shattered and he sat the base back on to the table.

She met his eyes. 'I'm still not leaving, Rhys.' She rose and moved, planning to search out another flannel. But before she left, she gazed over him to reassure herself he was not about to die.

He returned to the bed, stretched out lengthwise, his head at his pillow and his ankles crossed. 'Sweet, you may return to calling me Your Grace at any time.'

She spoke over her shoulder. 'You must recover. You would need a big spot to be buried in and the man who cares for the gardens would grumble if I asked him to dispose of you.'

'Bellona, you do not just dash a duke into a hole in the ground. You must have a bit of a ceremony first.'

'Yes, Rhys. I suppose it would take some time just to dig a hole for your boots.'

She could feel his eyes on her as he digested her words.

'Even if you address me as Your Grace, I suspect you've always seen me as no more privileged than one of the sailors on the ship that brought you to England.'

'That's not true.' She shook her head. 'I've always seen you as a duke.' She continued searching for a useful cloth, only stopping to look at him. 'But the men at sea are quite skilled in things that matter. You are skilled in books and learning, and I suppose that has a place besides writing letters.'

She found another flannel inside the washstand.

'Thank you.' He exchanged the reddened bandage he had for the new one, pressing it once more against the wound. He shut his eyes. 'Would you bring me a brandy glass and the bottle?'

She went for the drink, splashed some in the glass and then returned. He pushed himself upright with an elbow, his injured hand still gripping the cloth. He downed the liquid and held out the empty glass. She refilled it with the same amount. He looked at it, frowned and drank more slowly before handing the glass to her once again. The fresh blood smears on the flannel pressed to his injury caused her stomach to clench.

Putting the glass and bottle on the table, she returned to the dressing chamber and found another flannel for his cut. When she returned with it, he took it from her and placed it over the other one.

His eyes moved over her, reminding her of the way water in a stream followed the movement of the current.

'If you wish to get the dressing gown from my wardrobe, you may wear it,' he said. 'I would not want you to catch a chill.'

She moved to the dressing chamber. She didn't feel cold at all and she didn't think he'd been overly concerned about that. When she opened the wardrobe, she reached out, running her fingers over the silk and linen in front of her. Nothing looked as if it had ever been touched, but everything had rested against Rhys's body. She took the banyan, wrapping it around herself, amazed at how well shaving soap smelled. The garment drooped from her shoulders and dragged on the floor, but felt like a royal robe.

'This is so...' She snuggled into it. Then paused when she met his eyes. They'd narrowed, but she couldn't see behind them.

Padding back, she sat in a chair, looking across at him.

'You can't sit there all night and stare at me.' He pressed against the flannel. 'That will surely enough do me in.'

'If you die because I'm looking at you, I will take note of it, since I have never even been able to pain my sisters by giving them my harshest look.' An army couldn't have taken her from the room. 'I need to stay to make sure if you fall asleep, you don't get blood on the covers.'

'You sound like my mother. You have been spending too much time with her.'

'I think she will agree with you and so do I.'

He adjusted the pillow with his left hand. 'I suppose I should not have been traipsing about in the dark, but I have done it often in the past year. If I walk enough, then I sleep without my own dreams and I prefer that. The nights are so long after I have finished with my ledgers.'

'The dark frightens me. I always had my sisters close by when I was young. I had never been alone in the night until I sailed here. Sometimes I feel smaller than Willa. And now it has caused your injury. I didn't want to hurt you. I would rather my hand be cut.'

'I believe you. I didn't mean to grab the blade. I didn't know you had a knife in your hand until I reached the hilt. Then it was a little late to re-consider.'

'You could have been hurt much worse.'

'So could you.' His voice rose in exasperation. 'Granted, you did me an injury, but do you re-alise what could have happened?'

'It's better to have a knife than nothing. Even the smallest man is stronger than I am.' Rubbing her fingertips together, she examined them for red. 'It is important I protect myself.'

'Why? Why do you feel it is so important?'

She looked at his hand and let her gaze linger over the rest of him. Tall. Shoulders the same width of Stephanos's. But he tried to see her and not just the reflection of his power from the fear in her eyes.

She shook her head. 'It is…how I must be,' she said. 'How I have always been. At least for a long time.' She crossed her arms over herself.

'The ship?'

'That was the second time I knew I could die at a man's hands.'

The memories she kept in her thoughts always, of the island, and that day of violence, flashed in her mind. 'One day when I was young, I heard shrieks. But I thought it was happy noise. I wasn't close enough and I wanted to see what was happening. I ran to the people and saw them crying, but I could not go on.' There had been more than tears. There had been wailing—begging the heavens to reverse time and bring her uncle back to life.

'I could not see my uncle breathing his last,' Bellona explained. 'I could not believe that it was real. This time the truth felt like a dream. I could see and hear but I could not…feel. You cannot undo something like that. You wish for the moments to go back just the smallest time, but they will not. You long to know it didn't happen, but it did.'

She remembered stopping, and sitting, wrapping her arms around her knees. She could hear the words, and see the people, but they blocked her view of her uncle. More screams. Louder this time.

'So much noise,' she continued. 'Then Stephanos was walking away. Swaggering, away from everyone. Towards me. On the trail, he stopped and watched me. He was not even a true man yet, but he was tall even then. As big as the men. His eyes were evil. *"Your uncle is dead,"* he said. *"I killed the man who stabbed him."* He laughed. Blood was on his face and where his knife was tucked in his sash. *"I could kill everyone on this island and no one could stop me. Even you, little one. I could cut your throat."'*

She'd watched him and felt no fear. But she had known he was thinking of death as a prize—someone else's life a bounty. A proof of power.

'He laughed. He threw back his head and raised his fists into the air. Like a rooster crowing to greet the morning. He was not sad my uncle died. He was happy for my uncle's death because he could kill the murderer in front of everyone. He didn't care about justice. He cared that other people feared him.'

'Not all men are evil.'

'Stephanos was. And only one evil man can cause so much pain. And he liked it. Years ago, Melina was to marry him. She had no choice. He had decided to wed. He was going to marry one of us and he didn't care which one. Melos was too small to escape him. Melina sailed away to bring us funds to help, but when she didn't return, he noticed Thessa and would not stop watching her. She agreed to marry him to stop him looking in my direction. But then the ship came and we escaped. I still have dreams about it. About all of it.'

'Anyone could have nightmares after seeing such things.'

'I see too much in my dreams.' She wrapped her arms around herself. 'Again. I see a man's face with nothing in his spirit but death. The happiness of having power over others.'

'You cannot be feeling true danger from me. You cannot.' He pushed himself up. 'I could not hurt you. I could not.'

She shook her head. 'I don't believe you could. But there is something in your thoughts you are not saying.' Something she couldn't decipher. 'When you meet my eyes, I see… I am unsettled. If you are in the room, I know where you stand. I cannot think of anyone else when you are near.'

He shook his head from side to side. 'That is

just a… Something that happens between a man and a woman. It means little.'

'I cannot think it means nothing.'

'Not everything a person feels or thinks is to be spoken of. That is why thoughts reside in the head. Some things are to be kept silent. No one tells another person all the things inside.'

'My sisters and I, we did.'

'Perhaps women do. Men do not.'

'So they do not think of important things that need to be told?' She moved so she could see the light flickering on his face.

He closed his eyes. 'A man doesn't need to prattle on.'

'It is not prattle,' she said. 'I don't know what it is, though.' She shrugged. 'But perhaps it is not good. Your mother talks so much of death and hurting. And now you are injured. If you do not get well, your mother will never forgive me.'

'I doubt she will forgive you anyway if she finds out the truth,' he teased.

'My sisters and I had a saying, "There is the truth, and there is the truth we tell our mother."'

He smiled. 'My brother and I said it a little differently. "If you tell Mother, I will kill you."'

'I suppose they both mean almost the same.' She leaned closer, seeing his lashes against his cheek. The way the soft fringe and the strong jaw, lean nose and stubbled chin all formed the man.

'I am aware the duchess is on the mend,' he said. 'But I don't want to risk her learning of this.'

She rose and got another flannel and took it to the side of the bed, looking down at him.

He opened his eyes, peering into hers. 'Stop staring at me so.' He reached for the fabric. 'You might as well lie beside me. You're already ruined if anyone sees you here. It will probably look more innocent if we're on top of the covers, looking irritated, anyway. You might as well relax.'

She didn't want to go back to her room. To the dreams. She might have even talked to a pirate to keep from being alone. To be alone with Rhys, though, she would have fought sea savages.

She walked around the bed and sat on the other side, resting against the headboard, snuggling into the dressing gown. 'I wanted to make sure you are not hiding pain.'

'I'm not hiding it at all. It aches. But less than

other hurts I've had.' He paused. 'Where were you going when you were in the hallway?'

'The servants' quarters.'

'Were you searching for someone?'

'No. I sometimes sleep there. In my big room, sleeping is difficult. A few nights ago, I could not get the door to latch properly and I could not rest. My bedchamber seemed so large and open that someone could have walked in on me in my sleep and I felt that I had nowhere to hide. So I took the book to a smaller room I had found. I felt safer there.'

'You felt safer away…away from the rest of us?'

She nodded. 'The room is more like my home on Melos. A place so small no one could hide and a single lamp could light to the very edges of the room. In Melos, I would have thought it so grand to have the plainest chamber in your house. It is far better than what I once had.'

'Bellona, do you not respect the servants' world?'

'I do.' She smiled. 'Even your servants would think me far beneath them if they had stepped on Melos and met me right before I left my home. On

Melos, the animals lived under my home and the stairs led to the two rooms above, where we lived.'

'You'll never have to live like that again.'

'I miss it,' she said. 'I long for it every day.'

'How could you want to return to that?'

'I miss my sisters and my *mana* being together. The waves. The blue. The smell of the sea. The sand under my feet. But now I must be happy in England. I just do not know how to do that and it has been two years.'

'It takes a bit to recover when you lose what you hold dear.'

'I wish I could share with Mana and I wish she could see the riches here. The only thing I know is—if she had to choose and could, she would have chosen to be poor in order for us to have much. She would be so happy looking down from the heavens, although I don't know if it is possible.'

'Perhaps she does see this.'

'She would not be happy I hurt you.'

He chuckled. 'Of course not. A woman is not like that, especially a mother.'

'Gigia. You did not know her. She would think

it humorous or perhaps be angry that I let you so close to me in the hallway.'

'I can understand a grandmother not wanting her granddaughter to be close to a man in the dark.'

'Oh,' she said and chuckled. 'Gigia was not at all like you think. Not at all. She was not at all like the English and their proper ways. If she were here now she would be angry with me that I had not—'

Silence again. She knew he thought of the same thing she did. Gigia would have been angry that Bellona was not pushing her body against Rhys. But what he didn't know was that she would have been most angry to know Bellona had not been whispering a price in his ear.

Chapter Eleven

His hand hurt like blazes where he'd cut himself on her blade—which was the only thing allowing him to keep a decent thought in his head.

No, he didn't have a decent thought. But keeping his hand pressed against the makeshift bandage while reminding himself that he might still die of a fever kept him from pulling her against him.

She slept completely wrapped in his dressing gown, only her head poking from the top of it, concealed more chastely than any woman he'd ever seen.

She wiggled around, towards him, and the dip in the bed helped him roll ever so slightly towards her.

Miss Roman Warrior Goddess could have killed him with her very sharp knife, but he'd immediately wanted to reassure her when she'd discovered she'd accidentally sliced him.

Flames nicked at him everywhere, but he wasn't feverish.

His body still had the cravings of a youth, but his mind had advanced somewhat. He had rules. He had managed for quite some time to keep out of a woman's bed. He turned over. But now one was in his bed and she was sleeping peacefully.

He should have married before now.

He just wished… He just wished he had wed the previous year. He should have. Then his wife would have been settled by now. Most likely, a child would have been on the way and Rhys could have threaded his fingers through his wife's mussed hair and rested his cheek against her skin.

His boots were on so he couldn't get under the covers. He'd have to call his valet to be undressed. If he did that, she would have to leave. He wouldn't be able to sleep. He'd be lying there, bleeding and thinking of her.

She turned in her sleep. Her arm went around his midsection, jolting him, and he rested his clasped hands at the side, his arm just against her hand, keeping it snug to his body.

It would be for ever until morning, but the time would pass too soon.

Bellona awoke with a dim light flickering in the room and the sound of rain pounding against the house. Rhys sat in the overstuffed chair, which had been turned towards the bed. His left arm propped his head and she couldn't tell for sure if his eyes were open.

She pushed herself into a sitting position.

'It's morning,' Rhys said. 'Or it will be soon. You should leave before someone discovers you.'

'Your hand?'

He held it closer to the light. A blood-caked slice went from the bottom knuckle of his forefinger to the heel of his hand. He waved his fingers.

She put a foot on the floor, and looked at the night table. 'Will you return my knife?'

'Do you truly believe you need it here?'

'No.'

He reached to the drawer, pulled out the knife and handed it to her, the blade facing himself.

'I'll put it away,' she said. She held the cold

handle and looked at the weapon. The crumpled flannel, coloured with darkened red, lay on the nightstand.

The knife no longer made her feel safe or secure. Now it felt poisonous. The men who had frightened her in the past had hurt her from a world away.

Next, he picked up one of the shards of glass from the floor and put it on the table. 'You should take the real weapon from this room. My valet will believe the culprit was the broken glass. But I don't want him to see a knife in my room where there has been none before because he would surmise something. What exactly, I don't know, but I don't want to take the risk.'

He lowered his voice. 'Bellona, if you have fears in the night, I will check to make certain no one is there.'

'When Thessa and I were taken on the island, it was from our beds in the dead of night. I fear what happens when I sleep. But this time waking was the most dangerous course. I am sorry.'

She rose, reached for the tip of his fingers and examined his hand, putting the image of the injury into her mind as strongly as she could. This she would remember when she thought of the blood and felt fear, because this could result. She must control herself. She couldn't live in terror any longer. 'The hallway is long. If I have trouble sleeping, I'll sleep in the room below stairs. I feel safer there. If I shout, someone will hear. I don't want to see anyone's blood again and know I caused it. I can't.'

'You should not be below stairs. You are a guest. We have family rooms all about.' He waved his arm, then he dropped it to his side, grimacing. 'Just no family to fill them any more.'

She turned away. Only one person had the task of filling the rooms and she did not want to think about that.

'I will be leaving to go back to Whitegate soon,' she said. 'There I'll sleep in the nursery near the children if I need to. When I watch them, the world doesn't seem quite the same dark place. It seems like there's sunshine in the night.'

'I know how much better you've made the duchess while you've been here,' he said. 'I suppose there is a reason the mourning time is a year. Perhaps that's just how long it takes for everyone and I shouldn't have been so concerned. But after

Geoff passed, she crumpled, seeming to fall into the past, and even I could not rouse her.'

Bellona knew the duchess had been moving about Harling House more. She even talked of other things besides her grief. Bellona could leave without concern, and if she stayed it would be foolish. Being at Harling House when Rhys returned with a wife would not be wise.

'I am enjoying speaking with you.' He spoke softly. 'But if you don't leave soon, someone might see you. I'll walk you to your room. I don't want my dressing gown left about for the maid to see so I'll return with it.'

'We did nothing wrong.' She pulled the clothing tight around her, tying the belt. 'Except I did cut your hand.'

He moved to the door, waiting to open it. She stopped beside him. His hair had been finger combed and his shirt, rumpled, hung loose from his trousers. She reached, smoothing the sleeve, pressing a hand against it, but the wrinkles were fixed firm. 'You look like you have been in a war.' She didn't release his arm.

'It will certainly not be perceived as innocent if it is known you spent the night here. The talk would rumble about for the rest of our lives. You in my room. My hand slashed. Tales could get quite grand about that. Even I would have trouble believing it all innocent and I am here to see that it is. It might be assumed I attacked you. Or that you meant to hurt me and I had to restrain you. I don't know what would be said, but it would not be good. You'd be ruined. Quite ruined.'

She wouldn't admit the thoughts running through her mind, but she didn't care if she were ruined. She didn't. But for his sake she didn't want any tales put out about her hurting him and people speculating on what had really happened. She didn't even want to remember the night because of the pain she'd caused him and the fear that he might become feverish.

'I am so sorry,' she said.

He cupped her cheek in his hand. 'I see it in your eyes. You don't have to tell me.'

Everything shifted and it was as if his spirit stepped behind her, beside her and all around her.

'I'm leaving Harling House soon,' he said. 'And this will be the only chance I have to tell you goodbye.'

'You would vanish without taking your leave of me?'

'Yes. I would and I should.' He leaned forward. He brushed a light kiss on her cheek. 'I won't forget you.'

'You can't. I've put a mark on you.'

He moved, pressing another kiss on her cheek, lingering this time. His lips touched her as he spoke. 'You certainly have. Deeper than you know.'

He did not say he cared for her, though, and the knowledge washed over her in the same way a winter wind entered the cracks in the wall and enveloped everything inside. She had to make the feeling of unease disappear. She had to warm herself and only by stepping closer to him could she find any comfort at all.

She examined his eyes and he did not move, just looked back at her. Brown. Chocolate. Aged wood. Perhaps not as dark as the men on Melos. But a gaze softened by his lashes. He stood patiently, not speaking, and he didn't smile, but the small lines at the corners of his eyes relaxed.

Then he did smile. 'You shouldn't examine a man so closely. It does things to him… It is the same as if your fingers had swept over me.'

She reached out, putting her palm over his heart. The fabric didn't prevent her from feeling the strength of the man beneath, of the skin covering taut muscle.

He reached up, taking the barest grasp of her fingertips. He shut his eyes and pulled her hand up so that her knuckles brushed against the roughness of his cheeks.

No clock ticked. No sound from beyond the walls reached them.

He snaked the other arm around her waist, using the strength of his forearm to hold her against him, sending shivers into her that she could feel every place her body had ever touched anything and all those senses changed into something burning inside her.

His kiss was her first true kiss. His tongue, warm and hungry, took her, tasting her, melting her into his body and swirling her from her feet and giving her the feeling of when she swam just underwater and sunlight heated her back, only stronger.

He turned her, the door at her back, holding her up and himself, not ending the first kiss, but changing it to a treasure trove of smaller ones, moving to her jaw, her ear and burrowing down her neck, his left hand pulling open the top of the dressing gown, heated fingers pushing the barrier away to make a path for his lips over her skin.

He pulled back, released her, and her knees almost gave way, but as her body seemed to dip, his arm kept her upright.

His eyes stayed on hers, but when he opened his mouth, it took a second for him to speak.

'I am not myself.' His voice roughened, the words barely reached Bellona's ears. 'I do not know what is the matter with me.' He gave her a tight bow of his head. 'Forgive me.'

Bellona muttered. 'You have marked me, too.'

She stepped to the door, stopping only long enough to throw the dressing gown back into the room as she left.

Chapter Twelve

The palm of his hand tingled and burned. The cut had opened twice in the morning, but each time he'd cared for it and the bleeding had stopped.

His morning meal had not gone well. The rasher of bacon left a tallow coating in his mouth and he'd had to wash it away with a drink of chocolate—even that had not been quite right. He'd almost sent to have the cook try again, but he just was not hungry. Eating with his left hand made everything taste off.

The day's lashing rain splattered against the window and Rhys only had the ledger books in front of him so he could look busy if someone walked in. The sums were not terrible, but rather the way he'd hoped them to be. Everything soured before his eyes because of his thoughts concerning Bellona. The woman had injured him and he had fallen at her feet. If his mother had known how simple it could be, she would have been arming all the ladies of the *ton* with knives in their reticules.

This morning, he did not expect to see Bellona moving about the house. She wouldn't be going out to practise archery because of the weather and she'd not slept much.

The decision to leave for London had been taken out of his hands. The roads from his home would be difficult for a carriage and the trip wasn't a good idea. He would get stuck. But he was already mired.

How many times must he go wrong in order to recognise the right path?

His proximity to Bellona had merely misled him. Misdirected him. Natural enough.

He'd relived a certain kiss a thousand times and cursed himself a thousand-and-one times. What if he'd only kissed her because he'd been so long without a woman's touch? Or worse, what if he had kissed her because she was like a meandering stream, winding and winding and seeming to be just a trickle until it pooled into something so wondrous the eyes could not believe it?

He could not do this to her.

His father would have counselled him. He would have shaken his head and closeted himself in a room with his son. They would have discussed the events. Or rather his father would have guided Rhys.

His father's main responses would have been, *'I see. That sounds interesting. I hadn't thought of it that way. What of the other people involved? Your future children? What kind of mother will best raise your son to be a duke? Help your daughters to make the best marriages? This is not a decision for you. It is a decision for your future heirs. And what of Bellona? What is right for her?'*

He forced the thoughts away, determined to make the best decision for everyone.

His sister, his father and Geoff's deaths had pounded his heart into dust. He could not resurrect it and expect to have the strength to carry on with his father's legacy. To let the lands and the estate go to a cousin, while the remains of all those he'd loved would reside here for eternity, was something he could not risk.

He had no choice but to marry a suitable woman, and he had no true heart left to give her. Perhaps that was why Louisa was the perfect wife. He'd not seen any real affection for him in her eyes.

If Louisa died in childbed, and left a child behind, he would be able to care for it and continue on.

He had courted her quietly while his brother was alive, knowing that his brother wanted Louisa—and why not, she was the perfect duchess. Geoff was no fool. Louisa's head wasn't easily swayed. Her thoughts were not altered by a duke pulling her one direction or his brother tugging her another, determined, on this one thing, to win.

When Geoff had died, the letters Louisa sent Rhys had been written in almost the same tone he would have expected from his man of affairs and he had responded similarly. Letter after letter exchanged—with little more personal nature than those he might have sent to Simpson. He'd saved every letter. Every one, and read them over and over, and each one convinced him even more of her suitability. The guilt he felt at courting the woman Geoff had planned to wed only flared occasionally. Now he wanted her for another reason. After he observed the mourning period, he had told himself, he would ask her to marry him.

Rhys had once believed his heart was in the right place. Perhaps. He no longer needed to think about that or question himself. He needed to go forward. Perhaps putting his body in the right place would cause his heart to produce the right response. Louisa knew what was expected of her in the role of duchess. Knew the ways of society. She was pleasant. Kind. Thoughtful. Perfect.

He didn't love her. To love someone else—to release his heart to them, was impossible. He could not give what he no longer had.

'Rhys.' His mother stood in the doorway, whispering loudly. Rhys jolted as if caught in an illicit embrace.

He collected his ducal mien and with his left hand scratched a jagged figure on the page before him. His mother had not entered the library in a long time. 'Yes, Mother?'

'The maid said…' The duchess rushed to his side. 'She mentioned a cut on your hand. The footman saw it when you were eating.'

'It's nothing to concern yourself over.'

'Let me see it.'

He held out his hand, keeping the palm almost closed so the slice wouldn't open again.

She gasped, her thin fingers reaching out to hold the sides of his hand. 'How…?'

'It was just an accident.'

She clasped her hands to her heart. 'I cannot. I cannot lose you, too.'

'I am planning to stay alive for quite some time, Mother. Please do not try to get rid of me so quickly.'

'This is not a jesting matter. You—' She turned and reached to summon a servant. 'I am sending for the physician now.' Her voice rose to almost a scream. Her body shook.

'My babies. They cannot all die. I cannot be left by all my babies, Rhys. Can you not see that?'

'I am almost recovered now, Mother. It is not my time to die.'

'We must have the Prince's physician. We must.'

He took his time with each word, hoping to calm her. 'If my hand becomes infected, we'll send for the man, but the roads are too bad for him to travel.'

'It will be too late by then. Look at it,' she said,

again clasping her hands to her heart. She collapsed on to the sofa, her voice rising. 'I cannot live through this again. I cannot.'

Bellona ran into the room. 'Is he bleeding?'

'Bellona. He is injured. Badly. His face is feverish. His hand must be infected.' She clasped her head. 'My baby.'

'He is dying?' Concern flashed in her face.

'No more than I was this—last—yesterday.' He did not wish his mother to know the truth. 'I have a cut on my hand, Bellona.' He spoke precisely. 'A simple cut. That is all.'

'I did not mean for this to happen. I cannot live with myself if you die,' Bellona said.

'He is my only…' The duchess stared at Bellona in bewilderment. 'He is all I have left.'

'Ladies.' Rhys's voice calmed them. 'I am only slightly injured. Not dead. Please do not hurry my demise along by wearying me to death.'

His mother rose, pushing herself up. 'A mother should not outlive all her children and have no grandchildren to carry on. It is not just.' She looked at Rhys, but her question was directed to the winds. 'What have I done to deserve this?' She put her arms out. 'What have my children done?'

'Nothing, Mother.' He moved to her and held out his hand. 'See. A little cut. I'm fine.'

'You promise me you will not die. You must promise.'

'You have my word.'

She snatched his wrist. 'I will keep you to it.' Tears pooled. 'And you will give me grandchildren? Soon, Rhys. Promise you will give me grandchildren soon. I want to hold them before I die. You must go to London as soon as the roads are safe.'

'Yes, I will.'

Chapter Thirteen

Bellona put her hands over her ears even though no one spoke in the room and she was alone. How many times in how many ways had the duchess said how much she missed her family and how Rhys must wed someone from his own world? And how many times had his mother expressed her fear that he might now die if the cut in his hand became putrid?

Rhys had spent the morning calming his mother while Bellona listened, watching his hand to make sure it no longer bled. After he'd left the room, his mother had talked of nothing else but her younger son for hours. Then the discourse had travelled through each deceased family member and five handkerchiefs.

Bellona waited until the duchess tired herself into a nap. *Robinson Crusoe* was in the room at the servants' quarters. Perhaps she had found a man whom she could spend the rest of her days with, this Mr Crusoe, not that she particularly cared for him, but at least he did not have a mother nearby.

Rhys was in the library. She knew it. She could almost follow his movements inside the house without ever seeing him. He varied little from his usual paths and when he did she could tell by the activity that changed in the household. A different servant would be at the stair or she'd hear his horse outside, or a scent of some baked treat brought upstairs would waft her way.

He had told his mother the roads would be better the next day and he would leave for London. Bellona could not let him go without seeing him again.

She walked into the library.

Rhys sat at his desk. He didn't have the usual ledgers in front of him, but a chessboard with several pieces resting to the side and most on the board. His right arm lay on the desk and he moved a white pawn with his left hand.

He turned to her. Sensations of their kiss returned to her body, but this time, his eyes created the warmth swirling inside her.

She could stay at the door, safe, far enough away from him, or she could step inside. She moved forward, unable to do otherwise. 'The duchess was quite fractious today—your injury on the anniversary of Geoff's death.'

He nodded. 'I thought to leave so she might not learn of my hand, but decided it was not for the best, because of the date.' He moved a black knight.

'You have no opponent?' she asked.

'Not for this game.' He grinned at her. 'If you are unarmed, you may join me.'

'I have no knife,' she said, then answered the question in his eyes. 'Or weapon of any kind. Nothing that can jab or hurt you except my hairpins.'

'I suppose one must take progress where it is found.' He nodded to the board. 'Do you wish to play?'

She shook her head. Another thing she could not do. 'How is your injury?' she asked Rhys, stopping near his hand.

She waited, moving closer. He turned his palm

towards her. The gash was closed, the skin around it slightly puffy, but reassuringly healthy.

'The valet has told me he has seen a man recover after having his leg cut off,' he said, 'and that his own father died from a toothache. He said when it's my time to go, something will find me. But he said it's not my time to go. He knows this because he peered at the whites of my eyes and pinched the top of my foot. The best check of all, he said, was to slap a cold cloth across my face. I almost let him, but when I declined, he said I passed his test.'

'I have hidden my knife, even from myself. It is with my bow and arrows.'

'Do you continue with the nightmares?'

'I have had dark ones, but I'm fighting back with the knife in my dreams now. It's much better, and when I wake I tell myself I can shout for help. I remind myself I can scream out.'

'Is my mother treating you well?'

'Well enough. She asked me to read to her again. A letter she'd saved from your sister this time. I could read most of it, and when I did not know a word she was able to tell me without looking. She said I have progressed much with my reading.'

'She is correct.' Gently spoken words.

'As a mother must be,' she said. 'When I have my own children she assures me I will understand.'

'I think you understand perfectly well now.'

She stepped to the mantel and noticed a vase, not as tall as her hand, had been added. Primroses were tucked into it, their perfume so delicate she'd not noticed until she stood near the flowers. She brushed one yellow petal, feathersoft. 'Yes. I do.'

'You didn't want to leave your island. But you did. It was for the best.'

'Best for me?' She let laughter into her words.

'Yes. It has not turned out so bad, surely?'

'No. I cannot mind. I know how things must be.'

'I cherish those thoughts. I would not want you unhappy.'

'I'm not. Though I don't know that I wish to live on Warrington's estate any longer or live in London. I do not think I should stay here now. I want to have true contentment.'

'Do you truly know what you need for that?'

'Yes.' She met his eyes. 'I have known since I was a child.'

She went to the bookshelves and knew just where to find the *Cobwebs* book, seeing that she had placed it back there. She pulled the book out and looked at the title again. 'I thought about how Mana would have rejoiced to see her daughters so well placed. She would have bargained with the heavens that she would suffer so her daughters would not have to. And perhaps she made a bargain in another way to give us more. So when I feel sadness, because she could not share this life with me, I tell myself it is not so bad. She would have been joyous to know how bountiful my life is. And I will not let her struggles be for nothing. I will not.'

She traced a finger over the cover of the book where his hand had rested. 'I even know what would cause me the greatest of unhappiness. The union my mother had.'

Rhys had to gaze at her. He had no choice. He turned. That crown of hair she wore would topple around her shoulders some day and the man who could see it every day would fall to his knees and give thanks.

'What did your father tell you about love?' she asked. 'Your mother has mentioned it to me.'

'He said if the head could lead, the heart would follow. He said many men have lost their families, their lives and their world by trusting the most untrue organs of the body. He said the heart lies. A man's body lies. But he must separate himself from that and look from a distance. I thought them wise words, but he could not have known he did not need to say them to me.'

'The *Robinson Crusoe*. It was your father's book first?' Her lips quirked up and her expression nearly felled him. This moment was the most precious one of his life. He felt the strength of the world inside him as some mystical force flowed from her eyes, igniting a flame within him.

'I'm certain,' he said.

'Mr Crusoe. A man who wanted adventure and then spent most of his life alone. I don't think I will finish it after all.'

He looked at her long enough to see the smile in her lips and the sadness in her eyes. 'I want you to take the copy of *Crusoe* when you go. You may sell it if you wish. I will never read it again. It would always make me think of you alone on the island of Melos.'

'I would not sell this book. Perhaps I should read it at night when I cannot sleep. I could see how truthful the book is.'

At his side, she took his cut hand, examining it closely. 'I think you will live.'

'I think we both will,' he said.

He reached out with his other hand and let his forefinger touch her skin. She accepted the movement as one might let raindrops linger on the face. His caress slid over the contours of her cheekbone, feeling the silk. One fingertip was not enough. He stretched his hand so he could sweep more of her into his senses.

'I never thought dark colours could be so bright,' he murmured. 'Your eyes. They shimmer.'

His fingers moved to the valley at the side of her temple, where her cheekbone rose. 'They linger in my sight. They take my soul and hang on to it.' He ran his touch over her nose. 'You were created for a warrior god.'

She shook her head, but not enough to move

from his fingers, but to brush against them. 'I am blemished. More so than my sisters.'

He chuckled. 'Marred? That could not be possible.'

Her nod moved her closer. 'I have a longing mark.'

'That cannot be bad.'

'My sisters' marks are brown, almost the shape of hearts, but mine is red, more like a scrape that never goes away. With my sisters we believed my mother wished for love for them, but for me, we could not think what she wished for.'

He moved, the smallest bit closer to her. 'Did you ever ask her?'

'Yes.' She stumbled over the word. 'She said she had wished for love for my sisters, but by the time I was born she said she had realised her error. She told me the two red blemishes on my skin are where a heart was torn in half. She said she wished that I would never fall in love. She said it hurts too much. She thought like your father. Perhaps you and I are in agreement on the foolishness of possessing a heart.'

He'd touched her lip when she spoke. She could no longer move. This was not the same immobility of fear, but of an embrace of security. He was fire you could walk into and never be burned, just feel the tingle and caress of the flames.

Now the fingertips from both his hands rested on her skin and his breath whispered against her. 'Your mother was wise for you.'

'She was. I know. Because I already saw my father leave my mother and I want no man near who will not stay with me all his life. Who will not place me above everything and everyone else.'

His hands slid from her face and he closed his fingers. 'I hope to remember the touch of your face. You're the magic I will hold within me for the rest of my life. In a secret part of me that keeps me whole and gives me breath. But I cannot give you what you need most.'

She touched above her breast. 'And I must have a man who puts me above…his father. His mother. Even his children. Who loves me with all the intensity of the sun's heat and his love reaches to the stars.'

'You ask—'

'For what I wish for. Why should I ask for less? I am happy to be alone before I will be with a man who does not cherish me as I wish.'

'A man can say the words easily enough. Words, Bellona. But how will you know if he speaks the truth? And what if he's not sure about his own future? What if he does not even know if he can feel for a woman what you wish him to?'

'If he does not know—then he does not feel enough.'

He swallowed. He moved and his elbow touched an inkpot, knocking it askew. He caught it, but not before splashes destroyed the paper.

Turning, she moved to his desk. Ink had pooled on his work. She put the stopper back on to the empty bottle.

He shrugged and touched a blot on his sleeve and frowned, still staring.

She put her fingertip in the obsidian pool. She paused, studying the letters scratched on the piece of paper. Taking her time and reading. The list of things he planned to do in London. The places he would go and the people he would meet. She dotted her finger over the letters, obscuring them. Then she put another spot at the side of the first one, letting her finger drag over, smearing the lines into darkness.

She looked at his eyes.

Her index finger touched the back of his hand and she left a faint mark.

'Have a pleasant journey.' She walked out through the door.

Chapter Fourteen

A storm brewed, but not in the clouds. The sun warmed the morning, turning the day into a spring confection of promise. Bellona didn't want to go back inside the mansion. Rhys's carriage had just left the estate.

The air moved aside for her arrows, creating the perfect pathway for each tip, taking them so close they clustered together, fighting for room. One *thunk* after another. She stepped back to give herself more of a challenge. It didn't work.

'Miss Bellona.' The shout screeched into Bellona's ears.

She turned. The maid ran from the house, skirt clamped in both hands raising it enough to allow swift movement. 'She's fallen. She's fallen.' The maid stopped. 'The duchess. Down the staircase. She won't open her eyes.'

Fear leapt into Bellona's chest. 'Send a rider after Rhys's carriage.' She dropped the bow. 'Let Rhys know the rider will need to continue on for the physician.' She rushed into the house and found the duchess lying at the base of the entry staircase.

The cook's bulk bent over the older woman, with only the duchess's feet visible. The servant talked softly to the still form. The butler stood at the ready.

The duchess's eyes fluttered. Then she blinked, looked around and studied her surroundings. A puff of air escaped her lips. A sigh.

'Are you hurt?' Bellona knelt beside her, relieved she was breathing. The lifeless form had plunged the memory of Bellona's own mother into her heart like a knife.

The duchess pushed herself up, looking at them all, but not speaking.

'Are you hurt?' Bellona repeated.

The duchess held out a hand to Bellona. 'I had thought to see what heaven might look like. You are not it.'

Bellona smiled and put her arm around the older woman, her ribs feeling as though they were hardly covered by skin. The woman winced, but managed to stand. She reached up and touched her cheekbone. A bruise would be evident soon, but for now there was only a scrape. Then she clasped her wrist and wiggled her fingers. 'I'm fine. Fine.' She pulled out of Bellona's grasp and grabbed the banister. 'I'm going to lie down.'

She took each step up the stairs with great care.

Bellona followed behind her and the cook did as well.

'Just leave me,' the duchess said crossly. 'I fell. Simple enough. I didn't watch my feet. I stumbled. Others cannot stay alive and I cannot die. I cannot *die*.'

The sharp turn of Cook's head alerted Bellona that the servant was checking her reaction to the duchess's words.

Bellona schooled her face to show no emotion, but she didn't think it worked.

'I'll fix a purgative for Her Grace,' the cook offered.

'No. I'll keep my bile and whatever else I have inside me right there. I just had a fainting spell. I'm fine just as I am.'

The cook looked again at Bellona, and this time she grimaced.

They'd hardly settled the duchess into a chair, with a maid sitting beside her, when Rhys burst into the sitting-room door.

'How is she?' he asked anxiously.

'We don't think she's more injured than a few bruises.'

'What caused her to fall?'

'I am not sure. She said the world turned black around her.'

'She has never fainted before…'

'I fell, Rhys,' the duchess snapped, eyes closed. 'I fell. Do not worry about me. The house could burn around my ears and I would still be standing. Festering boils could appear all over my body and I would still see the sunrise every day.'

'Mother.' One strong reprimand.

She opened her eyes. 'I didn't mean for you to have to return. I am just sitting around every day, waiting for the end.'

He turned. 'You may slap her, Bellona. We will see if she can chase you.'

'Don't be ridiculous.' She shook her head. 'I just fell down the stairs.'

'An accident? Or on purpose?' Rhys said grimly.

'Neither. I was crying over Geoff. The tears were in my eyes and I had to go to the garden. I had to pick some honeysuckle. I'd almost forgotten to pick the honeysuckle for him.' She waved her arms about, her white sleeve billowing. 'I might not have done it on purpose, but I certainly wouldn't have minded waking up somewhere else. When I opened my eyes, I realised the truth. I am in a different kind of purgatory. My back hurts and my face aches. My wrist burns.' She sniffed. 'I would like some port.'

'How will I know you won't stumble again once you take a sip?' Rhys asked.

'Because I cannot die. A thousand times I have asked to be with my husband and children and I cannot. One year ago yesterday Geoff was taken from me. They are all waiting in heaven and cannot be happy without me and yet I cannot join them.'

'I would have thought you might wish to stay here on earth with me,' Rhys said quietly. He strode from the room. Bellona followed.

Outside the door, Bellona caught his sleeve.

'She is just distressed. She means none of it.'

He stopped, face stone. 'I understand that.' He pulled his arm from her grasp and strode to the stairs.

'Rhys,' she called at his heels.

He turned to her on the stairway. 'You don't understand.' His face rested near hers. 'It is not my title. It is not my estate. It was never meant to be. Never.' His words flowed faster. 'I do not know why Geoff did not marry and have children. I was not supposed to have it all. I don't know whether to feel guilty for taking it or angry that it's now mine and I cannot escape it.'

'That has nothing to do with this moment.'

'It is everything to do with it.' His eyes darkened. 'If he were here none of this would be happening. Things would be as they should be. They would be—controlled. The world was taken and torn like little scraps of paper and tossed into the air. All scattered and in bits that cannot be mended.'

'Do you wish to tumble down the stairs as well? Would that make it all better? Leaving a cousin to inherit. Would it be his destiny either?'

He raised his hand, the mark showing. 'I do not care at this moment. I must get to London, find a wife, bed her and produce a child. Hopefully before nightfall.'

'Oh…' She dragged out the word. 'More's the pity.'

He lowered his chin.

'From where I was born,' she said, 'even the people who cannot read have no trouble with that.'

'You witch. It is not quite the same for me.'

'I imagine you will find some way to have pleasure doing it. I have heard it can be done.'

'An unmarried woman is not supposed to know about these things.'

'And what turnip were you born under?'

'Not the same one as you, apparently.'

'Now go to London and do as you must.' She put a foot beside his and moved down the stairway, turning back to him. 'Safe journey.'

'Bellona.' He rushed after her and caught her arm. His voice softened. 'I cannot leave you like this.'

'Yes, you can.'

'I don't want to be alone now, and there is no one in the world I would rather be with than you. And perhaps you are right. Perhaps you are the one able to see this clearly without the heart being involved.'

She didn't answer, but her hand grazed her skirt, above the red blemish hidden from view.

Chapter Fifteen

She continued down the stairway and heard his footsteps behind her. She rushed ahead, moving to the servants' quarters where she could shut out the world above the stairs. No one was about and she moved to the small room she'd taken over.

Only the door didn't shut when she pressed it. Rhys's hand caught it and pushed it open again.

'So this is the room where you feel safe,' he said, stepping inside and shutting the door behind him.

'Yes. It is more my world than any other room in the house. You can see it for what it is.' Even as he looked around, she knew he could only see the room. He couldn't see the truth of her past. This room was a palace compared to where she'd grown up on Melos.

Nothing marred by salt from sea air. Nothing

marred by life. This room had belonged to a scullery maid and it was the closest she'd found in the house to what she'd had.

His eyes furrowed. 'I did not know such a place even existed in my home.'

The small bed had a washstand beside it. Resting on the washstand was a small mirror propped against the wall, a tallow candle and Robinson Crusoe's tale.

'This is how most of the servants' rooms are.'

The bed covering wasn't torn. The walls were solid. She raised her eyes to the ceiling and saw no stains. At the washstand, she pushed against it. No wobble. 'I am sure Mr Crusoe would have been pleased to have such a place on his island. I would have.'

Rhys sat on the bed, elbows on his knees, fingers steepled and his chin resting on them. He raised his eyebrows. 'I have been angry these last few years. Enraged that my sister died, my father and then my brother. Now I anger at even my mother, who suffers deeply.'

Brown eyes, more rich than any silk or sable, peered at Bellona. He smiled. 'But it doesn't matter. Nothing changes. I tried shaking my fist in the air. Pounding the wall. It changed not a thing. Didn't make me feel any better, only more angry because it was senseless.'

'I did not mourn my mother after she died. But I did not need to. While she was ill, I cried and thought my life could not go on. But she talked so much with us towards the end. We talked of everything and she prepared us. I missed her, but the hardest part was her suffering. The last week of her life. That was cruel. She hurt so.'

In front of him, she rested her hand on his shoulder and then let the back of her hand move upwards, along his cravat, to the skin above it, letting sensations engulf her as she talked. 'Your mother will get over this. It is just the valley before she climbs back up the hill of life again.'

'I thought if I went to London I might be able to put the loss behind me. But when I return, there will be even more. You will be gone.' His eyes flicked to her and one side of his lips turned up.

She brushed his hair from his temple. 'There is the duchess you must find.'

'Do not remind me.'

'Why not? You will do it. You have put your mind to it. Don't tell me you do not think of the woman. How you will approach her. What you will say. How you hope to feel something for her in the way you used to feel before Geoff passed away.'

'When I close my eyes at night, it's not her I think of. When I open them in the morning, she is nowhere in my head.'

'Truly?'

He turned to her. 'Look at my face. What do you think?' He touched the earring at her ear. 'I notice you always wear these.'

She nodded. 'Yes. I think it makes your mother feel better.'

His hands clasped her waist. Warm bands. Strength that made her feel delicate.

'I want to make certain you are provided for,' he said.

'It is not needed.' She held her chin up.

She shook her head and turned her gaze from his. 'When you wed, I will never again see or speak with you. It is for the best. I will not forget the past. The good or the bad. Yet I will not fall into the same trap of the heart that my mother fell into. When it is done, finished, it is over and done with.'

She didn't raise her eyes, but kept the expanse of his chest in her view. The cravat rested close to his heart, but she didn't know what emotions lay inside the man. No words of love reached her ears and only the warnings of her mother sounded in her mind. She would heed them.

Rhys's hand slid up, sparking eruptions she had only heard about in myths. He cupped her cheeks in his hands. One kiss. Then another. So light. Lighter than the one before. Soft. The barest moment of contact and then he pulled back.

She kept her eyes closed, her chin upturned, and savoured the softness of the lace on his sleeve against her face.

Opening her eyes, she said, 'You dressed so fine to go to London.' She grasped his wrist, trapping the thin cloth so that she kept it between them. His jutting wrist bone rested under her fingertips. Then she stepped back and let her hand fall slowly, and land on the buttons of his waistcoat.

'Bellona…' He said her name, but it wasn't really a word. More of a caress. He paused. 'I cannot. Not now. Not ever.'

'Cannot?'

The words sounded pulled from him. 'I cannot

touch you because I cannot...*touch* you. You deserve the promise along with the touch.'

Her gaze stopped at his face. She could see him more clearly than she had ever seen another person. Her eyes even caught the tenseness at the corner of his lips and the slight sheen of moisture at his brow.

His eyes darkened, but with an emotion that didn't frighten her in the least. But he still did not move one bit—even one hair closer.

Then she waved fingertips over the silken waistcoat. The fabric working as a barrier between the life of him and her hand. He took in a breath yet still didn't move towards her. Nor away.

He made her think of the statue of an armless woman she and her sisters had found on Melos. If the artist had carved a male, Rhys could have been the perfect model. His face. The stance. Unmoving.

She trailed her hand up, turning the palm so that the back of her knuckles moved past his cravat and caught the slightest bit of roughness on his cheek. He was strong enough to have moved away at any time, but she knew he couldn't. His eyes closed. The back of her fingers stroked his chin. His lashes rested just above her touch.

With the lightness of a feather, his fingers clasped over her wrist. Eyes still shut, he pulled her hand away. 'You must go to Warrington's estate.'

Slowly, his eyes opened. Her heart crashed alive in her body, flooding her with such pounding she could hardly take in air.

She had an arrow, of sorts, and she carefully aimed it. 'When I do, your mother has said there is a kind vicar…that you provide a living for… who might be looking for a wife. I should meet him.'

His lips barely moved as he spoke. 'I will see that he calls on you.'

'You do not have to. I will.'

She pulled back from his grasp but she couldn't walk to the door.

His body remained still, but his gaze didn't. The thoughts she couldn't touch were there, showing in his eyes.

It wasn't fear of dying without him that overtook her when she looked into the brown, but the truth of living without his touch. And she took the strength he used to stand still and captured it in her body to stand there immobile.

His hand reached to her face, but she flicked her head back out of reach.

'You must not forget, I'm not an English society miss,' she said, 'which your mother tells me is important to you. I have tried for two years to want to be one and I see I am not, and will never be. I will be always free. I may not be a lady by birth, but I *am* worthy to walk the same earth as you.'

'You are.'

'I saw my mother cry when my father left us and I swore I would never beg for a man's attentions. I would have them freely or not at all. Whether he is a vicar or a soldier or a carriage maker, I will find a man who falls to his knees and thanks the heavens for me. And when he speaks words to me, they will be true. How I feel for him is not so important—as how he thinks of me. I am not a goddess. I do not wish him to think I am such. But he will have me in his heart as if I am.'

'I would like to see you with your hair down…' His voice was a whisper with a rumble that could only come from a man's throat and hardly touched the air, but swirled around her at all sides, as if an artist with a thousand brushes had taken her as his canvas and danced his brushes lightly over her body.

She pulled one pin from her hair.

He took it and held it between them, letting it linger in their vision, and she couldn't take her eyes from the fingers that held it so lightly.

'Your hair always looks as if your next movement will tumble the locks around your shoulders. I catch myself holding my breath, waiting. The wisps dance with your body, but the rest of it stays, looking soft and…like you. But even with the pin removed—' instead of returning the clasp to its place he palmed it '—it doesn't fall.'

His hand fell away, as if he'd forgotten what it held. His gaze moved over her tresses before returning to her face. 'A meadow. Did you know, it is always as if meadows or forests surround you? When I was a child, I would lie in the grass and look up at the puffs of clouds, and then close my eyes. Sunshine warmed my face. The grass softened the ground beneath me.

'The world had the same scent of an oak leaf held to my nose. At that moment, if a bird flew over me, it was as if its wings brushed my face and I was alive and everything was quiet in a way it had never been before. I could feel the poetry of the world and now that same verse surrounds you. I can feel the warmth of your hair against this pin.'

She reached out, putting her palm on his chest, cloth caressing her fingers. 'You have been reading—too much of that man who writes about women walking softly at night. Byron.'

'I would never say you walk softly in the night. *"She walks in beauty like the night..."*' His eyes flicked back to her face. 'Those words I do recall and they do apply. I'm sure there's more after that, but when I look at you, I cannot even remember who I am.'

She stood so close she could even see the way his pupils seemed to fade into a softer colour at the edge. But she could not see herself reflected. She shook her head. 'I do not think Byron knows the true meaning of love either. Words. Perhaps that is why I have had so much trouble thinking of reading. It is bad enough when false words are spoken. To put them down on paper is even worse.'

'I admit, words do not do you justice.'

She stood immobile, and one edge of his mouth moved up. He took a step and reached up, and both his hands went to loosen her hair and she felt strands against her skin. Finally, her hair fell around her shoulders as he stepped away, but he wasn't truly moving from her. He was using his eyes to remain close, looking at her lustrous hair.

Taking her hand, holding it open, he dropped the pins into it. Then he closed his fingers over hers and pulled them up, dropping a kiss over her knuckles.

She put the pins on the table and stood with her back to him. The mirror reflected from his shoulders to his waist.

She took a breath, watching him worry the edge of his sleeve in his opposite hand. Then he straightened his fingers, flexed one hand, relaxed it and ran his forefinger along his opposing thumb, softly brushing back and forth.

She couldn't take her eyes from the mirror.

'If I were to choose one minute in my life,' he said, 'to live over and over again, it would be this one.'

'You say all the right words—almost...'

'I know. I say the easy ones. How hard can it be to tell a woman she is beautiful?' His fingers slowed, curling into a soft, unmoving clutch.

'But you are honest to us both.'

'A man must be more than his wishes, his dreams. He must set his path and follow it. He cannot let himself be swayed by what…he desires.'

'Words of your father.'

His reflection tensed, but his words held no emotion. 'True words. Words I believe.'

'I know. And I do not know if I hate you or love you.'

'Perhaps it would be best if you hated me.'

'I have seen how love withers when a man marries a woman who cannot follow him in his life,' she said. 'I know I am not your idea of a duchess and living that life is not what I see for myself. This simple room is how I wish to live. I am like my mother, except I know not to walk her path.'

'What are you trying to say?'

'Do not think if you lie with me, there will be a wedding to follow. I would not be compromised. I do not have to bow my spirit to anyone. The dowry I have has made that true for me. I do not have to listen to your society's rules and I am not staying in London either. I will find a small place and have a simple life. I will plant my own flowers and cook my own meals. I will work side by side with my husband to make a home that is ours alone.'

She stopped watching his reflection in the washstand mirror and turned, examining his eyes. Her lips turned up, but it didn't feel like a smile. 'I suppose I will feel differently when you leave tomorrow to find your duchess. But today I love you.'

Her lips were soft under his. She tasted of nature. Perhaps it was the spiced scent which always seemed to cling to her, or perhaps it was because she was so different from the women of his past and future. But he didn't care about the reason. Just for a few moments he wanted to experience her.

She clutched at him, pulling him to her. He ended the kiss too soon, leaving their faces pressed cheek to cheek, feeling their breaths mingle. Then he sat on the bed and took her by the bottom, skirts and all, pushing them up just enough so he could sit her astride him. He kissed her again and ran his fingers up her back, through the thin material of her gown, until he touched one of her shoulders. The feel of her under his hand captivated him.

He buried his face in the cleft of her bodice, awash in the heavenly sinful friction of cloth covering soft, delicate skin.

Keeping his lips against her skin for all but the briefest moment, he slipped the shoulders down on her gown, revealing a corset contrasting against the flesh that blossomed over the top of the stiff fabric. Her breasts, like her hair, barely stayed in their constraints, as if waiting for the smallest movement to free them.

Hooks unclasped under his fingertips. The corset ties hardly needed a tug, and when she stirred against him, the corset fell open and the chemise had already slid down her shoulders.

As he removed her clothes she slipped from one form to the next, becoming a woman from another land, a world he'd never seen, and a magical being, female, feminine and with the ability to hold him captive with her spirit.

His hands grazed over her back, taking strength

from her body, filling him with a sense of power. She arched against him.

He had not known it could be like this. To be inside this realm of another person, gaining strength from them.

She increased the distance between them just enough to capture this moment in her vision. To see him. His eyes were shut. Defenceless. Innocent. Never had she seen such a captivated look on a man's face. His nose, aquiline, and lips, soft. She moved, brushing her forefinger over them, and he kissed her and kept one arm at her waist while he pulled back the counterpane and watched as she slid into the bed.

He swept the coat from his shoulders, removed his waistcoat and pulled the cravat away in a silken whoosh. He whipped his shirt up and over his head—stopping her breathing for a minute. He tossed the garment aside. For half a second he stood motionless.

He sat beside her and the narrow bed, not made for two people, sagged with his presence. She placed her hand in the very small of his back, savouring the feel of his muscles beneath her fingertips while he tugged at his boots and then his stockings. The buff doeskin slid from his legs and he lay almost over her, propping himself on his elbows to keep his full weight from her, skin heating skin.

He kissed her and she could taste him, and her heart beat stronger, igniting the volcanic smoulder inside her. Her blood transformed into a lava heat, seeming to flow from her body through his body and returning to her.

His legs melded with hers, and his whole body surrounded her. The shaving spice on his skin mixed with the barest hint of wood smoke and she didn't know what kept her from actually igniting.

He twisted to his side, pulling her almost from the bed and into his complete grasp. The pillow slid to one side of the floor and the coverings to the other. The bed had no room for anything but them. His every movement against her increased the deepness of her breathing, and sent her higher into a cloud of pleasure. Molten.

Fingers explored her, claiming each curve of her body, and the feeling of his hand rolled over her so that even the places he did not reach responded as if he had caressed them.

He touched her softness, her wetness, and she erupted into spasms, lost to everything.

Rhys sat with his shoulders against the bed frame, looking at Bellona. Her hair wreathed around her—more appealing than any he'd ever seen graced with a tiara. He tapped her chin when she closed her eyes and let his knuckles rest at her arm when she looked up at him—sated, he hoped.

Twining his fingers through her hair, he lifted it and let the locks slide free. The second time, he brought them to his face, the delicate ends caressing his cheek. Savouring every strand.

And then something clattered outside the door, hitting the wood.

He knifed his body around, jerking the counterpane from the floor to toss the covering over her, and when he did his elbow hit the washstand, jarring it, skittering the mirror over, and the glass clattered to the floor. The fabric slid in place, partly, just as the door opened.

But it wasn't the aged housekeeper's head, the one with discreet quiet acceptance in her demeanour, who peeked around the door, but one of the underservants holding a wooden pail. Peering in with a question in her eyes.

Her expression changing, her eyes opened wide and her mouth fell into what appeared to be a near scream, but came out as a strangled gasp.

No, of course it could not be the housekeeper, a woman known for her silence.

He closed his lips and watched as the thoughts behind the girl's eyes embedded the scene before her into her mind for ever.

'Leave,' Rhys commanded.

The girl nodded, gave a gasped 'yes' with the uptake of her head and then she snapped shut the door.

He swore, words he'd never said in front of any female before, and the moment they fell from his lips, he knew as Bellona's head turned to him. He saw a different look in her eyes and he much preferred the servant's shocked gaze to the black one befitting a coiled snake about to strike.

He blinked to gather his thoughts because his next words were so very important, but before he could speak them, she pulled ever so slightly from his side.

Her eyes. He'd never seen a darker stare.

Chapter Sixteen

Her hands clenched. Trapped. But she would not be snared. She had lain with him, knowing he would go to London and she had not once asked him to stay. She had wished him well. She had been in his bed and then he swore when they were discovered.

He was not the one who would be destroyed by their actions becoming common knowledge and he well knew it. She was. But he swore. Because now he must do the right thing and offer for her hand. She'd seen how a man could be a treacherous husband and father when he did not wish to be wed. Her father had followed the dictates of his body and had then been angered because he blamed her mother for his lust.

'So, Your Grace, this is a first for you as well.' Soft words.

'In a sense.' Controlled, he said, 'I will instruct her that she is not to speak of this.'

'You may instruct her,' Bellona said calmly, 'but you know how the talk will travel. By the time we have dressed it will already be flying around the estate.'

'We will marry.'

'I would not wed you if you were the last duke on earth.' She reached for the pins at the bedside and in one quick twist she'd secured her hair and pinned it almost in place. She pulled the covers around her and moved from the bed. 'I can do better.'

'The Prince is taken.'

'I am not talking of rank, as you very well know. You trapped me like a hare.'

'No. I do not have to do something like that to get a wife and you know it. I can wed any one of a score of women. A fortnight of courtship and a proposal and I would be married.'

The words buzzed in her head so loud she could hardly think to form her own thoughts. They were true, but for him to speak them, unforgivable.

'Yes. But I am here. You desire me. Your head tells you I am the wrong woman, but your body does not care. And now you think I have no choice. That I must marry you because my reputation will be soiled for ever. You also have no choice—you can say that later, too.'

'No.'

'You heard the maid and you knocked the mirror askew.'

'That was an accident.'

'Accident.' She followed with an expressive gesture. 'That is what I think of your accident.'

He jumped to his feet. 'You cannot for one moment believe I did this to trap you.'

'Oh—' she shrugged '—why should I not? You had a brief moment to think and you didn't. You acted.' She cocked her head to the side.

'You are wrong.'

'I refuse. Refuse. Refuse. To let my children think their father was forced into marriage with me.' She could not control her voice. Let the world hear. 'That he purchased me in his own way. Oh, I have seen that. How many *drachmas* am I worth? Five hundred. Oh, but you have much more money. A thousand, then. And will you shout at me in front of my children to tell me how you paid too much for me? No, you will not.'

His voice softened. 'I would not.'

'No, you will not.'

She stood, securing the coverings, a Grecian goddess draped in white, as in times of old, proud as any statue. She brushed a tangle of hair from her lips.

'I will walk naked down St James's Street before I turn my back on my heritage and before I am trapped into a marriage I don't want.' She swirled the cloth and controlled her words. 'But thank you for asking.'

He inclined his head to her and reached for his own clothing, thankful she did not have a spear and that her bow and arrows had not been returned to her. That was the only thing from this situation which he could be happy with.

'I—'

Her words cut across his before he could finish. 'I will say, *Stubble it, Your Grace.* Or perhaps, *Rolleston, hold your tongue*, seeing that I can only call you Rhys when we are alone because we have no ties at all.'

'Except the ties of marriage,' he added.

'And this is written where?'

If he did not tread very carefully, he knew that not only the servants, but the tongues of the *ton* would get more than a splash or two of *on dits*. This would make the notorious tales of Lady

Lamb fall by the wayside. He slipped on the trousers that had been dropped beside the bed. He picked up the shirt he'd tossed to the floor and donned it. She stood draped in rough-woven bedclothes, and the small amount of light found her, sparkling on the earrings, cloaking her regally.

'In society's eyes,' he said, 'you'll be able to wed no vicar now. You will be a woman known to have been…been in my bed…in the servants' quarters…'

'What about you, Your Grace? If you ask another to wed you too soon, what will you think of her if she says yes? She will be marrying only your title. Your funds. Your estate.'

He continued with his shirt and trousers. 'Warrington will insist on our marriage. Your sister, the countess, will expect it. I will acquire a special licence before first light tomorrow morning.' He held his boot and sat on the bed. He stared at the leather. 'With Warrington and I both in accord, we can have this completed by nightfall. It is not unheard of for a man and woman to share a bed on their wedding day.'

'This is not my wedding day.'

He raised his eyes…waiting.

She smiled. At least her lips did. Her eyes, not at all.

'Yes. It is.' He paused, seeing steel in her face. 'You cannot…' He paused. 'You cannot *refuse*. Warrington has control of your dowry.'

'Yes. Warrington has control of my dowry. I cannot get it at the moment, but I am sure he will give it to me eventually. That was a mistake my father's wife regrets. She has promised she will correct it very soon.'

He knew where this was going. 'And your father's wife…'

Her shoulders flicked up and then down. 'We have talked. Her relative has the wealth so that my father cannot touch it. It was done that way before her father died because he did not want his money in the hands of her husband, my father. My father's wife can do exactly as she pleases because her cousin moves the funds as she instructs. And when I told her in the past of my wish to be free…' Her chin tilted. She might not have a spear in her hands but she could use her words as one. She tossed the words out and they landed as a challenge. 'My father's wife understands. She understands my need to make sure

I am safe at night and that no man can get near me if I choose not to let him. She has a spinster aunt in Scotland. My father's wife owns the house and she would like me to live there with her aunt. That is who I spoke of before.'

'Bellona. You must be my wife.' He looked at his boots again. The floor. The crumpled neck-cloth. The waistcoat lying beside it, but even they did not make sense to him now. Could she not understand? Did she not know how many ambitious mothers would put their daughters before him—a virginal sacrifice the daughters would willingly become? His wife would be getting the same life of wealth he shared. The same deference from the whole of society. It was the way of the world. He had no more choice in it than they did.

'I will cherish that request—those words—just as I cherished the words in the books I sold to the sailor.'

'It isn't a request as you well know.'

'And I am not refusing you.' She swept the cover around her as she turned, her cape of bed-clothes swirling, and he realised she was about to walk out of the room into the servants' area clad as a heathen goddess. He did not think she would walk quickly up the stairs. Oh, no. She would possibly meander. Every servant in the area was going to get to see her dressed like this.

'I am merely taking a lifetime to decide. You may wait patiently for my answer.' She opened the door wide and he was suddenly thankful he was mostly dressed.

She pointed to the floor. 'I will be sending someone for the dress.' She indicated the clothing he had removed from her body. 'Please do not let it be misplaced as I will be directing a servant to this room.' Her eyes. No woman had ever looked at him in such a way.

'You cannot go about like that,' he commanded.

The door closed on his words.

The mirror lay at his feet. Unbroken. He picked it up. Hair mussed. No cravat. He looked more heathen than she did.

He slung the mirror on to the bed behind him, put on his boots, kicked the pillow into the wall and looked around the room. Let the servants talk.

For the first time in his life, he was thankful his father was no longer alive.

Chapter Seventeen

Bellona bypassed the servants' stairs, fearing her covering might get caught in her feet on the narrow climb. In the main stairway, she bundled the covers closer and moved towards the family rooms. She reached the top in time to see the duchess open a door and stand with her hand at her neck, and a bruise on her forehead.

'I heard such shouting…' the duchess said.

The woman was not picking good times to leave her room.

Her eyes closed, opened, and then closed again briefly as she spoke the first words. 'My dear, you appear dishevelled.'

Bellona nodded. 'Yes.'

'As if you have been…' The duchess swallowed, examining her.

Bellona met the older woman's eyes. 'I was thinking of taking a bath.'

'It is always sensible to disrobe on such an occasion.'

'I should also like a carriage readied...' Bellona paused. 'I will be returning to Whitegate.'

'I agree.' The duchess nodded. 'But might I speak with you first?'

The duchess stepped back inside the door, keeping her hand on the wood. Bellona followed and sat, pulling the covering with her, kicking it with her feet to clear it from the pathway.

After shutting the door, the duchess stood across from Bellona. 'And should I...should I assume you have been walking about my house like this? And perhaps even been seen?'

'Yes. I heard the butler sputter just now so perhaps he saw me.'

'Were you bathing alone?'

'No.'

'Is there to be a marriage?'

'No.'

'My dear. Even being able to read, dance and embroider adequately will not rescue you from such actions if there is not to be a wedding.' The older woman's head tilted low, but her eyes remained straight ahead. 'You have no choice. You rather agreed to that when you decided to bathe.'

'No.'

'We must consider all options.'

'I am only considering the ones which do not include your son.'

She swayed and grasped the wall. 'It is worse than I feared. Rhys. Rhys saw you dressed such?'

'I assume he saw me quite well.'

'In the servants' quarters? The duke was with you in the servants' quarters?' She panted. 'Well, you certainly made a fine kettle of fish. To trap him into marriage is one thing. *But in the servants' quarters?*' She made a fist. Her eyes narrowed in a way that said she could have easily tipped a boiling cauldron on to Bellona's head. 'I should never have let you step foot in this house. You planned this all along.'

'Not all along. I waited until after I had met him.'

'So you *bathed* with a duke and then walked around in view of the whole household?'

'Yes.'

'Well, that explains nothing.'

'A maid did not knock…when I was unclothed. The bath was not a private matter any longer.'

'Did you pay her to open the door? In all my years a maid has never interrupted my bath. Possibly because a decent woman knows to bathe at night.'

'So do all decent men.'

The duchess raised her hand and reached for the bell. 'Do not move. I will send for your clothes to be packed. You will not believe how fast the servants can have the carriage readied when I am on a tear. You can dress or not for the carriage ride. It hardly matters.' The duchess's hand stopped. She struggled for words. 'And there could be a little…' She blinked. 'Have you and Rhys been *bathing* together…regularly?'

'I would not speak of such things with his *mana.*'

'Nonsense. I *am* his *mother*. It is not as if I did not instruct his father how to handle that little indiscretion Rhys had with one of the servants.' Her eyes narrowed and, this time, she used one finger to jab her own chest. 'And I was *wed* to *his* father and that shackle had to be kept clamped on *his* leg.'

'The duke and I have agreed not to marry.'

Rhys walked swiftly through the doorway, the door knocking back against the wood. His cravat was looped in the most unsettling knot Bellona had ever seen. His hair had somewhat returned to its place and his waistcoat was buttoned. He had her clothing draped over his arm.

'Mother, Bellona and I are betrothed. We must go immediately for the special licence.' He looked at Bellona's covering, took in a full breath and held out the dress. 'And she forgot what she was to wear—in her excitement over the marriage.'

'Rhys,' his mother said, voice high. 'We have more rooms on the upper floors than can be counted. You could have been in one of those where you wouldn't be seen. I cannot believe this of you. I cannot believe it of *her.*'

'However, it is done. Bellona and I are to be married. I have sent the maid to instruct the carriage to be prepared. Mother, please start writing notes to all your friends telling them how I could not wait a moment longer to make her my wife.'

'*Never.* I don't need grandchildren after all. In fact, I've decided I don't like babies at all. They're never well mannered. Cast up their accounts. Spit on silk. Then they grow up and—it—gets worse.'

Bellona took the chance to turn to the door, but Rhys was between her and the exit.

He spoke softly. 'We must wed.'

'I have never heard of so many proposals in one day.' She spoke more words, in Greek, and from the tightening of his eyes, he had certainly learned those from his tutor.

'Bellona. Consider…what we have done.' His words were soft and his eyes gentle, but she had heard the harsh tone from him when the maid had opened the door. The one that came from his heart. That one she agreed with.

'I am not thinking of the past,' he said. 'I am thinking of the future.'

'Mine is in Scotland,' Bellona announced.

'Sometimes travelling is very good for you,' his mother grumbled. 'It is a pity it just did not start soon enough.' She held her hands up. 'And none of this would have happened if not for my fall.'

'I must go.' Bellona struggled to reach out her hand while keeping her breasts covered. 'I need… the dress…'

He moved forward and she extended her hand,

taking care not to hold it out too far. He placed the garment near her and she fumbled to hold everything together. He frowned, waiting while she managed.

'I would have liked to have wed you, Your Grace,' she said. 'But—you will spend your days looking at me as if I am less than you. As if I trapped you.' She shook her head. 'I knew every moment we were together you did not plan to marry me. Only because of the maid outside the door did you finally consider it.'

'Rhys. Did you not learn anything from that past indiscretion with the servant?' his mother asked. 'Did your father not explain the word *mistress* means to pay and go away? One does not soil one's own home.'

He frowned at her. 'It is not like that, Mother.'

'You took advantage of Bellona.' The duchess swept forward as if she'd suddenly gained strength from all the disappointed mothers of the world, the silver knot of her hair shaking as she walked to him. 'You took advantage of…a woman practically alone in the world and her supposedly under my guidance and care. I can forgive her more easily than I can you.' She stared.

'You were not raised to behave like this.' With each word her voice strengthened. 'You know better. I cannot believe you did this.'

She stopped in front of him. Her hand swung out, palm open, and she slapped his cheek. 'Get out of my house.'

He didn't flinch and his expression did not change. 'As you wish, Mother.' He turned and left.

The loudest thing in the room was Bellona's thoughts. The duchess had her head averted and stood away from her.

'It wasn't like you think,' Bellona said to the duchess finally. 'He didn't take advantage of me. I needed… I wanted…'

'Do not say it. The two of you created this wrangle and I cannot slap you because you are not my child.' The duchess sighed. 'The only thing I want to hear from you is that you will leave immediately.'

'If the servant hadn't heard Rhys drop something in the room and walked in to discover what made the noise, no one would know. Nothing would have changed.'

The duchess turned to Bellona and the lines

at her eyes and mouth had deepened. 'And if the black plague hadn't happened—well, then we would have missed all that death and dying.' She put a hand to her chest. 'I would not usually compare this to the destruction of so many lives, but right now, it feels about the same to me. Get dressed. I have had enough of being a mother for one day. For one lifetime. I am going to have some wine and lie down. And *if* I wish to speak with you when I wake up, I will take a carriage to visit you at Whitegate.' She made a flitting movement with her hand, as if sweeping Bellona out through the door. 'I would not stand by the door and wait if I were you.'

Rhys sat at his desk, examining the black-ink mark Bellona had made on the page he'd kept. One smear, with another beside it. A heart, or rather two halves of one. Not joined. He tried to find the right oath for how he felt. There simply wasn't one strong enough and even stringing all the ones he knew together hadn't worked. Whoever invented swearing did not make words strong enough.

His father had once said that being a duke was

no different from anyone else except one had to always appear perfect. Wise words. Not quite accurate, however.

His father did not mention days when one did not know exactly how one could be so imperfect and not decipher any of it. He could not jump over a broom and then try to leap back to undo the action because then two errors had been made.

'Your Grace.' A footman stood at the doorway. 'The carriage is readied as you requested and Miss Cherroll—' His gaze dropped. 'She is also asking to be taken to Whitegate.'

Rhys felt no surprise. If he did not miss his guess from the flustered servants who had been darting to and fro, his mother was trying to manage the tales to reflect her family in the best light. Bellona would not fare well.

But he would change that. 'We will travel together,' he said. 'Let her know the vehicle is ready.'

The footman darted away.

Rhys stood and walked to the front of the house. He stepped outside and into the carriage. In a few moments, the door was opened. Bellona was half-inside the carriage when she saw him. She halted, but then continued and sat beside him, or rather as close to the other side of the carriage as she could get. She pulled her reticule into her lap and crossed her arms over it.

'Lovely dress,' he commented.

'Thank you for returning it.'

'I see your reticule does not have a blade poking from it.' The carriage jolted forward.

She ignored him.

'Are you going to London?' she asked.

'Eventually.'

'I'm going north.' She looked out of the window.

'Not in this carriage.'

'I do not need your carriage. I must tell my sister goodbye and arrange the trip.'

He grunted. Warrington might have other ideas. And he wagered her sister would as well.

'Are you…wearing a weapon anywhere about your person?' He watched her face carefully.

'Will I need one?' she asked. She didn't turn from the window.

'I might wish to borrow it from you. I don't think Warrington is going to be pleased when he hears of the recent…events.'

'I expect him to be more upset when he discovers his carriage missing and on the way to Scotland.'

'Bellona. Do not be surprised if he is aware something has happened before you even arrive. My mother had many servants scurrying to make sure she got in her side of the story first.'

'No.' Her head snapped around. 'Surely the news…would not travel that fast.'

'I think it moved as fast as it could be written on paper and carried through the woods by the fastest runner at Harling House. Accept that we are to be married.'

'I accept that *you* are to be married. That is no surprise to anyone. You have no choice, Your Grace.' She smiled and touched her earring. 'I do.'

He studied her. 'Well, it is best I find out your disagreeability before we wed. I would hate to be surprised.' He studied his palm before glancing at her. 'Again.'

He was not sure he wanted any wife at the moment. A woman could appear as sweet as the finest confectionery, but then one error at the wrong moment and she stubbornly refused to do the sensible thing and correct it.

'You know that no one can force me to marry you.'

'Fine. That might be safest,' he said. 'Don't marry me. But Warrington will not be pleased. Your sister will not be pleased. Your niece and nephews will miss you.'

'I can write enough words now to send them letters. It is how I will practise.' She tapped her hand to her head. 'Thank you for helping me read. It will be very useful now.'

The face which had been so soft in his hands earlier had changed. Her eyes no longer had the sparkle he'd seen in them before.

He tried to think how he would advise someone else to sort out this problem, after he'd told them they were an arse for getting in such a bramble.

Fine. He knew he'd been foolish, but he couldn't condemn himself for that.

He glanced at his puckered palm, wondering if his senses had bled out with his humours. The memory of her would go with him to his grave. And *if* he ever needed to be reminded he could simply hold out his hand.

'I don't regret what we did, Bellona. I only regret the knowledge of it being something for people to whisper about. If you wed me, and continue in the ways of a duchess, then society will accept you well enough. Your sister, the countess, is quite adept at moving in society. You can be as well.'

'No. If you think because we are sisters, that we are similar, you are wrong. To be a sister means only the faces are near the same. Our thoughts are our own.'

'What is wrong with you that you do not relish the chance to put yourself in the highest tiers of society for ever? To wed me?'

'As I said, I can do better.' She spoke. Quiet words. His second slap of the day.

The carriage rolled up to Whitegate and she jumped out before the door was properly opened for her.

She ran towards the steps. He would not chase after her. At a sedate pace, he followed. The groom watched from the corner of his eye. The servants would discuss this tonight. At least she had looked lovely draped in bed clothing. He hoped that had been noted.

The butler opened the door for her and waited for Rhys.

Bellona was not in sight by the time Rhys crossed the threshold. 'Summon the earl,' he said to the servant.

'I do not think it is necessary, Your Grace.' The butler spoke in the distant way of a well-trained servant, showing no awareness in his face of any upheaval in the household. 'He dispatched a message summoning you at half-past and he did not speak quietly.'

Rhys brushed by the man, not waiting to be announced, and moved up the stairs as easily as if the home were his own. He slowed at the sitting-room door.

Bellona sat on the sofa, not speaking. Spine firm—lips the same.

Warrington stood, arms clasped behind his back, staring at a painting of the three children playing. One chair was overturned.

'Rhys.' Just the one softly spoken word. Warrington didn't move.

'War.' He paused. 'Would you like to travel with us to procure the special licence?'

The pop of Warrington's jaw preceded his answer. 'I don't think you need do so, Rhys.'

'Why?'

'No one will expect you to.'

Bellona's chin tilted a bit, defiant, but her knuckles were white as she gripped the reticule.

Rhys stepped inside and shut the door.

Warrington exhaled sharply. 'She tells me she led you to the room. When you suggested marriage, she refused.'

'I will leave England,' she said.

'You cannot run away from this, Bellona,' Rhys challenged.

'My sisters and I ran from Melos.' She shrugged. 'It has not turned out too badly for them.'

'It doesn't have to turn out badly for you either.' Rhys gestured with his right hand for emphasis.

Warrington's eyes locked on his palm. The earl gave a sharp intake of breath. 'Arrow?'

Rhys immediately dropped his hand, turning the wound away from the earl's gaze. He shook his head in answer and kept his eyes on Bellona. 'Do not make this worse for yourself.'

'I won't,' she said. 'I'm leaving.' She paused for

a second. 'It will be best for you, too. You will not have to concern yourself that you could do better.'

'I have never said such a thing. You are the one who keeps saying that. Not me.'

'You don't have to.'

Warrington huffed. 'It is as if I have my children standing in front of me. You both need to listen.' He righted the chair, thumping the legs on the rug. 'I have known for a few days, but I hoped it would disappear. It hasn't. Lord Hawkins has been drinking. The man appears to be losing his mind—perhaps he is succumbing to some sort of illness. Unfortunately, it is also loosening his tongue. He claims Bellona has been trying to get money from him. Claiming she will say she is his daughter to discredit him unless he pays her.'

She jumped to her feet. 'He *is* my father. The funds have been organised by his wife and she gives them freely.'

'I know that,' Warrington said. 'But he is splattering every handful of mud he can in your direction.'

Chapter Eighteen

Warrington snorted. 'Don't look so…gutted, Rolleston.' Warrington's eyes narrowed. 'Neither my wife nor Bellona can help their birth. None of us can, *Your Grace.*'

Your Grace. He heard the sneer in Warrington's voice, but it reminded him of who he was. And he realised who Bellona was. He'd never cared about the *on dits* that Hawkins had a mistress he visited when he left England. When he found out Hawkins was Bellona's father he'd not really cared. But the truth had been secret for so long and now Hawkins was spouting it everywhere.

Warrington closed his mouth and paused before speaking to Bellona. 'Perhaps you should consider the special licence. Even Rhys can't change a marriage after the deed is done. His property joins mine. You would be close to Melina. And when Thessa returns from sea with Ben, you will be near to her as well. If you go away now to Scotland, it will be assumed there is a child. If you stay here and wed the duke—perhaps you can geld him.' He shrugged and gave a pointed look to Rhys's hand. 'Just a thought. I'm sure she'd eventually think of it on her own.'

'His Grace and I would not get on well.' She reached up, pushing an errant lock behind her ear. 'He doesn't even like the way I dress my hair.' She shrugged. 'He does not know how to live for himself, only for others. I do not know how to live that life. I have seen what happens to a woman who falls in love and marries a man when he does not love her back—or think her above his tracks in the dirt.'

'I would not treat you ill.' The duke's words bit into the air.

'But in your heart you would. Now you can promise—anything. Everything. That is easily done.' She looked across at him and slipped a pin from her hair, and tossed it to the table beside her. 'My father promised to return to my mother. He would hurry, he said.' She stared at Rhys. 'He promised most sincere *agape*, love, when he meant it the least. And do you know what my mother's last words were?'

Rhys blinked, forceful. Jaw firm. Solid, unmoving.

'She asked if my father was on the ship in the harbour. But he was not. He was never returning. I knew it.'

'You cannot judge other men by your father.'

'You judge other men by yours.'

He shook his head, causing a strand of hair to fall across his eyes. He put his hand to his temple and thrust the lock back into place. 'I know he was a stickler for convention. But that does not mean—' He used his flat palm to indicate himself. 'He *was* a good man and I can follow his example. All men make mistakes. Even him.'

'You made a mistake and now you must correct it?' She tilted her head.

'We must be married. You cannot hide away in Scotland.'

'I find it nobler to be a spinster than to throw myself under your feet. I do not care who you wed, Your Grace. As long as it isn't me.'

'You should tell him everything, Bellona. Rhys

isn't worth much, but he can keep his counsel,' Warrington advised.

Bellona stared forward. Rhys thought she'd looked much gentler when she'd held the arrow to his stomach.

Warrington left the room, his grumbles mixed with curses at her father.

Rhys stood, his face with so little expression she could not read it. Behind his eyes he was secured alone with his thoughts and she suspected they were not charitable ones.

She refused to discuss any more of her life with him. Warrington said Rhys could keep silent, but the earl didn't realise Rhys was the one person she most did not wish to tell.

'We are finished here,' she said. 'You've done as much as you can to help me. You've tried to correct what you see as an error. You should go about your duties and remove this from your thoughts.'

'Remove it from my *thoughts*? And how might I do that?' He moved to stand in front of the painting and pointed to the smallest girl. 'If I wave my hand over the canvas, will it make the scene disappear? Will it make the memories I have go away?'

'Memories are the past. Thoughts are what are in a person's head at the moment. I do not care what you do with your memories. You may polish them until they outshine the sun. But do not keep me in your thoughts.'

He whirled from the painting to look at her. 'You think I am so uncaring a person that I can bed you in my home and just toss that aside.'

'Did you not do that to a woman once before— a servant?'

'Even that was not as simple as the way you speak of it. It was not.'

'My mother loved my father so much. And she thought she could not live without him. But he was not to stay and she died. Perhaps she spoke the truth of her love. Which showed me so much. The warmth faded from her body while my father painted. I was not with him, but I know—at the very moment my mother died, my father had a brush in his hand, a canvas in front of him and more concern about the light than my mother. She never meant more than being a subject for a painting to him.'

'He will pay for that.'

'He cannot. It cannot be done.'

'You do not have to worry about your father, Bellona. I can ensure he has a set-down. It will be his word against mine. You and I can face this together and it will never be more than a rumour. A tale we laugh away.'

'No.'

'He cannot spread such tales if we are wed. It will be ridiculous for him to do so. I will take care of him for you, Bellona. He cannot cross a duke and get away with it,' Rhys said.

'No. Do not add more coal to the fire.' Bellona shut her eyes. She should have left England earlier. Now her father would feel he had successfully chased her away if she left, but she did not know how she could stay and watch Rhys wed someone else.

'It is not about increasing the gossip. I will see that he ceases it altogether. We all have our weaknesses, Bellona. All of us. And I can find his.'

'Searching them out will not be hard. They flutter about him like birds over grain. I do not want you to be pulled into his mire. He relishes such things.'

'I will relish this.'

'Do not meddle. I am his daughter.' If she confronted her father, he could tell more truths. More truths she did not want known. She could not lie away the truth. 'His actions do not truly surprise me. I do not wish to be near him and he feels the same about me.' She ignored the way the air seemed to have the scent of her home again and she could hear the waves. 'I am so much his daughter that we cannot bear each other.' Rhys could not get involved in her past.

'You are not like Hawkins.'

'Oh, I am.' She put her hand over her heart and patted. 'I do not use mine to guide my actions. It is to beat and keep me alive, nothing else.' She shut her eyes. 'The letters my father sent my *mana*… My sister read them aloud to her so many times we could recite them. Such words of love. Tears in Mana's eyes. Hope in Melina's voice. Thessa and I would later go to the sea, fall on to the sand in front of the waters, and repeat the words, each of us speaking with all the sincerity we could bring to the speech. None of the fish ever changed the direction of their swimming. The waters continued on as before. Gold did not fall from the heavens. The words were worth nothing. They were not love to Mana. They were words for himself. A painting he created on paper instead of canvas.'

'Words may disappear into the air, but a special licence is binding.'

'My father married twice. Two too many times, but he married for a reason each time. His first wife's funds and my mother's beauty. I will not marry you for your title. Or for your protection of my name.'

'You cannot tell me you do not care for me.'

'No. I cannot. I would say I care for you more than anyone in London does. But no matter what feelings I have, one person's love in a marriage is not enough.'

Chapter Nineteen

She held out a hand to brace herself against the thoughts buffeting her, but nothing fell into her grasp. Rhys stood there, not speaking.

But his past gripped him as strongly as hers held her tight. She'd been marked on the outside and the inside.

Her mother might have called the spot on her body a longing mark, but it wasn't. The mark was her strength. A reminder not to repeat her mother's broken heart. All her father's children had the blemishes—her father's London wife had told her how each of her children had been born with similar marks. They were a legacy, just as a title was. But where her sisters had brown marks, hers had red in it—like a scrape, as if the blood had risen to the surface on her hip and never healed. A heart that was broken.

Now she truly believed that her mother had wished for a torn heart for her daughter.

Better to have a broken heart than a broken soul from loving someone who could not love her in return.

If she didn't turn her back on him in that instant, she would not have the strength to do it at all. She turned. She could not look at his face.

She left him behind.

Rushing up the stairs, she went to her sister's chamber, not knocking but running inside. Melina sat in there, her son's toy soldiers arranged on the table, and Willa stood at the side, moving the toy men into rows. A governess sat in a corner chair.

When Melina looked up, Willa ran to her aunt and wedged herself against Bellona. For a second, the hug erased the pain deep inside her, but then when she looked at the little girl's tousled curls and cherub cheeks, she realised she had given up her chance to have a child by the one man she loved. Sharp spasms of pain hit her body and she forced herself immobile to let the hurt pass.

Melina looked at her sister's face. 'Take Willa to play in the nursery,' she said to the governess.

'Warrington told me about Rhys.' Melina stood as the governess and Willa left. 'When you moved to Harling House to be a companion to the duchess, I knew you were taking a risk, but how could I warn you?'

'You could not have. I already knew. When I met Rhys in the forest, I knew. No one had ever unsettled me the same way he did.' She'd pointed the arrow tip at him to keep herself safe, but not in the way he'd thought at the time.

She couldn't stay at her sister's house. Rhys had even taken that from her. To see the children grow and watch her sister's family flourish while she stood on the outside looking in would wither her spirit. She had to leave.

'You will survive,' Melina said, walking to put an arm around her sister's shoulder.

'How would you know?'

'You have no other choice.' Melina reached out as if to pat Bellona, but instead pinched her sister's arm.

'Stop it.' Bellona pulled away.

Melina reached out, fingers poised to nip Bellona again.

Bellona took a step away. 'You had better not.'

'It is only because I care for you.'

'Do not let us get in a competition to see who loves the other the most. Your children do not need to see such behaviour.'

'If you do not want me to hurt you, then you must remember that you would not want a husband who does the same.'

'I know. My mind knows that.' She put her hands to her head, pushing back the hair that had fallen at her brow. 'But my head cannot find a way to tell my heart. I do not understand why it will not listen.'

The man of affairs still sat in front of him, patiently awaiting the return to his duties. Rhys didn't know how a man could smell of roses and be content in life, but Simpson seemed to have mastered that. Rhys felt he could kick the chair legs from under the man and he would receive only an apology from Simpson for having placed his chair in the wrong path.

Rhys's jaw hurt from keeping his words careful and precise and all emotion banked.

He began looking over the ledgers again. He spotted an error. One he'd made. He crossed it out, irritated. He couldn't have been paying attention to have made such an obvious mistake.

Voice ever so solicitous, the man of affairs said, 'I wish to speak with you about a private matter, concerning a bit of rubbish currently being batted about.'

Rhys nodded. Apparently the man of affairs had heard the *on dits*. Rhys could sense a change in the man—an awareness of unsaid things.

'So—' Rhys relaxed his body in the chair, interlaced his fingers behind his head, and fixed his eyes on Simpson '—what is the talk?' Might as well get the words on the table, so to speak, and then get on with things.

'Talk?' The voice was just a tiny amount too shrill. 'I would not call it that. Only small minds repeating things heard. Embellished, I'm sure.'

Rhys didn't speak, but let his eyes pull out the words. He waited. And in the same manner of a gust of air blowing over his body, he viewed his physical self. He'd never sat in a chair in such an informal way. Rhys put his feet flat on the floor, hands on the desk, straightened his back and leaned forward.

'It's said the dark-eyed foreign woman had wild

ways, and you, well—' his head swiveled sideways '—did as a normal man would and partook
of her favours.'

'That's all?'

'It's said she's even claimed to be that Lord
Hawkins's daughter—the one who paints. Trying to disgrace him—though you know how he's
viewed by the *ton* as full of himself and rather
like a belch that's gone on too long.'

Rhys let his palms feel the smooth wood.

'And we all know,' he continued, 'that the sisters come from Grecian high-born people on an
island where the French have been claiming trea-
sures abound from the past. But people are sup-
posing the youngest one is unsettled.'

Rhys's lips firmed and he glared at the man.

'You asked.'

'Yes, I did.' Five heartbeats of silence followed
and Rhys reminded himself he had offered to wed
Bellona. She had refused.

'One other thing.'

Rhys waited again, wanting to throw an inkpot at the man to hurry him and strangely upset
at the thought that the man would not pick up the
tossed inkpot and hurl it back.

'Lord Hawkins, he doesn't seem to be taking things well and is blaming the girl. He's said she's hurt his children with her tales.' The man put his fist loosely to his upper lip, as if to blunt what was said next, concentrating on his words. 'Of late, it's said he can't even get along with himself.'

Rhys only response was his usual flick of the brows.

Lord Hawkins wasn't cracked. He knew him. The man didn't have an *un*selfish bone in his body. He could lecture for hours on a bird's beak, as if no one but he could see it. As if everything he saw, he saw in brighter colours and with more meaning than mere humans could digest.

'He's not doing...' The man's words trailed away.

Rhys met his eyes and forced him to continue.

'He's not doing her any good at all, Your Grace. He's talking about her in a way no lord should talk about a girl who has been a guest at a duke's home.'

Rhys placed his right hand on the desk, above the drawer, and knew that underneath lay a newspaper, with the words neatly printed, not only the reference to *a certain duke*, and most of the things his man of affairs had just said, but repeated several times, as if once wasn't enough.

Bellona was referred to as the Untamed Grecian Temptress from a land of Saturnalian delights, ready to leave a trail of women in tears as she danced about for their husbands.

The simple-lined caricature did not look like her, but a Gillray sketch, hair flowing as a brief covering swirling around her, while she held a tambourine, dancing. The goddess of beguilement. He hoped to be able to return a copy of the newspaper to the artist, personally.

'We're through for today,' Rhys said.

Simpson shuffled the papers together. 'You'll do fine, Your Grace.' He coughed. 'Not a life about doesn't have some struggle from time to time. You've just had more loss than most of recent. Time for a spell of good luck.'

Rhys waited until Simpson left and returned to his examination of the man's meticulous records. Truly, he wondered if Simpson hadn't managed better alone.

Rhys wanted to return his life to normal. To erase the impact of tales that might be told, before the whispers grew louder. To gauge the look in the faces of others and listen, and steer the conversation if they mentioned anything of the improprieties he had caused. But most of all he wanted to forget.

Folding his arms flat over his desk, he rested his head on them, closing his eyes and trying to trick himself into sleeping. In the night, whenever he'd lain in bed, his mind had darted alert, thinking of all the mistakes of the past few days, and the woman whose image he could not erase.

The sound of a rap on the door caused Rhys to raise his head. He brushed his hand over his eyes, uncertain of how long he'd slept. A servant stood there, holding a salver with a calling card.

Rhys straightened, and reached out. The tray was moved to him and he pulled the pasteboard card into view. Lord Hawkins. Bellona's father. He'd sent for him the day before. He tossed the card back on its resting place.

Rhys brushed a hand across his cheek, feeling the bristles.

The grimness of Jefferson's face alerted Rhys. Jefferson had been trained well. With just the briefest narrowing of his eyes, and the extra-precise steps he took as he moved backwards to the door, he told Rhys this was not a congenial guest.

'Show him to the sitting room,' Rhys said, 'and serve him cold tea. Collect me when he has reached a proper temperature to boil the water.' Rhys put his head back on the desk.

He felt he'd just shut his eyes when the sound of Jefferson clearing his throat woke Rhys.

He pushed himself up from the desk, stood, pulled his waistcoat smooth and reached for the coat he'd tossed on a chair, donning it.

'Would you care for a comb, Your Grace?' Jefferson asked.

Rhys shook his head and walked out through the door, running a hand to smooth his hair, but not really caring.

When Rhys walked into his sitting room, the scent of a painting just completed lingered around the man, perhaps linseed oil or painting pigments.

Bellona's father sat, holding a cane, gnarled fingers grasping it, a birdlike flutter to his movements. It felt as if someone had left a raptor in the room and it had flown from place to place, leaving feathers and droppings about. A chair had been moved a bit. A tea cup sat half-empty with crumbs scattered. Rhys examined Hawkins's face, looking for a resemblance to Bellona. He saw none, except perhaps a bit of the chin. And they both tilted their head to the side when showing displeasure.

Hawkins stood. 'Rolleston.' His bow was more the semblance of movement than anything else. 'I have wasted near a day waiting on you.'

'Greetings to you as well, Lord Hawkins. I am going to make you pay for what you did to Bellona. It is nothing personal, you understand. It is justice. You left your daughters to fend alone. You left a family without funds to live in little more than a shack on an island while you lolled about here.'

'I did no such thing.' His lips twisted. 'My only family has always been in England.'

He thumped his walking stick on the floor. 'I hate Warrington for giving refuge to those women when he should have packed them back on the ships they arrived on.'

'They're your daughters, no matter how much you deny it. You know it and I know it.'

'I know no such thing.' He chuckled. 'It's possible I spent some time with their mother while I was away from home. So I can understand how they might be under the impression I am their father. Ridiculous as it is.'

'You make this easier for me.'

'You let her gull you. You couldn't keep your hands off her.' He frowned and looked to the ceiling. His voice softened. 'Not that I don't understand. I had the same problem with her mother. Couldn't leave the woman alone. I'd sail from Melos thinking I'd never see her again and then I'd go back. I couldn't stay away.'

'You were a married man.'

He chuckled, shrugging. 'Only slightly.'

'You are going to *only slightly* pay for deserting your daughters.'

Hawkins raised a pointed finger and softly shook it in the air. 'Oh, no, no, no. You cannot do a thing to me or I will remind everyone how you soiled her. I am no different from other men. I even kept my number of visits to the island to a reasonable amount.'

A flush of intensity blasted Rhys's body.

'You would do well to follow my example.' The

voice hit Rhys's ears with a clatter that rang on and on.

Rhys's stomach churned cold.

Hawkins strode past Rhys. The walking stick brushed Rhys's leg. Hawkins looked back over his shoulder. 'She's been nothing but trouble since she arrived. Calling on my wife. Not settling into suitable English society as her sister did. She's nothing to me. My children—she let my *real* children see her. My daughter cried. Un…for…giv…able.' He dragged out the syllables as if he spoke four words.

Hawkins stopped in the doorway. 'And you…' He pointed the cane at the painting over the mantel. A work by Lawrence. 'Wouldn't know a good painting if you fell over it.'

Rhys didn't speak. He didn't want to give the man even the smallest response, afraid of what his voice might reveal.

Hawkins's walking stick crashed against the door frame. 'You lie to yourself, Rolleston. You think you're better than me, but you're not. Your brother was born to be duke—not you. If he'd been wise enough to wed and sire a son before he died, you'd be living off your nephew's whims.

Now you toss crumbs about instead of scrabbling for them. Your dead brother's crumbs. I bet every morning you say a prayer of thanks that he died.'

Hawkins left, pulling the walking stick up and putting it under his arm.

Rhys didn't move.

The foundation of his life cracked, turning into rubble.

Chapter Twenty

Rhys went to a soirée. Louisa was there. She turned her shoulder to him when he walked near and relief surged along with guilt. The relief won when she danced twice with someone else and her eyes shone on her partner. Watching her, it was as if he'd never *seen* her before. This woman he'd hoped to marry, but had never really seen for who she was—because, he now realised, he'd never truly loved her.

He forced his attention to the man who was speaking to him, Lord Andrews.

Lord Andrews leaned closer, winking and smiling. 'So what of the bit of muslin you—?'

'Stop.' Thoughts pummelled Rhys from the inside, causing him to need a moment to sort through even half of them. 'I asked her to marry me. She refused.'

Lord Andrews stared. Rhys didn't think he'd ever looked at Lord Andrews properly either. The man was commanding, of fair face and quick-witted. Yet, Rhys would have compared him to a toad, waiting, watching for insects. They'd shared brandies more times than Rhys could count.

'I am pleased we spoke,' Rhys said. 'But I must be away.'

On his way to the door, he dropped the brandy glass he held on to a footman's tray.

He had to wait for his carriage outside, the unseasonably cool air brushing his face and waking him up to feel even more.

How many times had he truly looked at himself through his own eyes? Possibly never. He'd always used the eyes of others to gauge himself. His father. His older brother. His mother. The things he did privately were deemed to deserve no judgement. No censure. No introspection. After all, he was the second son. It did not matter. Nothing mattered until after Geoff died and then everything tilted in a different direction.

The town-coach door was opened. Rhys stepped inside and made himself comfortable. Even in darkness, he knew exactly what the crest on the door looked like. He'd had the colours corrected as they faded. But he didn't know the face of the man who'd held the door. Didn't know his name.

Rhys touched his cheek with his marred hand.

He had thought, when he'd first discovered that Bellona was not the offspring of someone in the Greek upper classes, that she was scarred by her birth. Perhaps in a way like the statue without arms the sisters had found on Melos. The one that Warrington had told him about and said the sisters thought an ancestor of theirs had posed for. Supposedly, the statue favoured their mother.

But blemishes and perfection did not always appear in the expected forms. The white line at the top of Bellona's nose made him want to kiss it. Her hair tumbling about called to him in a way perfection never would.

He was marred. Bellona had risen from a world of struggle and became someone of strength. He had been handed the world and only had to continue on the path already cleared for him, yet he'd been unable to choose the right steps. She'd made her own path and tossed her head back and fought with all her strength to survive, becoming stronger.

He'd become weaker. Softened by the world giving him his wishes as he indicated them. He supposed—but he would not wish to repeat it—if he had true strength, it had been gained when he'd watched Bellona follow the rules she created for herself.

The feeling of a funeral surrounded him, and now he felt he knew what it would be like to attend his own last service, and see the crypt surround him on all sides, with the grim knowledge that he had done this to himself.

Bellona sat in her room, the needle slowly going into the fabric and moving out on the other side. Her eyes not rising once. Holding the embroidery high into the light, she examined the stitches. She would be better letting the maid sew while she attended the washing. Cleaning she could do well, which no one wanted her to do. Embroidery, which everyone expected of her, was a tangle of threads.

If not for the war with the Turks, she would be wishing for a return to Greece. She couldn't safely sail to Melos now. Or ever. If she did, she'd not be able to see her nieces and nephews grow. She'd not see her sisters again.

Warrington's voice didn't carry through the walls any more. She wondered if her sister had finally quieted him or if his throat had simply given out from the exertion. This was the one time he seemed to have forgotten his rule about servants not hearing family matters.

She looked into the grate. Only ashes left. No more of the vile newsprint.

She wished for more words to burn. Burning the papers somehow seemed to ease the ache in her heart. She could not even look at the mark on her body any more. Once, it had made her feel stronger, the memory of her mother—a trace of the past. Now, even the blemish ached.

Just like her heart and all the rest of her that mattered.

Ruined. That word had carried through the walls a few times.

'She could not be more ruined.' That had spewed into the air and cloaked her with a feeling of being unwashed.

The needle jabbed her finger and she didn't spare her grumbles. She could be more ruined.

Warrington was wrong to think otherwise. If not for her sister and niece and nephews, she would be finding out where the scandal sheets originated and marching there with the largest hammer she could beg from the stable master. The printer would be having a holiday from his work long enough for repairs. Then he could write about the angry woman who'd smashed his press and stopped him from being able to put his cruel words on paper.

Rhys could not be sailing easily through this either. He could not.

'A visitor for you.' Her sister spoke from the hall.

Bellona's heart pounded. Rhys. She thrust her sewing to the side.

The quick sideways shudder of her sister's head paused Bellona's movements.

'The duchess.' Melina frowned. 'She's…'

'She's in quite high dudgeon,' the duchess said, walking in behind Melina. Melina rolled her eyes and left.

The older woman's skin hardly covered the bones of her face.

'Embroidery again?' She walked closer, the

black crepe of her skirt reminding Bellona of a raven's wings fluttering about. Her reticule matched the clothing and her bonnet completed the effect.

She peered at the sewing while opening her reticule. 'You should conquer reading first. Then dancing. Perhaps leave the sewing to someone else.'

She held up the folded paper and tossed it on to Bellona's sewing. 'I received this unsigned note, but I believe it is from Rhys's man of affairs.' She knotted the ties of her reticule. 'I believe the words are simple enough for you to make out. I brought it for your own good.'

'Your *kali thelisi*, good will to me, is kind.' Bellona forced her lips into a smile and refused to touch the paper, uncertain if she could read it. Refusing to let the duchess see her stumble. 'But I was going to send my sister to tell you I am not at home.'

'Oh, my,' the woman said. 'Neither am I. The stairs weakened my knees. I'll be in bed the rest of the week.'

'You shouldn't overtire yourself.'

'You'd like that, wouldn't you—if I left?'

'Yes. I don't wish to be near you.'

'The house is quiet without you. The servants seem to miss having you about. One of their own has left them.'

'Your maid was very kind to me.' Bellona glanced at the messy fabric beside her. If she'd known what was to happen, she would have stolen a piece of Melina's perfect embroidery and worked on it, pretending to complete it.

'I'm sure the staff here is also kind to you.' The duchess looked around the room. 'The maid does know where her loyalty lies, though.'

'As you know yours.'

'True. I do.' She held her head up, again reminding Bellona of a bird. 'I'm a duchess. I'm well suited to it. But I am a mother first and I only have one offspring left.' She sighed. 'Are you with child?'

'It is a little soon to know.' She shrugged. 'And when I do know, I will not inform you.'

'I will raise the child for you.' The duchess picked a bit of fluff from her gown.

'I will bear that in mind.'

'I'm excellent at selecting nursemaids. I have a gift for it.' She lowered her lids. 'I made sure my children had the best of governesses. Ones that suited them.'

'Perhaps you should have cared for the babies.'

The duchess frowned. 'Child. Think about it. If you were a babe, would you want me or a governess comforting your tears? I am not suited for that duty.' She raised a brow.

Definitely, Bellona would have chosen a servant. 'I see.'

'Even now, I know to put the needs of my son first and let someone else handle the task of giving him direction.' The duchess's chin bobbed. The lines at her eyes deepened. 'You must go to London and speak with Rhys. He's causing a disgrace to our name by lowering himself to squabble in public. He is not maintaining his dignity at all. You caused this by your presence and you can correct it.'

'But it would not be—'

'Proper?' the duchess inserted. 'Child. You two lost that chance already. I would hope that you could be a bit discreet. Perhaps leave your bow and arrows behind and travel in darkness.' She examined Bellona. 'I'll send a quiet servant with you and you can wear my veil and dark clothing. If anyone sees you, they'll assume I'm visiting him.'

Bellona didn't speak. She shook her head.

'It's not that I particularly like you,' the duchess continued. 'But I think I could—even though I cannot imagine you would ever be a true duchess. But I must have grandchildren and I want them now. There is only one way I know to get them and I will have to accept someone, so it may as well be you.' She shrugged. 'No one's good enough for him, but then no one was good enough for my daughter or Geoff either. You see where that has left me.'

She shook her head. 'I could accept someone as unschooled as you because of the grandchildren.' She leaned towards Bellona. 'I have decided I want the babies strong most of all. I want them to survive. You would have a spirited child.' She sniffed. 'You're tolerable for short lengths of time. And you sing well.'

'I doubt I would let my child meet you. Rhys is not going to be in my life again so you must pick out someone else to breed the next heir.'

The duchess chuckled. She examined Bellona toe to head.

Fingers splayed, the duchess put her palms together and then she interlaced her fingers. 'The butler did the unthinkable. He started a betting book with the staff concerning Rhys and you. Even taking in the possibility of an heir. I am not supposed to know of it, but my maid understands the importance of her duties.' She extended her forefingers towards Bellona. 'All sorts of wagers are being bandied about. I plan for my maid to do quite well. The maid has been informed that she is to wager on you marrying Rhys inside the month and that the first child will be a daughter, because I know you will do that just to spite me.'

'I liked you better when you were crying,' Bellona said.

'Well, child, you should have thought of that earlier. You should have thought about the consequences when you…bathed with my son. The butler has not yet recovered his senses or he would not have started the betting book.'

'You have no say in this.'

'Fine. But you need to alert Rhys that you mean nothing to him.' Unclasping her hands, she stood.

'I have.'

'You have not convinced him.'

'He's a grown man. He can do as he pleases.'

'Oh, he is,' the duchess said. She smiled. 'I have it on good authority—since the staff in London knows I must be informed of events—that an interesting tale could be bandied about at any day.'

'What about?' Bellona couldn't help herself.

The older woman's lips turned up. Bellona thought of Gigia.

'I shall win that wager,' the duchess said.

She didn't walk to the door like a woman with a sore knee. She looked back. 'My son has to have some tenderness for you or he would not be so bound on destroying your father.'

Bellona paused two steps from the room's entrance, listening as she brushed the black veil from her face. A murmuring voice, a male, answered Rhys's bursts of command.

She took a deep breath, moved to the doorway and saw Rhys and a smaller fellow. The diminutive man, face wan, needed a razor, although he had been near one much more recently than Rhys.

'Your Grace,' Bellona spoke, pulling Rhys's eyes to her.

His eyes showed no reaction to her presence. He stood. 'I beg forgiveness that I cannot entertain you. But as you can see we have much to finish.' Papers mounded his desk and a small stack rested on the rug.

She tossed her reticule into the empty chair. 'So no shop owner may dare exhibit any of my father's paintings or they will have the Duke of Rolleston's wrath visited upon them. Even the tradesmen are afraid to sell any artist's supplies to him, for fear of reprisal. His every step outside his house is noted, and should anyone extend any favourable notice to his art they are warned away.'

This time, his face turned directly towards her and his eyes sparked an inferno. Then he switched his attention to Simpson and the man jumped back in his chair. Even Bellona could see the guilt in the face of the man of affairs.

'Rolleston.' She snapped the word out, pulling his gaze. Even though she did not fear him, she didn't like the look he gave her—the calmness a bit too scorching.

'My dear. I am impressed.' Then he pointed a pen to his man of affairs. 'Simpson. For your tale-bearing you are let go without a reference.'

The man's jaw dropped and he gathered his papers as he stood.

She stepped back into the doorway, feet firm. 'Stop,' she commanded Simpson.

'Oh, I could not, miss.' He caught a paper that had slid from his fingers, grasping it before it hit the floor.

She put a hand out, palm against the wood. No one could move through the doorway without pushing her aside.

Simpson stood, looking at her, eyes wavering but feet immobile. 'Pardon, miss?' His eyes begged.

'Tell him,' she commanded the duke. 'Tell him there will be no repercussions for his actions.'

Words knifed the air. 'There will be.'

'Then he may wed me for my *proika, my* dowry.'

Rhys coughed. 'His wife will object.'

She shook her head in frustration. 'You cannot blame this man for his concern—if he did write to Harling House to mention your behaviour towards my father. You have a houseful of servants here and I have noticed that your staff at Harling House cares for you. Or perhaps they just fear the duchess and only pretend affection for you.'

'I am quite well, thank you.'

Her eyes raked over him, and she pressed her palm tightly against the door frame.

Well groomed, he looked like a duke and commanded a woman's attention in a discreet way. Unkempt, his appearance made a woman's hands beg to straighten his clothing. Or loosen it some more. His eyes looked into the depths of her being.

Rhys need never question whether a woman would only want him for his title and his wealth. But he should always question whether she wanted him only to pleasure her senses. The days Bellona had not seen him had taken her strength and weakened her for his touch.

Simpson needed to stay in the room. She needed to keep him there, for her own well-being. The granite in the duke's eyes told her he would not back down and she could not lose her strength.

'It's said you have been about town, seeing that no man near you has a parched throat, and you've been more affable than people are used to seeing.'

'I see no reason to hide from anyone. My life is my own. To live as I—' Then his breath swooshed on the last word, echoing it in her ears. 'As I wish.'

'Your cravat is a sight,' she said.

'Well, dash my wig,' he said, words light. 'And I have been wearing it in public all day.'

Silence dragged.

'Miss…' Simpson said tentatively. 'Might I pass by you?'

'Not until the matter of your employment is settled.'

'Simpson.' The duke's voice was a commanding boom. 'You will return in the morning to take up where we left off.'

The man took a tentative step towards Bellona.

She left her hand at the door.

'Bellona—' Rhys spoke low, voice curling about her '—must I toss him out of the window?'

Predatory eyes snared her, but she wasn't afraid. Well, not in the mortal sense, anyway.

Rhys made sure he truly looked at her. He needed to see past the hair, the memory of her body and the opinions of other people.

Her fingers slid from the wall and Simpson snaked out through the door before she had fully stepped aside.

'So you are here to tell me all that I have done wrong. You do not have to. I am well aware. More so than you, I suspect.' Rhys put the chair against the desk, but did not release the wood.

'You have enraged my father.'

On that he had not been blinded by any foolishness of his heart. On that one thing he knew he was absolutely right. 'Surely you cannot have concern for that man who did not even give you his true last name, but one he simply pulled from the air.'

'I have no care for him,' she said. 'But his wife has been as kind to me as any *mana* would. I care for her. She suffers with him. It is the way of the world.'

'She's strong. She will survive.' He gave the chair an extra shove.

'If he shoots you, as it is said he has threatened, you might not.'

One side of his lips went up, a smirk. 'It is not in his best interest to be near me. If I die merely from choking on a bone, he will hang. If he does try to do me in and I live, he will be hanged. I have seen to that already.'

'You have convinced people to speak ill of his paintings.'

'I have viewed a considerable amount of them

in the past few days as I visited most homes in London where I knew the owners had his drivel displayed. I could not help but notice the subtle flaws in his work, which of course, I asked about before I viewed them. I only spoke the truth. Had he not had the funds of his wife as his patron, he would not have been able to survive on what his paintings earn and he is certainly not worth notice as an artist. Not only my opinion, but the men I talked with.'

'It is in the scandal sheets that the Duke of R. mused about whether this artist painted with his toe or his elbow and suggested he be shown what a brush looks like.'

His lashes flicked down and then up. 'That is actually a compliment compared to what I truly think. They would not even improve the look of a dust bin.' He looked at her.

'Not all of them are that bad.'

'Enough are. Most are. Someone should have taken pity on him and broken his paintbrushes long ago.'

'You are trying to do so now.'

'Yes. The man had left you alone for years. He should have continued to do so.'

'You brought even more attention to the situation.'

'If I did not stand against him, I could not have lived with myself.'

His gaze locked on her so hard she might have become afraid, except something deeper behind his eyes showed a private agony. 'I would not have injured you for the world and yet I live with, every day, how I caused your name to be sullied.' He looked at the ring on his finger. The one passed from duke to duke.

He changed the direction of his gaze. 'What does the crest on my carriage look like?'

She shrugged.

'Tell me about the servants?'

Her eyes tightened. 'Why do you change what we are talking of?'

'Just tell me about the servants.'

'Fenton, I do not like at all. He broke the scullery maid's heart. Thompson makes sure to keep him in hand, though. He thinks of all the women on the staff as his daughters.'

'And the maids. What are their names?'

'Julia. Honour. Susan. Eliza, although she prefers to be called—'

'Enough.' He raised his hand.

'Yes. I know their names. I saw them daily at your house. How could I not?'

'That is just it. How could you not? I dare say you have no thought of the art in the house which could fund a small country.'

'I do have some notion of the paintings on your walls,' she admitted. 'I have never imagined paintings could be so beautiful. Before I left the duchess, I walked through the house to view the art and that took her grief from my mind.' She lowered her chin for a moment before looking back at him. 'Days after I refused you, I realised I had turned away a chance to live with those works.' She shook her head as if she could not believe it.

His response was half-chuckle, half-snort. 'The art tempted you to say yes more than I did.'

She didn't answer.

To speak took more strength than he could immediately garner. Words choked inside him in a way they'd never constricted before. Then everything vanished from his mind except for what mattered most. 'I love you.'

Chapter Twenty-One

He'd not expected the deep intake of breath and the way her lids dropped causing her narrowed eyes to spear him.

He wondered if perhaps he'd been right to let his thoughts be directed by the opinions of others. He could not see what Bellona thought or meant or wanted.

'You say that. But you have not shown it. You have made things so much worse.' Quiet words from soft lips, but with fervour attached.

The words. He had to roll them around in his head to make certain he heard what she was saying.

He struggled to sort things in his mind and then he spoke again. 'I believe that my art collection is one of the best in a private residence anywhere in the world.' He watched her face. 'In case you are wondering.'

'Stubble it, Your Grace.'

'Yes, sweetness.'

She moved within arm's grasp and he could not help it. He moved enough to brush back the hair that had fallen to her temple.

The puff from her lips censured him, but she didn't retreat.

'You are trying to destroy my father and his family,' she said. 'You have no right.'

'I have every right.' She'd taken all his resistance to her and reduced him to the rank of a schoolboy. But then, she'd truly done that days ago. 'The man—he may not have meant to, but he could have caused your death. He left you on that island to fend for yourself.'

'You had no cause to interfere. I told you not to hurt him.'

'His arms and legs are all attached, as well as his head. I would say he is unhurt.'

'How my father treats me is my concern. I will deal with him, but how can I do that now when you have struck out at him and reduced him?'

'And just what were you going to do—thank

him for nearly causing your death by deserting you on Melos with no food? Forcing you to use whatever means you might find to survive.'

Rhys was taken aback that she was not more grateful to him, but he didn't care. He cared that she was standing in his house and thought enough of her father's wife to be concerned.

'You are not my protector. You have no right to my life because we kissed.'

'We did more than just kiss, Bellona.'

'And the women before me—did you jump to their aid in this way, too?'

'They did not have such problems as you, but I did not abandon them without a thought. Perhaps the first I did not stand by when I was very young and that cured me of the inability to do so again. I cannot hold a woman near my heart and then forget she exists the next day.'

'That is a poor excuse.'

'Really, sweet? I feel you owe me a bit of understanding. We shared something together I have never shared with anyone else.'

She raised her brows.

He lifted his palm, the cut towards her. 'A very

painful bloodletting. I should think you'd have some tolerance for me for that reason alone.'

'You know that was not intended.'

'Just as my actions towards your father are not intended to bear you any ill will.'

She shook her head. 'You have meddled.'

'Meddle? I did not meddle. The man, he needed to be punished. Any man who can cause such harm to a woman should suffer.' He stared at her. 'And you are here now—why? To what purpose? I cannot undo anything that has already happened.' He held his palm where he could see it. He gave a dry chuckle. 'This memento. It will never go away.' He raised his eyes. 'I suspect the true mark you have left on me is not on my palm.'

'That does not give you the right to denigrate my father.'

'I let him off lightly.'

'You destroyed him.'

'He still can sit at a fine table and drink fine wine. I feel no pity for him.'

'You do not even tell yourself the truth.'

He turned from her, shaking his head, and then faced her again. 'If someone strikes at me, Bellona, they can expect me to strike back. It is the nature of the world. It is how one survives.'

'Revenge. That is what you did.'

Her words rasped against the inside of his skin. 'I make the heritage I will pass on to my children. With that in mind you can understand why it is so important I uphold the beliefs I hold close to me.'

He had upheld them. Most of them. Until his world had become fodder for the tongues of the *ton*. But he could trace his madness back one step further than that. When a woman had put an arrow tip to his stomach. 'I had thought to make amends to you by holding your father responsible for his actions,' he said.

She merely shook her head. 'You took away his belief in what he loves most.'

He whispered, 'What he loves most should be— *you*.' He walked forward. He grasped her arms. 'We have both abandoned you, Bellona. He and I.'

'No. I only thought I needed him. I did not. My life is better without him. I did not need his love. I did not. I did not need his presence in my childhood. I only needed food. The funds he did give us came from coin his wife had given him, though I did not know it at the time. When I had nothing, she agreed to give me a dowry, which I now have. She has been my friend even though she could view me with distaste. I do not want her hurt. And you have added to her disgrace. The woman who gave me all she could and asked for nothing. She has treated me with the same kindness as my own *mana*.'

Just like the chimes of the clock sounded too loud in his ears, Rhys heard the pounding of regret in his body.

He loved the woman who had taken away every part of him he believed in and put a mirror in front of his soul.

'I did not tell you all the truth either. My father could hurt me even more and I did not want him to decide to tell you everything.' She stood in front of him and when she moved, the shoulder of her dress drooped. She pulled it back into place. 'My father came to Melos to paint my mother,' she said. 'He had heard tales of her beauty and of the island's. My mother had no funds and had been forced to sell her body so when my father decided to keep her she insisted he marry her. He did not mind the fact that he was already married. As far as he was concerned it was just words.'

Unthinkable.

The old duke would not even have welcomed Bellona as a guest in the house once he discovered her origins were so tainted. Her mother, selling her body, and her father a bigamist.

The tousled goddess stood in front of him and, like the shattered statue recovered from her homeland by the French, she was indeed more marred than only a dent on the bridge of her nose. But also perfect in a way he'd never seen.

'I don't care about your mother, your father or your grandmother.' Rhys reached out, his forefinger looped under a lock of her hair which barely remained constrained. He slipped the brown strands free. They fell to her shoulders. 'I wish I could be perfect for you. I'm not. Who your father married, or what your mother did to survive, does not matter to me.'

'Rhys, your mother told me how angry you were when a servant did not wear the proper livery once.'

'I was very young when that happened. I was trying to… I don't know what I was trying to do, but I was not acting as I should. That was not the correct way to handle it. I was in error. As I have been many times.'

He held out his left hand. 'Forgive me?'

She didn't step forward right away, but when her body swayed in his direction he moved to her.

'It is not idle words,' he said. 'I do not do that. It is not who I am. It is not what I believe in.'

He rested his forehead against hers. 'I am sorting out who am I to be. What I am to think. All I believed about myself has been a lie. I thought I could forgive myself anything. I was the second son. A second son did not have the responsibility of the first. I am still the second son by birth. I will always be, and yet I am the duke. The thing I wanted most of all, but knew I could not have. Knew I was not worthy of. If I married the perfect duchess, she would hide my flaws. Instead I found the woman who would show me my weakness. You hold it to my face, Bellona.'

'I do not. I would not do such a thing.'

He moved back. His eyebrows rose.

'I could be wrong on that,' she muttered. 'Before you met me, you imagined yourself too grand.'

'Yes. I did want to be grand. Every day I thought of my father and how he would act, or Geoff, and what he would do, and then I did as if they directed me. Mostly. Until you. I could not keep you from my thoughts.'

'What of the woman you courted?'

'She has not even missed me this past year nor I her. But, if I married a woman such as her, without my heart involved, it would be the same as your father did when he wed Lady Hawkins. He married the woman who could give him funds and increase his status, but he could not forget the island woman. I am like the man on the other island. The one in Defoe's book.'

'Crusoe.'

He shook his head. 'No. The one who lived to serve him. I can't be rescued without you, Bellona. I need you every moment of my day.'

'You do not think me good enough for society.'

'Bellona, it is not you that is not good enough. It is me. It was fine for me to be in a woman's bed if the doors remained closed. I felt no guilt at all. But the minute the door opened and others could see me for who I was—then it was different. I didn't ask for marriage to protect you. You were closer than I to that truth. *"Ah, the duke is caught with a woman, but of course His Grace married her. Noble man.'"* His words were a sneer. *"'Sacrificed himself to protect a woman.'"*

'It is no surprise to me. I told you near the same.'

'You may have told me, but I didn't listen.'

She curled into his chest. 'Put that as another flaw of yours. Along with not listening. But you are very appealing to the eyes...'

'You could not say, *Oh, Rhys, you are perfect just as you are.*' He couldn't help pushing her.

'I do not lie.'

He circled his arms around her, putting a soft kiss on her cool lips before moving back. 'You are here. Why not stay? As my wife?'

Eyes, darker than the darkest stone flickering in the bottom of a pool, looked up at him.

'How do I know you are different now than you were only a fortnight ago?'

He shook his head, letting her slip from his arms, but taking her hands in his. 'Perhaps I am not. Perhaps I cannot truly change. But now instead of using the eyes of my father and brother and mother to look at the world, I wish to use your eyes. I wish to see people the way you see them. Even how you see me.'

'I will think about it.'

'Take the time you need,' he said. 'I am not going anywhere.'

Quite without asking, she moved into his house with the same amount of fuss a mouse made when taking up residence. She found her own room and changed it as she wished. A chamber with the best light which now smelled of linseed oil and paints. She said she wanted a painting of her homeland and wanted to create it herself. He'd instantly sent for a tutor and she'd not said one word against the man.

No one could see evidence of her anywhere else about the house and he did not think she went out often, but contented herself in the room.

She did not come to him in the night. Not once. So finally he went to her. He could not help himself.

Rhys looked in her chamber. All her paints were scattered about and the canvas was there, but he could not find her and the hour was late.

He puffed a breath out through his nose, knowing it could not be a good thing for her to be gone. His jaw tightened.

Rhys returned to his bedchamber and summoned his valet.

'Your Grace?' the servant asked when he walked in through the doorway.

Rhys realised he'd been standing with his hand still on the pull. 'Miss Cherroll, is she about?' He released the rope.

The valet's long face became even longer. His words were spoken as he breathed out. 'I believe you are the only resident of the house, Your Grace. Miss Cherroll received a message and had to rush away.'

'Where did she go?'

'I believe Lord Hawkins has taken ill and she was called to his bedside. It is not certain if he will recover. If you are to request a carriage, I am to instruct you that her father's wife does not want attention called to the matter and it has been suggested that you not follow.'

Bellona stared at the face of her father, noting the bluish tone around his lips. Her oldest sister had already visited him—a quick discreet visit in the night. Their middle sister, Thessa, might never see him alive again because she was at sea. But the ship could dock any moment, or a year hence.

His condition was uncertain. She had asked his wife if she might stay a bit longer and her father's wife had agreed. They had sat, side by side, watching him breathe.

Lady Hawkins wore a dressing gown and no rings or jewellery of any kind. Her face had little more colour than her husband's. Her shoulders stooped. 'This is the end of our years together, I suppose. He is falling more and more away each day.' She took the cover and tucked it closer at his side. 'I don't think he is here any more.'

Bellona tried to think of questions she would ask her father if he roused, but none mattered. The answers would not change anything.

If he hadn't acted so badly, she wouldn't have been given life.

But it had seemed uncaring of her to leave him. Much like he had left them on the island. She stayed at his bedside, if only to prove to herself that she would not do as he had done.

She'd met her half-sisters and brother, and knew

they'd only spoken to her begrudgingly after their mother had insisted. She'd felt no kinship for them at all, and yet, for his wife, she did.

'There are no secrets between him and me any more,' his wife said to Bellona, looking at the wan face of her husband. 'They were his secrets, yet he was the one who could not accept them being displayed.' She shook her head. 'The truth of his skill, though, that is what concerned him the most. When he discovered he had no true gift for painting.'

'I am sorry for my part in that.'

'Nonsense.' She waved the words away. 'It's not as if he'd not had it pointed out to him a thousand times before. He just finally accepted it now.' She leaned forward and let her hand rest on the bed. 'His paintings have rarely sold for more than the price of the canvas and frame. The best ones, oddly enough, were the ones of his children and your mother. If he has any talent, it is for capturing people, and of course, he thoroughly detests creating anything but landscapes. Endless landscapes. He doesn't like people. To paint them would mean he might have to look at them. Spend time with them.'

She put her hand on the counterpane covering his arm. 'He lied as much to himself as he did to everyone else. He sneered at the knowledge of others—only believing himself capable of thinking correctly. If he had gleaned from others and used his dedication in the right way, then perhaps he could have had what he wanted most. No one worked as hard to destroy his talent as he did.' She shut her eyes. 'I am only sorry for the pain of my children. For all his children.'

'I cannot begrudge him the past,' Bellona said. 'If I did, then I would be saying he changed me and he does not have that honour. I am who I am because of my *mana* and my sisters and myself. I thank you for what you have done for me.'

'I hated the thought of you children living with nothing. I am sorry he told such lies of you and destroyed your chance of marriage to Rolleston.'

'He did not. Rolleston asked me to wed him. I told him I could not. I was not sure.'

'Bellona.' Her eyes opened wide and she leaned forward to look in Bellona's face. 'After... When you were discovered together, the duke proposed?'

Bellona nodded. 'Yes, but I did not wish...'

'Oh, you may be a bit more your father's daughter than I realised,' she said. 'He turned down his chance to create art because he did not wish to follow his talent of painting portraits. And you turned down a chance to become a duchess—because?'

'I thought he felt he was doing me a boon just asking for my hand.'

The woman took her hand from her chest and clucked her tongue. 'Well, you have the attitude of a duchess already.'

'I will not be married because of pity, or duty or any reason I do not like.'

'Something—perhaps my knowledge of this world—tells me that Rolleston could have tumbled his choice of women into bed and yet he chose you, and then he had the brazenness to ask you to wed him. The cad.'

'He told me we should be married.'

'Perhaps he's a bit fonder of you than you think?'

'He could be. He thinks he is.'

'I've known his family my whole life. Rolleston is, or was, rather a stick. Much more the saint than most. Pleasant to look at, I thought, but as interesting to talk to as a land steward—'

'He is actually very interesting to talk to,' Bellona snapped.

Her father's wife paused before continuing. '…And quite the duke, until the last fortnight when your father began to denounce you as an extortionist. Then tales about Rolleston's fury began to blossom like weeds in a garden left untended. He became terribly unsettled for a man who'd never caused any kind of stir before.' She raised her brows and looked at Bellona. 'Terribly unsettled.'

'But he was included in the tales. It was said I was using him for gain as well.' Bellona could not keep the pique from her voice.

'He could have easily shrugged it off. Perhaps you should go to him and ask him what madness has grown in him that he had to be restrained in White's because a man dared speak slightingly of you.'

'I had not heard of that.'

'My sister has tried to schedule as many soirées, nights at the theatre and morning calls into her world as she can the past few days to keep me abreast of all the *on dits* because she considers it her duty to know what is being said about her family. Particularly when it concerns my husband. The duke, whether he means to or not, is not letting the talk wither away. His anger over you causes people to note you even more.'

'Rolleston can do as he wishes. I don't know that he cares enough for me even though he says he loves me. I don't know that I can love him enough for both of us if he does not.'

Lord Hawkins's wife looked again at the bed. 'Whomever you marry is a risk. If you don't marry, it is a risk, too. You might look back later and have missed so much.' She took her eyes from her husband and looked at Bellona. 'At least the duke doesn't like to paint.' She smiled.

Bellona didn't nod, or acknowledge the words with anything more than her eyes, but the next morning, as she walked to the carriage, she longed for Rhys more than she'd ever longed for anything in her life.

After directing the servants away, Bellona stepped into the duke's library and saw him at the desk with his man of affairs. He looked up and twisted a pen between his fingers, his eyes fixing on the movement. 'Leave us, Simpson.'

The man stood and hurried by Bellona, but his eyes flashed concern as he passed her.

'I don't think you need worry yourself about my father saying anything bad again,' she said.

'Are you well?' he asked.

She nodded. 'I left before the end came. His children did not want me there. I knew his wife understood. I do not need to be present. As I sat with him, I realised that when he sailed from Melos the last time, he died in my heart. It is as if he is someone I hardly know.'

The duke placed his pen atop his papers. He shifted in his chair and his knee hit the desk leg, but he caught the ink bottle before it tumbled over. 'Blast it,' he muttered. 'I can't keep these things upright any more.'

Still he held the liquid in his hand. He looked at her. 'That never used to happen before.'

She walked to him and took the bottle, their fingers brushing, shaking her in a way she would not let him see.

He put his elbow on the desk, his jaw on his fist,

and his eyes flicked her direction. 'What day of the week is it?'

'I'm not certain,' she answered.

'Simpson would know,' he said.

'You can always ring for one of the servants.'

'And let them know I am unaware of even the date? If they have not surmised it already, I will not enlighten them that I am completely distracted.'

'Rhys, why did you ask me to marry you?'

'If you had said yes, we could have discussed it in detail. For years perhaps. But as you said no, I decline to even think about the moment, much less speak of it.' He stared at her, then he took the ink bottle back off her and set it aside.

She put fingertips under his chin and guided it in her direction. 'I have tried to sketch you, but I don't have the skill. I'll learn, then I will always have a likeness of you.'

Eyes, weary with sleeplessness, watched her until his face turned into her hand and he pressed a kiss to her skin. 'You will always have me in person, Bellona, if you wish it, wedding or no. I have committed my heart to you and you will always hold it. You are truly my first love. My only love. If you do not plan to marry me, I understand. That does not change my heart.'

'You think you can continue in your life without a wife?'

'I have not been married in the first decades of my life and have managed very well, and when I look at you and know that it leaves me free for you, I'm very thankful.'

He pushed the chair back as he stood, his body brushing against hers. His hands rested on her hips. 'I will only ask you once more, today, but the question will remain open every day for the rest of your life, if you do not say yes now. Will you marry me?'

She nodded.

Epilogue

Bellona could hardly believe the change in her sister. Thessa had returned from her sea voyage with a young son and enough tales to keep them all laughing for hours, but somehow the talk had changed from the voyage to the husbands, and had become something of a verbal competition to see who had married the most delightful man.

'He talks in his sleep,' Thessa said of her husband, Captain Ben. 'And I find it most entertaining.'

'Rolleston… Well, I do not know if he talks in his sleep or not,' Bellona admitted, covering a yawn, and then aimed a smug smile at Thessa. 'He does not sleep.'

Melina grimaced. 'You are not learning how to be a proper duchess and he is acting more like you every day. You both disrupt all around you.'

A young female shriek of laughter sounded from outside the room.

'See what I mean.' Melina shook her head. 'Willa,' she called out, standing to move to the door. 'Do not—'

Warrington walked in, carrying his daughter under his arm, snug against his side and grasped around her middle, her hands and feet flailing as she laughed. 'I don't know what we will do with her. She thinks she is as big as her brother Jacob,' he said, bending enough so she could put her feet to the floor and right herself. 'Willa, you must not shout when I toss you about. Jacob does not.'

'He does,' she said. 'And he has a pail of worms hidden under his bed.'

'No,' Melina said, rushing to the door.

Warrington put out an arm, catching his wife at the waist. 'Don't worry. I have told him we will go fishing. I'll see to the worms.' He gave his wife a kiss on the forehead.

Ben walked in behind him. 'Rhys and I have decided to teach Jacob how to fish. We cannot trust his father to such a simple task. And we all know—' he looked at his wife '—that I am very good at catching things from the sea.'

Warrington snorted. 'But we will be fishing in a pool and you always claim the fish are not biting.' He looked over his shoulder at Rhys. 'And you claim the sun is in their eyes.'

Rhys shrugged. 'That was when we were children. I say now that the fisherman who fares worst will be tossed into the pool by the other two.'

'Challenge accepted,' Ben said.

'Wait.' Warrington held out a hand. 'I will be the judge of the winner. You two can compete.'

Ben looked at Rhys and winked. 'Certainly, War. We will see that you do not fall into the pool and get your cravat wet. But I suggest you wear old boots.'

'You could use a dunking as well. You hardly look like a sea captain,' Warrington said. 'You are all Brummelled.'

Benjamin shrugged. 'I had a portrait sitting in the library. Thank you, Bellona, for recommending your tutor.'

'I think Ben looks quite dashing,' Thessa said. 'And the blue waistcoat matches his eyes so.'

Warrington made a choking noise. 'A good reason not to choose it.'

'I'm only too happy to wear it for my wife, even if it is a bit tight under the black coat.' Benjamin's smile broadened. 'It was worth the trade—worth standing for my own portrait just to have a painting of my wife as I saw her the first time.' He straightened the sleeves of his coat. 'She'll always be my mermaid.'

Melina frowned. 'I've seen that painting on your ship of Thessa in the water. Not something that didn't happen every day on Melos.'

Warrington turned to the artwork above his fireplace of the three sisters on the island. The old painting created in their childhood. 'That is the one I cherish.'

'This is the artist I cherish,' Rhys said, putting a hand at Bellona's back. She looked into his eyes. He often sat near her, reading aloud while she sketched or practised with oils.

She'd never expected to love painting and she didn't care if she ever became any good at it, but strangely, it made her feel closer to her mother's memory and her homeland. During her childhood, their house had always smelled of pigments and she'd learned to mix them quite young.

Her sisters did not see painting the same way,

but they had all agreed to travel to the museum in France when their children were older. They wanted another look at the statue they'd found—now that the armless woman had a home—and they wanted to show their children the woman from Melos.

Melina turned to Bellona. 'I will have a picnic prepared and brought to us at the pool. The nursery maid can watch the children, but we will watch the boys.'

Melina and Warrington left the room, followed by Thessa and Ben. But Rhys lingered a bit, looking into Bellona's eyes.

'Do you wish to go with the others?' he asked. 'I'd prefer to visit the pool in the moonlight with you.'

'Oh, that would not be a good idea,' she said, shaking her head. 'Ben and Thessa are planning a stroll there tonight.'

'Well, then,' he said. 'When we return home, we can visit the small room in the servants' quarters. I've had a good latch put on the door.'

'You did not,' she said, slapping at his sleeve. 'The servants will...'

He laughed. 'I did. I will take a book with us—

to give us something to do, of course. I gave strict instructions to the servants it is not to be disturbed. A good book should not be interrupted—ever.'

She shut her eyes and put her hand to her temple. 'What must they think of us?'

He reached and snatched a pin from her hair and palmed it as she tried to take it back, then he trapped her close for a soft kiss. 'I hope they think we are rather fond of each other.'

Her face was not that of a goddess—well, perhaps it was the face of his goddess. But to him, she was his angel. And when he bent to kiss her he did not care if all the doors of the world opened and everyone saw them together. For ever.

* * * * *